Enjoy!

Di Johnson

11 12/06

QUEST FOR THE CROWN

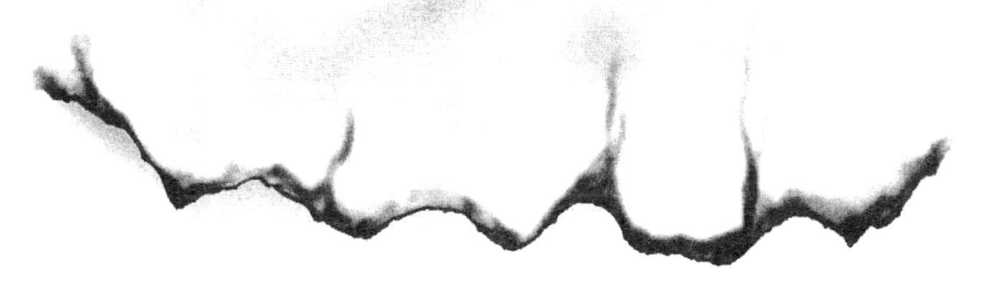

Also by Diana M. Johnson

Destiny's Godchild

"A medieval legendary beginning
for the House of Charlemagne"
B.P.S.C. IRWIN Award in Fiction, 1999

Pepin's Bastard

The Story of Charles Martel

Quest for the Crown

the story of pepin the short

a novel by

Diana M. Johnson

SUPERIOR BOOK PUBLISHING COMPANY
PO Box 8312
Van Nuys, California 91409

This book is a work of fiction. Names, characters, places and incidents are either products of the author's imagination or are used fictitiously.

Printed in the United States of America.

Library of Congress Cataloging-in-Publication Data
Johnson, Diana M. 1935 –
Quest for the crown: the story of Charles Martel: a novel/Diana M. Johnson

1.Pepin the Short. d.768. Mayor of the Palace for the Franks of Neustria 741-746. Mayor of the Palace for all Franks 746-750. King of All Franks 750-768 — Fiction.
2. Carloman (son of Charles Martel) d.755. Mayor of the Palace for the Franks of Austrasia 741-746. Monk 746-755 — Fiction.
3. Bertrada (Big-footed Bertha) d. 783. Daughter of Charibert, Count of Laon, married Pepin the Short 740 — Fiction.
4. Gisela, abbess of Chelles — Fiction.
5. Charles (Charlemagne) d. 814 — Fiction.
6. Childeric II, King of all Franks 743-750.
Boniface, archbishop of Mainz, d. 754 — Fiction.
7. Pope Stephen II — Fiction. 8. France—History 740-768 — Fiction.
9. Donation of Pepin — Fiction.

Library of Congress Control Number: 2001117023

ISBN 0-9661504-2-2

Author Photograph by William R. Johnson

To Betty Freeman, my mentor in the California Writers Club, San Fernando Valley Branch, for her unwavering support and assistance both personal and professional. And, as always, to Bill, the love and mainstay of my life.

Acknowledgments

Many people have helped in the writing of this novel. I especially thank my husband, Bill, and my mother, Grace Pyle Ellerbrock, for their unstinting love and support of everything I do.

In addition, my appreciation to Jean Akers, Millie Grey and Howard Goldstein, of our Monday Morning Writing Group whose comments and suggestions were, as always, invaluable. To my friend, Tina Farrell, my gratitude for her professional editing job of the completed manuscript. Her suggestions were right on target and greatly appreciated.

I happily give credit to Pastor Barb LeFevre-Lyons for her timely and dramatic sermons; two of which inspired scenes in Pepin's story.

Finally, I would like to recognize my debt to the San Fernando Valley Branch of the California Writers Club. My many friends there have helped me, personally and professionally, in ways great and small. Information I have gained at the meetings and state conferences has both improved my writing and illuminated the way from manuscript to published novels.

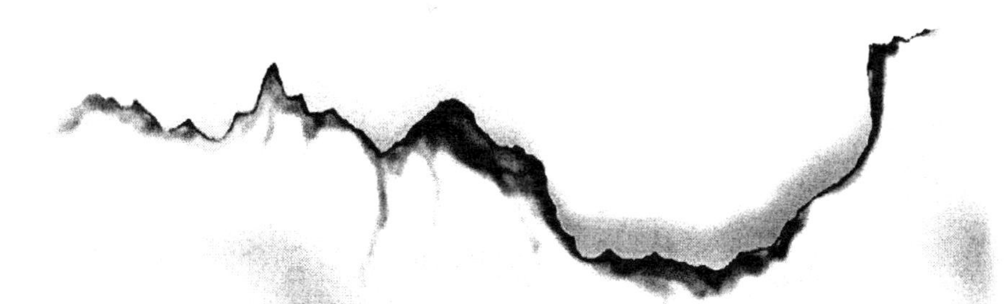

QUEST FOR THE CROWN

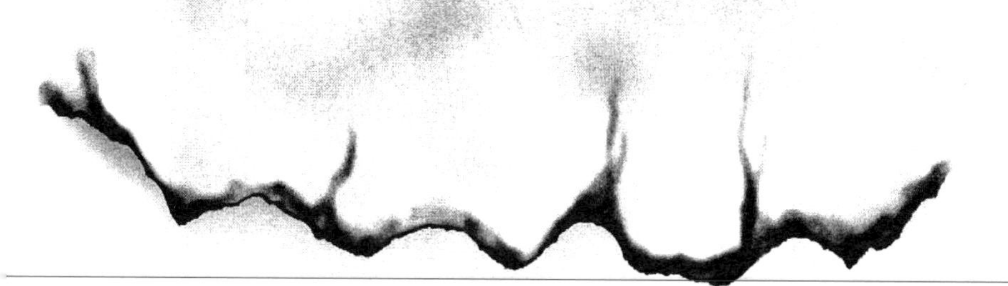

Family of Pepin de Vain

Destiny's Godchild

pepin de vain m. itta
d. 639

grimwald
(son) killed 661-2

childebert
(son) killed 661-2

bega m. ansegisel
(daughter)

pepin de gros
(son) b. 635-38

Pepin's Bastard: The Story of Charles Martel

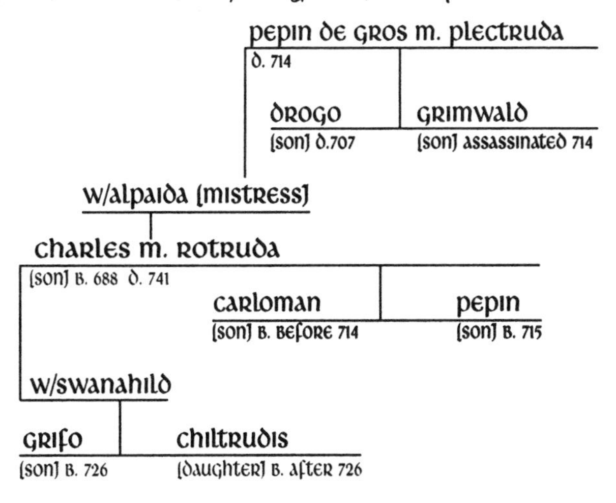

Quest for the Crown: The Story of Pepin the Short

pepin m. bertrada

rothaide	charles	giséle	carloman	adélaide	pepin
(daughter)	(son)	(daughter)	(son)	(daughter)	(son)
b.c.741	b.c.742	b.c.743	b.c.745	b.c.747	b.759 d.761

Frisia
Saxony
Thuringia
Swabia
Austrasia
Neustria
Burgundy
Alemannia
Bavaria
Auvergne
Aquitaine
Gascony
España
Lombardy
Middle Sea
aachen
herestal
cologne
rhine r.
soissons
st. denis
paris
seine r.
metz
moselle r.
danube r.
alps mountains
tours
loire r.
cher r.
bourges
saone r.
chalon
lyon
vienne
rhone r.
saintes
bordeaux
garonne r.
albi
toulouse
narbonne
monte casino

Alemannia

Burgundy

Bavaria

pavia

Lombardy

Ravenna

Rimini

ancona

Adriatic Sea

Rome

Middle Sea

monte casino

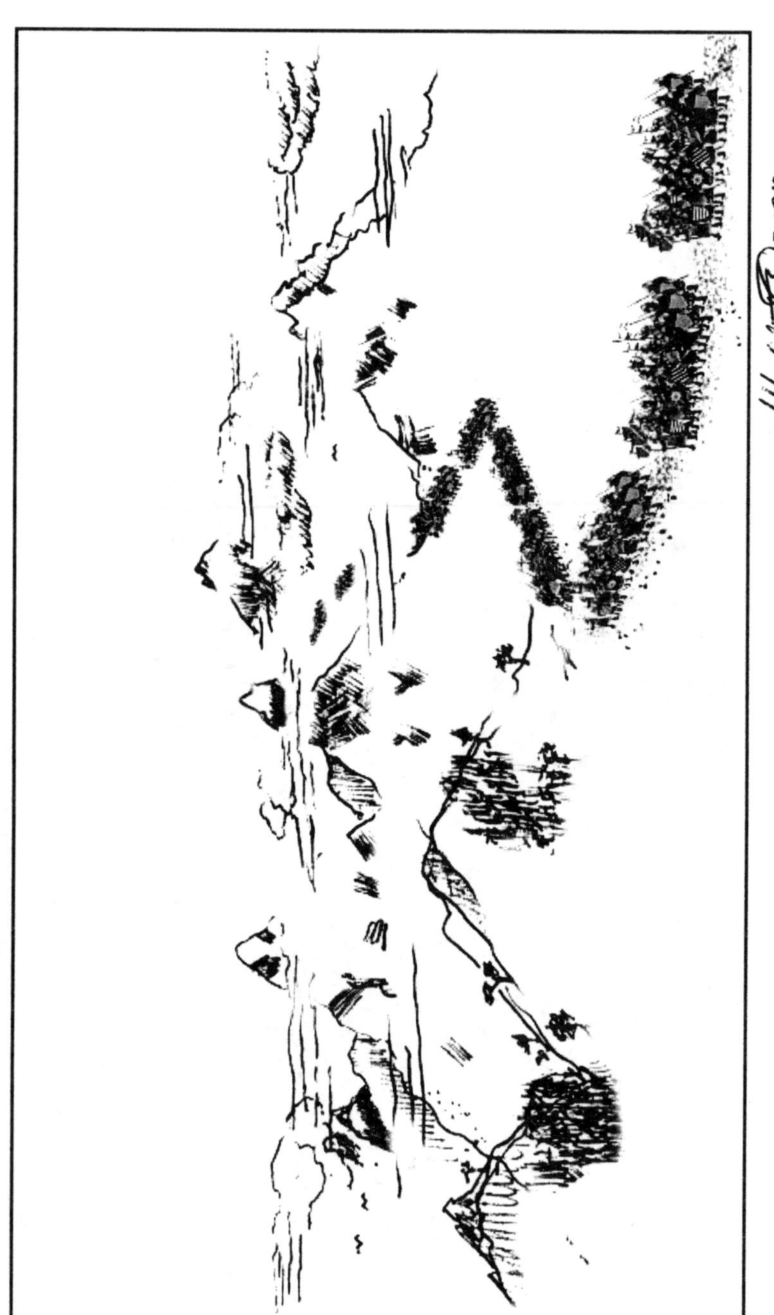

Chapter One

October 21, 741 AD

Pepin paused before the closed gate to the monastery. A sudden gust of chill wind swirled a shower of leaves around him. The nearly bare trees formed an intricate pattern of silhouettes against the overcast sky. He sighed deeply, then pulled firmly on the bell rope.

A black-robed brother opened the gate. "Pepin! God be praised you are in time! They wait for you in the infirmary. He has not long, you know."

"So I have been informed." Pepin felt his heart lurch. He shivered as cold air probed with icy fingers down his neck and inside his sweaty clothing.

"Someone will take care of your horse and put your belongings in a guest room." The brother pointed. "Go you directly to him, yonder."

Pepin walked with dragging steps. Dry leaves blew across the hard-packed courtyard with the sound of scratching cat's claws.

Inside the infirmary, Pepin saw a large, dimly lit room lined with empty narrow cots. They would fill soon enough as winter deepened. Sounds of low murmuring drifted from an open doorway to his right. Of course, Charles Martel would be placed in an alcove of his own.

Inside the curtained doorway, Pepin blinked. Those present, when they noticed Pepin, saw a short, broad-shouldered fellow, his clipped hair appearing more red than blond. A ruddy complexion spoke of someone who preferred the out-of-doors to a cloister.

The end must truly be near, Pepin thought, as his glance took in not just any priest, but Archbishop Boniface, himself. He and a scribe sat at the table, quietly discussing a parchment held up to the faint light entering through a wind opening.

Standing on the other side of the bed, Pepin made out the form of his older brother, Carloman. Tall, slender, his pale blond hair cut short. Pepin hoped Carloman would notice him, but his brother had eyes only for the dying man on the cot.

From the corner of his eye, Pepin became aware of a person standing in shadow at the foot of the bed. Not nearly so tall as Carloman, but equally slender, the young man's fine features were spoiled by a scowl. A look of hatred radiated toward Pepin from his fifteen-year-old half brother,

Grifo. Out of habit, Pepin stared back, challenging Grifo to back down.

A movement from the bed caught their attention. Finally forced to acknowledge the reason for his hasty trip to Quierzy sur Oise, Pepin looked at the bed and gasped. Who *was* that man? Surely not his father! He recognized nothing.

The head above the coverlet looked worse than death. Hair, once burnished gold, lay lank and gray upon the pillow. Once brilliant blue eyes hid behind closed lids, on a face that was sunken and lifeless. Where had gone the energy that drew men to him like dogs to a bitch in heat? Where the voice of command in the fever of battle or the hearty laugh when the joke was on him?

Tears filled Pepin's eyes. He wiped his sleeve across his face. The movement broke the spell.

"Brother!" Carloman reached across the narrow bed to grasp Pepin's arm. "Well come you. Though for a sad purpose I fear."

"What happened?" asked Pepin.

"Old age," replied Carloman. "He has been failing for almost a year. After all he *is* fifty-three."

Archbishop Boniface spoke a quiet word with each of the three brothers. Pepin felt a swelling of emotion as his boyhood religious mentor took his hand. The look of sad compassion and the pressure of his handclasp imparted comfort and reassurance.

"My lords," Boniface said, facing them all, "now that you are all in attendance, I must tell you of your father's wishes concerning Frankish Gaul. As mayor of the palace, Charles has divided the kingdom between you."

Although not unexpected, Pepin was taken aback at the anticipation which suddenly welled inside him.

The priest read from the parchment handed him by the scribe. "To Carloman, my eldest son by my wife Rotruda, is given the office of mayor of the palace for Austrasia, Alemannia, and Thuringia, with suzerainty over the Duchy of Bavaria."

Carloman smiled and Pepin felt a stab of envy. Austrasia! Their home province. Having been born in Metz and raised between there and Cologne, Austrasian noblemen there were among their staunchest supporters.

"Pepin, my second son by Rotruda," the priest read on, "shall be granted the office of mayor of the palace for Neustria, Burgundy, and Provence, with suzerainty over the Duchy of Aquitaine."

Pepin sighed. Romanized Neustrians held little love for their more Teutonic cousins from the north and east. His would not be an easy area to dominate. And exercising control over Aquitaine had always been a problem. Pepin could only hope his marriage to Bertrada, from a noble family of Neustria, would help rally the people to follow his new leadership.

"To Grifo, son by Swanahild, shall be given estates in Neustria, Austrasia and Burgundy as vassal of his brothers. These are—"

"God's death!" Grifo glared at Carloman, Pepin, and the unconscious form of Charles Martel in turn. "Will I *never* be an equal son to that man? Doomed to be forever subservient—never to rule as mayor over my own lands? I vow to see it will not be so!"

With an effort he snapped his mouth closed. His expression twisted into a grimace of hatred. Without further word, he spun on his heel and left the chamber.

"We shall outline his holdings when he is less distressed," said the priest, gently. "You may remain here alone with your father, though I doubt he will awaken." He rolled the parchment then turned to leave, the scribe scurrying at his heels.

Carloman had just opened his mouth to speak when their father opened his eyes and gestured weakly for them to come close.

"I... have something... of great importance to tell you," he rasped, the words barely audible.

Pepin felt a tingle of apprehension.

"Not now. Come back, both of you, when the priests celebrate matins at the darkest hour of night. Tell... Grifo. His mother and sister, too." With a sigh, Charles closed his eyes and fell silent once more.

Gaining courage, Pepin reached out to touch his father. Taking Charles' wrist, he felt for a pulse. Found it at last, weak and uneven. His throat tight, Pepin gently brushed the hair from Charles' face.

They watched for a moment, then Pepin followed Carloman out of the infirmary. The clouds had settled darkly on the tops of the nearby trees. The damp cold penetrated his backbone more deeply than ever.

He pulled his cloak more tightly about him. "I wonder what father has to tell us that is of such great import. And why we must hear it in the middle of the night."

"We shall just have to wait until matins to find out," replied the ever practical Carloman.

"Well, and so that is that," Pepin said shortly. "We are to be mayors of the palace. With no one to say us nay."

"Who would contradict Charles Martel?" asked Carloman. "With the throne empty these past few years, who else wields the power?"

"Grifo was none too pleased."

"I doubt not he will fight for greater influence."

"By Mithras, I would like to see him try!" Pepin felt a warm glow of satisfaction. What a pleasure it would be to put that scapegrace in his place!

Chapter Two

Some hours later, Pepin blinked as he followed Carloman into Charles' alcove. A single candle stood on the table, sending its uncertain light flickering into shadowy corners.

Propped up against pillows, Charles, though weak, smiled in recognition. Pepin fought the urge to gather the frail old man in his arms—to draw his sword and fight death in one-on-one combat. Instead, he gripped Charles' hand and was rewarded by responding pressure.

Carloman, standing next to Pepin, placed his hand on his father's shoulder, eyes brimming.

A rustle at the doorway drew their attention. Grifo's mother, Swanahild, paused at the threshold. His thirteen-year-old sister, Chiltrudis, edged around her mother. Grifo urged them to enter, allowing the leather curtain over the doorway to close after him.

Swanahild at once dropped to her knees, grasping Charles' hand. "Do not die! You cannot leave me alone. How shall I survive without your protection?"

Charles held her hand. "Hush," he whispered. "You are safe now. The danger was gone... long ago. No one here... wishes you harm."

Pepin's gaze shifted from his father to Swanahild. Much younger than Charles, her heavy, honey-colored hair scarcely showed gray. She had an ageless, fragile beauty. But on the rare occasions when Pepin found himself in her presence, she seemed—strange. One moment bubbling over with girlish gaiety, the next given to weeping and hand-wringing, or worse, completely unaware of those around her.

Pepin swallowed the protest that rose, unbidden, in his throat. How could Charles say no one wished her harm? *He* wished Swanahild harm. He wished she had never been born. Wanted nothing more than that his father had never returned from Bavaria with her as a second wife—with their infant son, Grifo. They had brought nothing but trouble, causing his mother, Rotruda, great grief.

"I have asked you here—" Charles licked his dry lips "—to tell you something of great importance."

Pepin caught Carloman's eye. A slight shrug reflected his own puzzlement.

"Carloman and Pepin will remember Egar, their tutor.... Many years ago, when Carloman was but a babe... and Pepin not yet born, Egar—a magician and ancient even then—told of a prophecy affecting our family."

Charles sat straighter against his bolster. Gathered strength. "You must know of it. But, I warn you, keep what I am about to tell you secret to the grave and beyond."

A chill swept over Pepin. Carloman and Grifo stood rooted to the spot. Swanahild stared quietly into a shadowed corner of the room. Pepin wondered if she understood one word Charles was saying.

Pepin's look rested at last on his half sister, Chiltrudis. Tendrils of dark blond hair escaped a braid to frame her face in gentle curls. The tip of a pink tongue came out from behind small white teeth to lick at her lower lip. Her eyes glowed in the reflected candlelight. She shrugged one shoulder and looked pointedly below Pepin's waist.

He closed his eyes to rid her from his vision. Strumpet! He could not abide her. Yet he felt his male organ begin to harden and a flush creep from his groin upward until he knew his face glowed with telltale ruddiness.

He opened his eyes. Chiltrudis gave a tiny smile, one eyebrow slightly raised. Then she directed her attention to Charles with exaggerated innocence.

"Many years ago," his father began, "Egar told us of a prophetic vision of a great king of the Franks. Egar said a young sorcerer saw the apparition, but I have long felt it was Egar, himself, who first had the vision."

Charles gestured toward a cup. Pepin leapt to grasp it. Held the cup while his father sipped, water dribbling down his chin.

Sated, Charles pushed the cup away. "Egar told us then that the great king would come from *our* family. How he knew this, I have no idea. But he was most firm on this point.

"The king has not yet come, but his day has been foretold.... Is drawing near."

Charles looked at Carloman, Pepin, then Grifo, in turn. "It may be one of you."

Pepin's chest fluttered with a thrill of excitement.

"Or it may be a child of your loins." Charles' eyes turned to Chiltrudis. Her look of petulance changed into a gleam of anticipation.

"How can that be?" asked Carloman. "None of us has a drop of royal Merovingian blood."

Pepin felt the elation burst. The prophecy, whatever its import, could not apply to one of them. "None," he blurted, "but members of the Merovingian family have reigned over the Franks since the beginning of time!"

"Not quite *that* long." A ghost of a smile played at Charles' lips. "However, nothing lasts forever. Not even the reign of the Merovingian family."

Pepin tried to recall what a king was for. The last of them, the child Theodoric IV, had died some four years ago. No one seemed to notice when Charles did not search for a replacement. Nor did he make any attempt to place himself on the throne. He had simply left it empty and continued administering the king's rule as if there were one.

Pepin thought he understood. Why would anyone want to be king when he was already mayor of the palace? In contrast to the unremarked passing of the king, the Franks would certainly notice when *Charles* died!

Pepin pressed his temple between his hands. Why then did he feel such a strong urge to be king, himself? Wear the crown? Sit the throne? What *was* it about the kingship that caused Egar to see visions concerning it?

Perhaps the legends surrounding the Merovingian monarchy elevated the king above mere mortals. After all, the Merovingians were known to be descendents of a sea serpent.

But, thought Pepin, if even the *rois fainéant* 'do-nothing' Merovingian kings were held in such high esteem, how much greater would be the Franks' awe for a strong, warrior king such as himself?

Or would his superstitious followers require legendary beginnings for any family entrusted with the crown? Perhaps Egar's prophecy was doomed from the start.

Pepin looked once more at Chiltrudis and was filled with resentment. She plainly wanted to bear the king. She could not! *The crown was his!*

Guiltily he looked about the chamber. Had he said anything aloud? Were his thoughts so clear they could be read from his face? No one looked in his direction. All eyes held fast on his father.

"What does the prophecy require of us?" Carloman seemed unexcited by the prospect of a crown. Merely curious about what might be expected of him.

Of course, as eldest son, Carloman would be king. Pepin regarded his brother. Tried to visualize the short blond hair grown long, a symbol of Frankish royalty. As a captain under Charles, Carloman had already proven himself a good soldier. He would competently succeed at anything. Pepin envied Carloman his two-year age advantage and his height. The sharp goad of desire twisted even stronger in his belly.

"You must build upon the power of mayor of the palace. Add to the might of this family until it is so great that the king of the prophecy might fulfill his destiny."

Charles' gaze swept each of them in turn. "In the meantime, should any word of our family's design on the Merovingian crown become known, every member of our line would be put to a painful death. Until they are ready to accept such a drastic change in the royal family, the Franks will fight to keep the rule as it has always been."

Pepin's heart thudded against his chest. For anyone other than a Merovingian to even think to grasp the crown was clearly treason. Cause enough to be killed by torture. Tied to a rack. Disemboweled.

Pepin pictured himself watching as the knife cut into his stomach. Saw his guts being taken out and laid, warm and bleeding, outside his body. All this while he was still alive.

Charles looked old. Once again drained of life and power. "Go you now. The future is in God's hands."

Chapter Three

Pepin and Carloman sat in high-backed chairs near the altar in the church of Saint-Denis. Grifo was nowhere to be seen. Not that Pepin had searched for him.

A cold, damp wind blew in through the narrow slits in the thick outer walls. Rain had fallen for three days without letup. In the gloom, Pepin could barely make out the mighty columns separating the aisles from the nave. Even the high clerestory windows of the nave let in too little sunlight to illumine the colors painted on the timbered ceiling.

A murmur of low voices and the sound of booted feet on the hard dirt floor filled the vast space with quiet sound.

Men stood shoulder to shoulder—indistinct forms in the gloom—packing the nave to overflowing.

Carloman leaned over to whisper into Pepin's ear. "Do you believe the story?"

"What story?"

"About Saint-Denis."

"Oh. You mean, during the Roman persecution of the Christians, he was beheaded in Paris? I believe it."

"But," persisted Carloman, "do you believe the rest?"

Pepin paused, remembering the tale. No sooner had the bloody head fallen with a "thunk" to the ground, than it began singing Christian hymns, all of its own accord. Then Denis picked up his severed, hymn-singing head and began walking. The singing stopped and Denis fell dead at last, on this very spot.

"You mean as actual fact?"

Carloman nodded.

"I never gave it much thought. I suppose I took it as a mysterious legend. Extolling the virtue of faith in the face of great adversity. But that it *really* happened? I doubt it."

"Doubt you God could have made it happen?"

"No. But why would he?" asked Pepin, puzzled.

"To prove his power once again to the Romans. To comfort and strengthen the Christians." Carloman looked troubled. "To test our own willingness to believe."

"I suppose the legend *could* be true. Why? Is it important to you?"

"Yes!" Carloman's eyes glistened.

This strange, whispered conversation made Pepin shiver. What had come over his brother?

"I believe. Oh, God help Thee mine unbelief," Carloman murmured, his head bowed.

He turned to Pepin once more. "I always envied you, you know. I could not figure out why father allowed you to study here in Saint-Denis while I got no farther than the cathedral of Metz."

Pepin was startled. He had spent his entire life trying to equal his older brother's prowess in soldiers' training. His bravery in actual battle. His knowledge. His ability to act appropriately in every situation.

"You? Envied *me*?"

Black-robed Benedictine monks entered their wooden quire stalls behind the altar from where they would sing the mass. The sanctuary with the tomb of Saint-Denis stood behind them. The monks moved so quietly, they seemed little more than shadows.

An acolyte lit the candles on the altar. The dancing flames reflected on golden candlesticks. Shafts of brilliant light pierced the darkness as the candle glow penetrated the jewels encrusting the silver chalice. In this sudden burst of radiance, Pepin was forced at last, to acknowledge the long wooden box in front of the altar.

Kyrie eleison, Christe eleison, Kyrie eleison
Lord have mercy, Christ have mercy, Lord have mercy

The familiar words, set into haunting chant by Pope Gregory, floated down from the quire. Coming from the darkness behind the candle-lit altar, the notes seemed to emanate, not from the throats of mortal men, but to descend from the stone of the cathedral itself.

As Archbishop Boniface followed the censer to the altar, the sweet smell of incense overcame the strong odor of wet wool issuing from the masses in the nave.

Pepin swallowed, willing his face to show manliness rather than grief. He remembered happier days as a student here in the monastery of Saint-Denis.

He relived the mind-stretching studies—Greek, geometry, Aristotle. Worshipping here, surrounded by the strong colors and brilliant gold, he had been awestruck by the majesty of Almighty God.

He realized now, by sending him here, Charles had begun Pepin's preparation for becoming the Neustrians' mayor of the palace. Even then his father had known!

By having himself buried here among the tombs of the Merovingian kings, was Charles Martel preparing the people to accept his sons as future kings?

How did one go about choosing a king? Pepin could not remember the coronation of Theodoric IV. There must be an accepted process. He would ask Father. Charles Martel would know.

With a stab, Pepin realized his loss. He could never again ask his father anything. Panic welled. How could he be mayor of the palace, much less king? He had no idea how to go about his newly inherited duties. The people loved their hero, Charles Martel. A mere son could never compete with the legend his father had become.

Haunting notes floating down from the monk's quire drew him back to the altar and the sarcophagus before it.

Requiem eternam,
Grant rest eternal,

dona eis Domine.
Lord, our God, we pray Thee.

Reguiem eternam.
Grant rest eternal.

Chapter Four

Following his father's funeral, Pepin returned to the villa at Quierzy sur Oise. Here he and Bertrada would spend the winter waiting for spring and the beginning of his life as mayor of the palace. Of all their holdings, this one brought him the most delight. Perhaps because Carloman had nothing like it in *his* realm. Not the typical Frankish wooden square palace, with its large, dark, smoke-filled great hall below, small living cubicles for the noble family above—the villa, part of Bertrada's dowry, was Roman in style.

Several large light, airy rooms flowed into one another, forming a square around a central courtyard. The lower rooms of stone supported an upper story of wattle walls daubed with plaster. The courtyard was bare now, but come spring, trees would sprout new leaves and bright flowers would bloom.

The sight of his wife standing in the entry vestibule, filled Pepin with a sense of peace that had been sorely missing these last few weeks. He endured the large meal with the household in attendance. Endured, too, the handclasps and expressions of condolence.

At last he and Bertrada escaped to the solitude of their chamber. Letting clothes fall where they might, Pepin led his wife to their bed. Buried his grief for his father, and anxiety for the future, in her love and comfort.

Afterward, Pepin stretched and sighed in the darkness. He could not remember the last time he had felt such contentment. The heavy hangings on their bed frame held in heat generated by vigorous lovemaking, creating a toasty cocoon.

He reached over and caressed the form lying next to him—heavy breasts, slightly rounded stomach, firm hips and thighs. "You have warmed me to my toes." In the dark, he found her face and gently brushed the hair from it. "I could not have a better wife."

She took his hand in both of hers and kissed his palm. "Truly?" Pepin could hear the smile in her voice. "What a lovely thing for you to say."

He could well understand her question. He had not always thought of her so. When first he saw her, mere days before their betrothal, he had found her unattractive. She looked so—*Roman*. Dark hair, brown eyes, dominant nose. Too tall, of course, and her feet were too big. He could picture some scribe in the distant future referring back to them in his chronicles as 'Pepin the Short' and 'Bertrada Big Foot'.

Pepin understood why his father had arranged his marriage to a Neustrian, daughter of Charibert, Count of Laon. At the time, he only wished she looked more Frankish. Pepin preferred blond curls, blue eyes and rosy cheeks. It would have been nice to have a wife he did not have to look up to. While that was doubtless asking too much, surely, her feet could have been smaller.

More than a year later, Pepin barely noticed her height or her feet. He still thought blue eyes and fair hair entrancing, but these thoughts had nothing to do with his wife.

"What did you think of when you were a young girl, dreaming of a husband?"

Bertrada stilled and the bedchamber seemed to wait. She shifted and said, "Why, what every young girl longs for, I would imagine. Someone tall. Dark. Strong and mysterious."

Pepin laughed. He knew in asking Bertrada a question, he would receive an honest answer. "And instead you ended up married to someone short, blond—"

"But strong and energetic," she interrupted, "which is far better than mysterious. I could have been married to a man old enough to be my father. Or someone who thought a good beating would keep me pliant and agreeable."

"Surely, your father would never have betrothed you to such a man!"

"He would not have intentionally put me in harm's way," Bertrada agreed. "But he needed to make the best alliance for our household with my marriage."

She fell silent, pondering perhaps. Pepin gave her time to think.

"My father spoiled me for most other men," she mused. "My birth was, by all accounts a difficult one. Whatever the reason, I was the only child. My mother did her best to train me as a docile, obedient daughter. But my father treated me as an equal. Nearly like a son in discussing affairs of our estate and the court in Paris with me."

Pepin realized his wife was certainly far more than a mere bedmate to *him*. During his long absences, Bertrada managed their many estates with competence and calm diplomacy. The major domos regarded her with favor. She maintained well-stocked larders. Their looms produced cloth of the finest quality. The villeins who worked the crown's land along with their own, treated her with a deference born of respect.

She never complained, but welcomed him back with dilight. Best of all, she was fruitful. Already their daughter, Rothaide, ruled the nursery, and Bertrada carried in her womb the seed of their second child.

Pepin felt a smile curve his mouth as he leaned over to nibble Bertrada's ear. "Now that I am mayor of the palace for Neustria, Burgundy and Provence, I will need your help even more. It will doubtless be some while before the noblemen believe I am a worthy successor to my father. After all, who am I to take the place of the great Charles Martel?"

Pepin could feel the mattress shift as Bertrada raised herself on one elbow. "How can *I* help? Surely my responsibility remains the same—manage your households and bear you children, hopefully a son."

"I have no fear you will produce a son." Pepin placed his hand on her stomach. "This one. I sense it already.

"No, what I need is your presence with me. As soon as the roads are passable I plan to travel to every corner of our realm. Would you accompany me? With you at my side, they will see I value the Gallo-Romans of Neustria. Will realize I am not trying to impose Austrasian domination on them.

"Sooner or later I must needs deal with Aquitaine. Even my father could not quell their fervent desire for independence. Eudo, their duke, betrayed him time and again."

He rolled onto his back, his hands behind his head. "I want not to face his son Duke Hunald and his Gascons with half-hearted troops at my back. I dare not ask the noblemen's support until I have gained their confidence."

He turned. "But only if you feel well enough to travel with me when I go."

"Whatever my mother's problem with me, except for the birth itself, I felt well enough to travel when I had Rothaide. But, could my being at your side truly make a difference?"

"*I* think so."

"Then I will, and gladly. My greatest desire is to please you in any way I can."

Pepin let his mind wander to the even larger possibilities of the future. "If what Egar prophesized comes to pass, and should it concern me, I may well need your support more than ever."

"Tell me of this Egar."

Their curtained bed was filled with shadowy darkness. A perfect setting to remember his elderly, somewhat mysterious tutor. "Egar joined the court nearly every winter. He would arrive just before snow made travel impossible—without fanfare—riding a horse and leading a donkey loaded with his pack and a travel harp wrapped in its bag."

"He played the harp?" Bertrada sounded intrigued.

"Yes. And sang ballads of Merovingian legends and Frankish might in an amazingly youthful voice."

"I would like to have met him."

"Egar had a unique way of standing very still in the shadows. With the hood of his travel cloak pulled over his head, we forgot he was there and he simply disappeared! Or else he would emerge from some dark corner of a chamber, as though he had been there all along. I have never known anyone else who could do such a thing."

Pepin shrugged. "He taught Carlo and me languages. History. Mathematics and astrology."

"What were *you* like as a boy?"

Pepin snorted a mirthless laugh. "I was too young, too short, and too slow.

"In soldier's training, long-legged Carloman beat even some of the men in foot races. He held his own in one-on-one combat. And he rode a horse as though he were one with the beast. But I... *I* was last in everything. Except for throwing the *Francesca*. I could occasionally hit the tree trunk we used as a target when I threw the double-bitted hand ax."

Bertrada took Pepin's hand in hers.

"But even then," Pepin continued, "Egar would sometimes talk to me. Just *me*, alone. I can remember his warm brown eyes. They seemed to look into my head—and my heart—as though he could see everything that was contained therein. The slightest breeze would blow his silvery hair like a nimbus about his head.

"When he talked to me thus, he made me feel as though I had—buried deep within myself—value I could not even guess at."

Pepin squirmed, tangling the bedclothes. Embarrassed at giving voice to such personal recollections.

Bertrada drew his face to hers. Her kiss told him—louder than words—that she accepted him, just as he was. And spoke of her gratitude that he would so freely confide in her.

Chapter Five

Winter passed. With spring Pepin and Bertrada made plans to travel in Neustria. Before they could begin packing, a page announced, “My lord Pepin, your brother, Duke Carloman, arrives. He would meet with you.”

“Show him here. And then fetch us some ale.”

“Yes, m’lord.”

Pepin glanced at Bertrada, seated on a bench near a wind opening, doing handwork. She looked like one of the Roman women in the faded frescoes painted on the wall.

Pepin felt a glow of satisfaction. Where else had a villa such as this survived from long-ago Roman times? Pepin particularly relished the large day room with its floor of pink marble, imported from Italy some six hundred years ago.

Pilasters of the warm marble, topped by graceful Ionic capitals, framed the doorway through which Carloman appeared, dusty from the long journey.

“Brother! What brings you to our humble villa?”

Carloman nodded to Bertrada then clasped Pepin’s hand. “We have trouble, you and I.”

"Trouble?" Pepin's joy plummeted.

"Grifo. And that minx sister of his, Chiltrudis. For all I know, their dear mother, Swanahild, has her hand in it as well."

"Grifo?" asked Pepin. "He is but fifteen. What trouble can he offer?"

"More than enough. Already he gathers his own troops to wage war on my domain of Austrasia."

"And you come to *me* for help? What has he, a score of armed men? And he, a pup at best, to lead them? Surely you can box his ears, with all the resources of Austrasia at your call!"

"Grifo is not the only one. Armies gather on Austrasia's eastern borders from Frisia, Saxony, Swabia and Alemannia as well."

"God's death! They waste no time, do they?" Pepin felt a churning in the pit of his stomach. "You say Chiltrudis has some part in this?"

"It would seem our 'chaste' young sister has run off to Bavaria, where she mates Duke Odilo. Mark my words, Bavaria will soon join the pack of wolves snarling and snapping at our heels."

"I feel sorry for her." Bertrada spoke for the first time.

"Sorry!" Carloman and Pepin burst out.

"You do not know her as we do," Carloman said.

Pepin walked to his wife and gently touched her cheek. He shook his head. "By the light, you would not say that if you were a man!"

"True. I am not a man. But I feel for her as one woman to another. She is what, twelve, thirteen? Ready for marriage. But what man of importance in her life has shown her affection? Charles?"

Carloman was quick to jump to his father's defense. "By the time Chiltrudis came along, father was not often with either family. Fortunately, Pepin and I were of an age to accompany him on campaign by then."

Pepin chimed in, his voice ringing with righteous indignation. "He chose, naturally enough, to spend what time he had with our mother rather than Swanahild and her brood. Why should he not?"

"No reason." Bertrada took Pepin's hand into her own. "I was just looking at it from Chiltrudis' view. Her father had no time for her. What of her mother? Grifo? Her much older half-brothers? Who gave her the attention she so obviously needed?"

"Not Swanahild," Carloman said, thoughtfully. "She always seemed obsessively dependent on Father. And her son. She thinks Grifo walks on water."

"*We* could not help her," Pepin added. "We had no association with Father's other family. I laid eyes on her no more than a score of times while she was growing up." He paused. "But, whenever I did, I found her disturbing."

"So now she has run off," mused Bertrada. "Returned to her mother's people. Mated the Duke. Ignored by the Franks, she may have thought the Bavarians would treat her better."

Carloman gave Bertrada an appraising look. "Perhaps, Madame, there is some truth to what you say."

Pepin strode back to his bench by the table. "Perhaps Chiltrudis did it to spite Grifo—and to spawn a worthy candidate for Egar's offered crown!"

Two pairs of startled eyes bore into Pepin. He felt heat flush his face. He quickly looked around to verify no one outside the family could possibly overhear them. "God's death! If she cannot *be* king, she can whelp one, can she not?"

"Whatever Chiltrudis' problem," Carloman said at last, "we can do nothing to solve it. We have enough facing us as it is. Grifo. And the eastern tribes massed at our borders."

"Where is Grifo gathering his men?"

"His estate in Laon. Within your realm of Neustria, but close enough to the Meuse River to cross easily into Austrasia from the west."

"You want me to take on Grifo, while you do battle with the others?"

"No. I propose we join forces. Show them we are not like the Merovingians, who in times past wasted precious men and treasure fighting brother against brother, nephew against uncle, losing much in the process." Carloman laid his hand on Pepin's arm. "Come with me, little brother. Fight with me back-to-back, side-by-side. You have my pledge I will do the same for you."

Pepin's chest swelled with pride that his brother had asked his aid. Promised his own as well. "But, what if the noblemen will not follow me? You know, as well as I, the Neustrians dislike bearing the yoke of an Austrasian such as myself."

"Father was Austrasian," reminded Carloman. "And to a man, they would have followed him to the gates of hell."

"True. But he was Charles Martel." Pepin smiled sadly and shook his head. "I am but his second son."

"Call a *Champs de Mars*. Tell them to come with their armies, ready to go to war at the conclusion of the meeting."

"Shall I tell them we go to join you against Grifo and those who threaten your eastern boundary?"

"No. Tell them only to be ready for war. They more than likely will think you plan to wage battle *against* me. They may even *like* that idea. Once pledged to you, they can learn the truth."

Pepin slumped. "What if they will not then go as gladly?"

"You will make them. You must!"

Bertrada helped Pepin pack for war camp as his own men from Quierzy sur Oise gathered in the meadow beyond the town. "Think you Carloman wants to be king?" She stood beside him, folding a tunic.

Pepin stopped. His coat of chain mail—small, interlocking metal rings—dangled from his hand. The crown, once his dominant thought, had receded over the winter. Concern for gaining the support of his far-flung realm as mayor of the palace to a non-existent king supplanted that obsession. "I suppose so. Though he has said naught to me about it. What man would not?"

"I cannot say. I know only *my* man would." She smiled her pride and Pepin felt his face grow warm. "But I think

Carloman would never be mayor of the palace in service to his younger brother as king."

Pepin's pleasure waned. He felt himself once again the small boy tagging after his older brother. "No. That could never be."

"And to divide the realm, with Carloman king of Austrasia, while you ruled Neustria, might strain your relationship beyond repair."

"Well, if that were to happen, we would both need to declare for the crown at the same time. One could never sit the throne of one realm, while the other remained mayor of the palace of the other."

Bertrada gave him a steady look. "What would you do, in order to gain the crown?"

"Do you mean, how far am I prepared to go?"

"Yes."

Pepin felt himself drawn to the edge of a chasm. Ambition and desire lay buried in its black depths. He could not bring himself to look. Did not want to know the answer.

"I am glad the question gives you pause," said Bertrada.

"What would you have me say?"

Bertrada smiled and shook her head. "The answer must be yours, not mine."

Pepin sat upon his favorite horse on a rise, looking over the fields outside Soissons. Heart thumping against his ribs, a strange combination of emotions churned inside him. Pride, excitement—and terror. Open-air tents dotted the meadow where yellow and white flowers bloomed in the green spring grass. Colorful ensigns snapped in the breeze.

A cacophony of sounds rose to surround Pepin. Horses neighed, men shouted rallying cries, "St. Denis for Lorraine," "To Burgundy," "St. Martin for Tours," cheering on their own men as they participated in foot races and mock one-on-one combat. Thwacks sounded where men threw their double-bitted casting axes, the *francescas,* from which the Franks took their name. They competed now for pride. Soon it might well be for their heads.

Held each year since ancient times, the *Champs de Mars*, named for both the god of war and the month in which it was held, reunited the nobles of the realm. Bishops, abbots, dukes and counts led their armies, from tens to hundreds. Only the noblemen took part in the debate. But they knew the views of their supporters and villeins.

Pepin rode into the middle of the melee toward the table, benches, and chair of authority that had been set up in the middle of the field. On horseback, he was as tall as any and—he knew—more commanding than most.

But as he dismounted, panic engulfed him and he felt suddenly diminished. Although undeniably short, he hadn't *felt* small since his youth.

I can ill afford now to dwell on something about which nothing can be done, he told himself, firmly.

"Well met, Pepin!"

"Martel's son for us!"

As the greetings surrounded him, Pepin dared hope.

Soldiers ceased their activity and gathered closer to watch the ceremony.

Standing tall, Pepin accepted the oaths of fealty. One by one the noblemen knelt, bareheaded, swords and axes laid aside. With hands between Pepin's, each one promised, "homage and fealty with hands and mouth to thee, my lord, and to defend thee and thy lands against all invaders, so help me God and all the saints."

Gravely, Pepin accepted each pledge.

He could not help but overhear muttering. "We pledge ourselves to our nobleman, and he to Pepin. To whom does Pepin pledge when the throne remains empty?"

When Pepin, ignoring the murmurs, revealed that their campaign would be against Grifo, in combination with Carloman and the Frankish Austrasians, the noblemen balked.

"By Mithras!" shouted a nobleman, pounding the table with his fist. "We would fight to extend our Neustrian domination. But why risk lives and treasure in support of those who already have more than their share?"

Pepin searched his brain for a rejoinder. "Look around. All have come to join forces but my half-brother, Grifo, he the son of the Bavarian princess Swanahild."

"Grifo be more Saxon than Martel's son," a soldier in the field blurted.

"Saxons be hardly even Christian. They be not Franks like we," added another.

Pepin felt a flutter of encouragement. "Grifo, the half-*Saxon*, has encouraged his kinsmen and the pagan Frisians to gather on Austrasia's border. They expect us to fight Carloman from the west while they attack from the east. When we meet in the middle, over the bones of dead Austrasians, we face them alone."

Pepin pointed to the nobleman who had opposed his plan. "How much better to face the enemy side by side with our cousin Franks. They will join us when it is the Aquitanians we face."

Another nobleman commented from across the table, "We can beat Saxons, Frisians, Aquitanians, all. We need not Austrasians to back us up!"

Pepin stared, searching in vain for a name to put to the man. This, his first *Champs de Mar,* was turning out to be every bit as daunting as he had feared.

"Neustrians to the fray," someone in the crowd cried out.

"Yes!" Pepin shouted. "Neustrians to the fray, but against the foreigners, not our cousin Franks. Neustrians *are* equal in strength to my brother Carloman and his Austrasians. And well they know it. By the bull! Carloman asks, nay *begs,* our aid. If we agree, no foe can defeat us."

Silence. Pepin looked from man to man around the table. None would meet his eye.

"My half-*Saxon* sister, Chiltrudis has run off, denying my offer of a dowry, to marry Duke Odilo of Bavaria. The Bavarians have failed to pay taxes due the Franks. *Now* they will join our enemies to the east."

A buzz of speculation spread through the crowd. Most had not heard of Chiltrudis' defection.

Pepin grasped this advantage. "Swanahild, mother to Grifo and Chiltrudis doubtless encourages this treachery. The Bavarian princess would have her own offspring in power over Austrasia *and* Neustria. We Franks *must* prevail. With Carloman we defeat Grifo first, *then* those who threaten our borders."

"I pledged my fealty to Pepin. My men and I will follow him wherever he leads!" Chlodomer's words carried well beyond the noblemen, even though he seemed not to have raised his voice.

Pepin sent his closest friend a look of gratitude. Would the others listen to Chlodomer, who was a Neustrian as were they?

The soldiers looked toward the noblemen to see which way they would vote.

The noblemen spoke heatedly among themselves, heads together, voices low.

Pepin grew hot, then cold, watching them. He wished he could make out what they were saying. But feared what he might hear.

At last they stopped talking. In the shuffling of noblemen, two groups emerged. They faced Pepin and the gathered footsoldiers. The larger group, perhaps two out of three, scowled. The others looked resigned. None looked completely happy with the outcome.

"We return home," declared Villicus, Pepin's most vocal critic among the Neustrian noblemen. He stood at the front of the larger group. "We have pledged to defend Pepin against all invaders, but we fight *not* to aid the Austrasians against those who invade *them,* not us."

With that, he and all of the noblemen with him turned and walked away towards their own encampments.

Silence fell on the footsoldiers. None of them had ever witnessed such an outcome to the *Champs de Mar.* No one would have refused to fight for Charles Martel!

Looking uncertain, men began leaving the field.

"We join Carloman in fighting the Saxons," announced a nobleman standing with the smaller group.

A faint cheer went up from the remaining footsoldiers.

Pepin took a deep breath. He wiped the sweat running down his face. His worst fears had come to pass. Most of his army was leaving.

But not *all,* he reminded himself. Some remained true. They would follow him in battle. He must prove himself to be his father's son and make the best of it.

Pepin walked on stiffly wooden legs toward his remaining noblemen. His face threatened to break like over-baked pottery with the smile he forced upon it. He clasped their hands. Gave thanks for their loyalty.

That done, Pepin took a shuddering breath and looked about. A fresh breeze blew out of the blue sky. The sun played hide and seek with fleecy clouds.

Looking across the meadow to the cluster of buildings on the banks of the Aisne River, Pepin reflected on the significance of this place. Dating back to Roman times, here Clovis, founder of the Frankish monarchy, had defeated Syagrius in 486. More recently, Pepin's father, an Austrasian, won his first decisive battle here, routing the Neustrians in 719. And here, Pepin admitted, he had been accepted as mayor of the palace of Neustria, and then lost the better part of his armies.

The men drifted to their various encampments. The air soon filled with the scent of roasting geese and chickens turning on spits over several fires. The sounds of drums and flutes mingled with shouts and laughter.

Pepin used his hunting knife to cut a thick slice of bread to use for a plate. On it he piled several slices of meat, fresh from the spit, and a crunchy wedge of crisp, white onion.

For the moment he was alone within the mob of men. The few noblemen and bishops whom he knew personally had returned to their own clusters of tents and cooking fires.

Chlodomer joined him, with a wry smile. "Well, old friend, where go we from here?"

"To join what is left of our men with Carloman's Austrasians." Pepin clasped Chlodomer's arm. "I thank you for speaking up."

"For all the good it did."

"Without your support, they might *all* have left."

Chlodomer slapped Pepin's shoulder and left to rejoin his own men.

From Soissons to Laon was little more than an easy day's march to the north and east. Pepin felt some chagrin as he observed his army. In the end, just eight noblemen had chosen to bring their footsoldiers and follow him to meet his brother and the Austrasians against Grifo and his Saxons.

"Why is it," Pepin asked riding next to Chlodomer, "that only the young noblemen with few followers joined us, while the older men with large armies returned to their estates?"

"The young ones with but small holdings have little to lose and much to gain, if by following you they earn more land. On the other hand, those with large estates gain more by returning home to increase their yields whether in crops or goods produced by their skilled craftsmen."

"Do they fear nothing by displeasing their new mayor of the palace?"

"On the contrary." Chlodomer turned to look Pepin full in the eye. "They wait to see how well you carry out your job. No doubt hoping you will fail, become vulnerable. They wait like vultures, to pick your bones clean and claim leadership for themselves."

Pepin grimaced. "A comforting thought."

Chlodomer winked. "But we will catch them at their own game. You will *not* fail, my friend. And we shall laugh to see them scramble all over themselves, to curry your favor."

The two rode on in companionable silence for some time. The narrow dirt road entered a dense forest of skeletal trees, just beginning to bud. The rest of the army walked behind them, only the creaking of the supply wagon wheels and the jangle of a half dozen horses' bridles reminding Pepin that, for the first time in his life, he was leading an army into battle.

"Remember when first you came to the monastery school at Saint-Denis?" Chlodomer asked.

"As though it were yesterday," Pepin replied. "In a new place, filled with strangers, you offered to share your bench with me, and by that act alone, gained my eternal gratitude. Though I have no idea why you should have done such a thing."

"I sensed a power in you that I wanted to be a part of. At first your red-blond hair and blue eyes, so different from the rest of us, caught my interest. I soon found that you were smarter by far than any of us. You could read and write, not just speak, Greek and Saxon as well as Germanii and Latin. And you understood mathematical equations I never have been able to comprehend."

"That is no credit to me," Pepin protested. "Our tutor, Egar, taught us. Carloman and I just learned what was set in front of us."

"And in the rough and tumble of outdoor contests, you might not have been the fastest, but you *were* the strongest." Chlodomer paused. "But..."

"But what?" Pepin felt a niggling of discomfort.

"All the while you seemed deeply unhappy. Your face held a permanent scowl. You seemed to regard everything, whether scholarship or games, as some sort of competition. Were you sent to Saint-Denis against your will?"

"You are right. I was more than unhappy. I was angry beyond all reason. Though not at coming to Saint-Denis."

Pepin recalled those turbulent years. "I was still a child, though on the verge of becoming a man. A difficult age, no matter what the circumstances."

Chlodomer gave Pepin a knowing look. "True."

"I worshipped my father. The great Charles Martel, though he had yet to win that appellation, could do no wrong. Could prevail over any enemy. He was the center of my universe.

"And then he returned from a lengthy campaign in Bavaria with *her*." Pepin made a face as if to vomit. "Swanahild, as a second wife, and their infant son, Grifo. And my universe was turned upside down."

"Your mother was still alive?" Chlodomer's brown eyes looked pained for his friend.

"Yes. Very much alive. And hurt to the center of her soul by what she saw as her husband's betrayal. I swore I would never forgive my father. Turned my back on him. Tried to make up to my mother for his lack."

Pepin felt, yet again, the anguish he had borne years ago. "No son, certainly not one as young as I, could have brought my mother comfort. Our once loving household became a place of chill silences and hard, properly formal verbal exchanges."

Chlodomer reached across to grasp Pepin's arm in sympathy.

Pepin continued. "So then, my father sent me to Saint-Denis for schooling. I was glad to leave, but felt cowardly for abandoning my mother.

"And I *never* forgave that she-devil, Swanahild, for bewitching my father into marrying her and fathering her children."

Chlodomer looked at Pepin, comprehension lighting his face. "So *that* is what this campaign is all about! You have risked the disaffection of your newly won noblemen to join your brother against *Swanahild* and *Grifo!*"

Pepin gave his friend a half smile. "I have never thought of it in quite that way. But you may be more right than not."

Chapter Six

The next day, Pepin and his brother sat their horses at the head of their armies. Carloman had been none too happy with the few men who had followed Pepin. But Pepin reminded him that the Austrasians had more men than they would have, if no one at all had come with him.

The footsoldiers of Austrasia, Neustria and Burgundy stood in lines, bristling with spears and throwing-axes. Here and there a mounted nobleman or captain sat above the rank and file.

Pepin squinted in the early morning light at highly fortified Laon, situated on its rocky height. "By the light! It looks a beastly place to take by force."

"Are you worried, little brother?"

"Not at the eventual outcome. Surely we have army enough to prevail. But how many men will die in the process?"

Shading his eyes with his hand, Carloman gazed at the walled city. "What think you? Should we siege the city? I doubt they will forsake their safety behind the walls to wage battle here on the flat."

"What would Father have done?" asked Pepin.

"I have no idea. I never could guess why he waged one kind of battle here, and another there," Carloman admitted.

Pepin was taken aback. He had counted on following his older brother's lead.

Pepin swiped sweat from his brow with his sleeve. Thought hard. "A siege would take longer than I suspect my half-hearted troops would stand for. And I doubt even Grifo is crazy enough to move out of his fortification."

He turned and looked at the army waiting for orders. "However..." He tried to shape his errant thoughts into a cohesive plan. "Give the word to remain in battle formation until mid-afternoon. If no one comes down to fight, we shall set up camp to look as though we are settling in for a long siege."

"And then?" asked Carloman.

"Under cover of darkness, we shall climb the mountain. And..."

Late that afternoon, having seen no glimpse of the enemy, the Franks set to work at putting up camp. Tents sprouted. Supplies were taken off wagons and neatly piled. A pen for the leaders' horses grew from cut trees. By the looks of it, the Austrasians and Neustrians planned to stay forever, if necessary.

Campfires blossomed as evening fell. The smell of game birds roasting on spits wafted through the air.

As darkness set in, men rubbed hands and faces with charred wood from the fires. Wearing their darkest clothing, and taking nothing but specially prepared arrows, casting axes, and their hunting knives, the armies of the Franks began their assault on Laon.

Silently, the men walked the steep uphill edge of the dark road. To Pepin, climbing among them, they stood out like beacons in the moonlight. He fervently hoped, if any sentries happened to look out over the wooden palisade, the trees, rocks, and shadows would keep the Franks from being seen.

Exhilaration overcame trepidation as Pepin watched their followers draw closer and closer to the walls of Laon. He held his breath as his foot slipped, sending a cascade of small rocks skittering downhill. Would the sentries hear and know they were there?

Pepin and the others crouched among the boulders and bushes as they spread out to surround the settlement. All seemed quiet within.

Removing the lid of an earthenware pot he carried tied to his belt, he blew carefully on an ember from the campfire until it glowed red-hot. He touched the straw-and-rag-tipped arrow to the ember and blew again, until flame appeared.

He shot the arrow into the air, signaling the others to set their arrows aflame and shoot them over the walls into the huddle of thatched-roofed huts inside.

From their positions surrounding Laon, the Franks shot small comets of fire through the dark night sky. In what seemed a mere heartbeat, the glow of burning roofs lit the entire mountaintop. Sparks shot into the air like a swarm of falling stars in reverse.

As soon as the arrows had taken flight, Pepin, Carloman, and the rest of the soldiers made haste to get as far from the conflagration as possible. Their retreat was followed by the hue and cry of people within.

A shower of rocks catapulted down from the palisade walls. Pepin heard a thud and a cry. Looking over his shoulder, he saw a man had fallen.

"By Mithras!" Pepin exclaimed under his breath. Like a fish swimming upstream, he struggled to climb the mountain through the mass of soldiers hurrying downhill.

Pepin reached the fallen man and felt for signs of life. Although the dark wetness of blood seeped out from under the man's helmet, Pepin felt his chest rising and falling. He was breathing!

Pepin grabbed the man and began to stagger downhill. The swishing sound of a missile shooting through the air was followed immediately by pain as a rock hit Pepin squarely in the back.

Pepin dropped the man, collapsing heavily on top of him. Straining to catch his breath, Pepin groaned. Shaking to clear his head, he began crawling downhill once again, dragging the man behind him. Anything to get out from under the onslaught of hurtling stones.

The Franks took turns keeping watch over their encampment throughout the remainder of the night, tense with the possibility of retaliation by Grifo's followers.

The injured man proved to be one of Pepin's own followers. Watching as the soldier's head was wrapped, Pepin felt his own chest fill with relief that he had been able to save him.

Next, the physician probed the swollen bruise on Pepin's back, causing him to gasp. "I fear the hit has cracked a rib. Just *here*."

Pepin groaned again. "Yes," he agreed through gritted teeth. "Just *there!*"

The next morning, Pepin and Carloman gazed once again at the palace of Laon on its rocky crag. Wisps of smoke from fires set by their flaming arrows climbed straight into the still, crisp air.

Pepin took a deep breath, wincing as he did so. "How many men think you we will lose in fighting this day?"

"Not one, I should guess," responded Carloman. "Look you there!"

Pepin followed his brother's pointing finger and saw the soldiers of Laon walking through the open gate and descending the twisting mountain road. Their hands were empty. No spears. No throwing axes. Even hunting knives had been removed from their sheaths. In place of the war gonfalon of Laon they carried a white banner denoting a lack of allegiance to Grifo, or any man. They had lost all faith in their fifteen-year-old insurrectionist leader.

Swanahild huddled on a bench in the great hall of Laon. Her weeping and wailing grated on Pepin's senses almost as harshly as the smells of the room. He did not mind the acrid scent from a hundred years and more of smoky fires ingrained in the timber walls and ceiling. If only that could have masked the noxious stench of rotten straw covering the earthen floor. Nearly April, and they still had not swept out last winter's threshings! A stable was better tended. In the depths of the straw, Pepin could smell rotted meat and the decomposed bodies of more than one rodent brought in by proud felines.

"Charles! Return from the grave and help me!" wailed the distraught Swanahild.

She turned haunted, red-rimmed eyes to Pepin. "Do not kill me. I beg you."

She held out thin, white arms, fingers grasping the air. "I want to live! How could it have come to this?"

Pepin's temper snapped. "For God's sake, woman. Will you stop that caterwauling? No one is going to kill you. You are hardly worth the effort."

Pepin glared at Grifo who stood, rigid with fright. "Though your son might well be another story."

"My son! My baby! Spare him! I *plead* with you."

Pepin felt the strong urge to strangle. "One more word from you and I will take back what I said and kill you both here and now. With my bare hands!"

Pepin turned to Carloman. "What *shall* we do with the two of them?"

"If you escort Swanahild to the nunnery of Chelles, I shall take care of Grifo, personally."

To his credit, Grifo had disdained to beg or cry for mercy. He stood silent. White-faced. Biting his lips, no doubt to keep them from trembling.

"Think you the city gate of Laon would look the better with his head on a spike for decoration?" Carloman asked. Even Pepin could not tell if he was serious.

Swanahild shrieked and Grifo looked ready to swoon.

"We might well keep him around for entertainment," Carloman continued. "Though we would have to cut out that scheming tongue of his so he could not talk others into joining him in another insurrection."

Pepin joined Carloman in the game. "And cut off his legs, or at least break them to keep him from running off and getting lost."

"I wonder how he would look with his nose cut off that handsome face?" Carloman pondered.

"And what is he? Fifteen or so?" asked Pepin. "Methinks we should cut off his man part quickly before he begets others so treacherous."

At that, Grifo succumbed to the taunting and threw up violently, adding a new stench to the already villainous odors of the hall.

Carloman stroked his chin, pulling the incipient grin downward, then looked at the boy. "For now I shall simply imprison him in Neufchâteau. It is stout enough and more or less on our way to meet the forces he has so thoughtlessly encouraged to mass on our north and eastern borders."

Once Swanahild and Grifo had been securely locked in nunnery and dungeon, Pepin and Carloman rejoined their armies to face the Saxons. Riding shoulder to shoulder with his brother brought Pepin memories of their shared childhood.

He recalled an incident when he had been perhaps six years old. Just beginning to learn to ride a horse. He remembered being frightened at sitting up so high off the ground. Without warning the horse threw itself up on its hind legs. Before Pepin knew what was happening, wham! His back slammed onto the hard-packed earth.

Terrified, all he could do was gasp for breath.

He looked up and saw Carloman, leaning over him. "Don't cry! Be strong, Pepin," Carloman had urged. "If you don't cry, I'll give you one of my wooden soldiers!"

Pepin had no air inside him to cry—or speak. The thought of owning one of Carlo's treasured soldiers surprised him beyond feeling pain.

After their riding lesson, Carloman, as good as his word, silently handed Pepin the much-loved soldier.

Now, looking across at his tall brother, fully-grown and handsome astride his horse, Pepin was suffused with an overwhelming love for Carloman.

Combining their armies and ruling their realms together was the *best* idea Carlo had ever had.

But what of his brother's indecision in forming a battle plan in Laon? Pepin pondered the moment. Perhaps that had been a God-given opportunity for Pepin to prove himself in front of the noblemen and footsoldiers who had followed him. After all, Carloman's armies were already committed, heart and head, to *their* new mayor of the palace.

God-given or another generous gift from his brother? He couldn't ask. Would never know.

Chapter Seven

Autumn found Pepin riding in the midst of a small contingent of soldiers.

Grifo had done him a favor. The thought brought surprise followed by wry amusement. First, the treacherous half-brother gave the Neustrians who followed their new mayor of the palace a chance to see his leadership in battle. Then, because of Grifo's quick surrender, the border tribes called off their campaign, granting Pepin the entire summer to become known to all in his realm—not as Martel's son, but as their mayor of the palace.

The fact that those who followed Pepin to Laon returned singing his praises hurt not at all.

At first Bertrada accompanied Pepin, acting as a bridge between her Austrasian husband and his Neustrian followers. She knew, instinctively, which detail of a nobleman's life would best serve to allow trust and friendship to spring up between them. With quick whispered comments, she steered Pepin past shoals of conflict into quiet harbors of acceptance.

This last journey had been taken without her as the time to deliver her child drew near.

Pepin urged his horse forward, overcome with the need to see how she had fared. The men matched their pace to his. The horses pounded down the dusty road through dense forests, past vineyards heavy with grapes, and along fields where villeins labored to gather the harvest.

Pepin stood just inside the curtain to the chamber he shared with Bertrada. The sight of her—smudges of fatigue beneath her eyes as she gazed in wonder at the babe suckling her breast—brought to mind the timeless image of the blessed Madonna.

As she looked up, her face broke into a radiant smile. "My love! You have returned. Come. Meet your son."

In a thrice, Pepin was kneeling at the bedside. The baby, sated, slept, his eyelashes resting on rosy cheeks. With trepidation, Pepin touched the downy head. The infant stirred. His tiny hand sought Pepin's great, callused finger.

"For such small fingers, he holds me with uncommon strength."

"He must recognize his father." Bertrada smiled. "I put off naming him until you arrived, though I assume, as your son, he will be called Pepin."

Pride burst within the vicinity of Pepin's heart. Tearing his gaze from his son he said, "No. Let us call him Charles, as the first male child born after Martel's death."

"A worthy name for our first born son." Bertrada kissed the downy head. "Charles he shall be."

As she took Pepin's hand into her own, Bertrada's nose wrinkled. "You smell of dust, sweat and horses."

In his rush to see them, Pepin had thrown the reins to a servant and dashed to the chamber without so much as pausing at the water trough to rinse the dust of the road from his face and hair.

He smiled his apology. "And you, my love, smell of the sweetness of mother's milk. No rose is more fragrant."

Later that night, Pepin and Bertrada shared a tankard of rich red wine while propped against the bolsters of their bed. The heavy hangings had been removed at the start of summer, and the lighter ones tied back to the bedposts. A shaft of clear white moonlight streamed through the wind opening, illuminating their chamber.

"Remember you, when first we met?" Pepin queried.

"Every detail." Bertrada took a sip, and then handed the cup to Pepin. "You have no idea the excitement that raced through the estate when word reached us that the famed Charles Martel and his sons were coming to visit."

"Why so?"

"Every spring father rode off with his army, to fight with the great Charles Martel. At the end of each campaign he returned, and for the entire winter all we heard was, 'Charles said' thus and so, or 'Martel and I' fought this way or that. My father's greatest satisfaction came from the trust your father placed in him.

"That he would come and bring his family made the visit a personal friendship, not just a duty call."

Pepin swallowed a mouthful of wine. "My father *did* respect yours. Depended on him in battle. Was grateful to him for his unconditional support in the early years."

"If only you could have seen the preparations," Bertrada continued. "I had never experienced such a dither. The majordomo gave orders as though for a battle. Pages ran hither, thither and yon, bearing platters, fetching supplies. Of course, the hall was swept clean and new rushes laid. Wall hangings were taken out and the dust beaten from them.

"Workmen set up every trestle table they could find. The majordomo, himself, carried in the salt cellar and set it to mark the line between where nobility would sit and those whose place was below the salt."

Pepin, picturing the chaos, chuckled in delight.

"And then, trumpets and drums announced your arrival!" Bertrada paused, remembering.

"The great Charles Martel, flanked by a son on either side, headed the entourage. We knew your mother had passed away, just over a year before."

Pepin sighed at the memory.

Bertrada took his hand in hers. "Her death seemed a connecting link between us, as my own mother had also died, just as I was on the brink of womanhood."

Placing the tankard on the floor, Pepin gathered Bertrada into his arms.

Bertrada snuggled into his embrace. "Although my mother had been an invalid for some time before her final release, I could at least talk to her. Ask her questions. And then, with the biggest decision of my life facing me, I found myself with no one in whom to confide."

"Decision? What decision?"

"Which of you to choose, of course. Or, I suppose, whether to agree to marry either one of you."

Pepin heard the smile in her voice. "Your father gave you such latitude?"

"Yes. Though I knew what the alliance between our families meant to him. And that a better choice would never again be found."

"And you chose me?" Wonder that such could be true, filled Pepin. "But Carlo is so much..." Pepin shook his head in bewilderment, "better in every way. More skilled. Handsomer. Loved and respected by the men."

"He is pleasing to the sight," Bertrada agreed. "But, remember, I sat between the two of you during the banquet. When the musicians arrived, we danced. I had opportunity to experience being with each of you.

"And while Carloman did and said all that could be expected of him, his response *to me* seemed pallid. Disinterested. In contrast, *you* sought out my views on subjects not usually broached with females."

Bertrada kissed his lips and Pepin tasted wine and a hint of spices.

"You were far more your father's son," she said, "and from that evening onward, my one and only choice."

A year passed like the flash of a falling star—there one moment, gone the next.

Now, whenever Pepin returned from his travels, two-year-old Rothaide ran to hug his knees. Squealed in delight as he tossed her into the air. Demanded to ride on his shoulders from chamber to hall. Even baby Charles grinned and giggled, his fat cheeks rosy, when papa tickled him.

But, following this last meeting with his brother, Pepin had dismissed his noblemen and their armies to go to their homes for the winter. Surrounded by none but his mounted personal guard, Pepin galloped toward the villa, his fury growing with each pounding beat of the horse's hooves.

Worst of all, he could talk to no one but Bertrada about the situation. Only she would understand.

He rushed to Bertrada to give vent to his frustration.

He paused at the entrance to their chamber. She rested, nestled in the pillows of the bed. Yet another babe, a girl this time, named Giséle, suckled at her breast. Pepin marveled at the magic of a new life, whole, perfect in every tiny detail.

Bertrada appeared as capable of producing a child every year as the fields and vineyards were of crops. And with nearly as little fuss.

She raised her eyes to meet his. "Well come home. How went your gathering with Carloman?"

Bile surged in Pepin's gorge. He strode to Bertrada's bedside. "He wants a king!"

Pepin glanced around to make sure they were alone and prudently lowered his voice. "Not *me*. Not even himself. A *Merovingian* king!"

"A *Merovingian* king? Are there any of that ancient royal family of the Franks left?"

"Carloman has found a royal relative, son of Chilperic II, in heaven knows what obscure monastery. And my brother wants to give *him* the crown, naming him Childeric II."

"But why?" Bertrada pushed her hair off of her forehead.

"I asked the same question." Pepin paced the small chamber. "Carloman said it would quiet those noblemen who resent us. Some, not just our Neustrians, but Carloman's Austrasian followers as well, regard us as upstarts. In reality no better than glorified servants to a non-existent king."

"Noblemen like Villicus," commented Bertrada.

The image of the Neustrian filled Pepin's mind's eye. Tall, olive complexioned, with short-cropped dark hair and a beak of a nose, Villicus had opposed him from the start. "Exactly!" Pepin rolled his eyes.

"And then there are those," he continued, "who see the Merovingian royalty as some sort of good luck token. 'As long as a Merovingian sits the throne, the Franks shall prevail.' Jupiter's balls! What a pile of rot!"

Bertrada lay the sleeping babe between two pillows and pushed herself up straighter against the headboard. "As mayors of the palace, you and Carloman have done well between you."

Pepin smiled. "We *did* take the palace of Loches from Duke Hunald of Aquitaine, did we not?"

Bertrada nodded. "And you both, along with Bishop Boniface, called the church synod. If it were not for you, the church would never have granted a portion of its wealth to finance the expense of your wars."

Pepin eyed her thoughtfully. In return he and Carloman had promised not to interfere with the church's right to weed out the illiterate, militaristic bishops Charles Martel had appointed. "Boniface *was* pleased with the resulting ecclesiastical reforms."

Bertrada looked at Pepin, clearly puzzled. "What more could a *king* do?"

Pepin struck fist into palm. "All thanks to Carloman, we are about to find out!"

On the day of the coronation, a ground-hugging, bone-chilling mist caused the trees beyond the meadow to fade like ghosts into gray nothingness. Standing with Carloman outside Childeric's tent, Pepin hunched his shoulders against the penetrating cold, their breath puffs of cloud.

As Pepin understood the process, the candidate was to be presented to the assembled noblemen and bishops at the annual *Champs de Mars.* They would ratify the choice. Why should they not? He was a Merovingian.

Pepin recalled once again their dying father's last words, telling of Egar's prophecy that one of their family would be king. At that time Carloman had asked what part they should play and Charles had said they were to gather the power that the great king would need. To Pepin's mind, Carloman was giving *away* that power!

The noblemen and bishops sat on benches around trestle tables pushed together in the center of the meadow. Their captains stood behind. Foot soldiers and priests massed beyond them, the outermost indistinct in the chill mist. All waited, murmuring quietly, for the royal claimant to make his appearance.

The tent flap rustled. Childeric II stepped out. Some four or five years younger than Pepin's twenty-eight, Childeric seemed not just slight in build, but 'inconsequential' came to mind.

Childeric smiled uncertainly. He grasped each of them briefly by the forearm, then turning to face the assembly, sighed, and squared his shoulders.

Pepin and Carloman escorted Childeric across the uneven ground. Pepin felt his thick boots sink into the churned mud. He dared not look down, but kept his eyes forward, his face a mask. Slowly the three of them approached the wooden throne at one end of the tables. Since being selected by Carloman as the next king of all Franks, Childeric had let his flaxen hair grow. Already it brushed his tunic collar, nearly touching his shoulders.

Pepin wondered idly, how *he* might look with long hair, symbol of Frankish royalty. Would he ever know? He glanced at his brother. Both of them wore their hair as was the custom—close cropped on top and shaved in back.

Childeric sat gingerly on the edge of the chair of authority. His pale blue eyes searched the crowd, seeking a friendly face. His long-fingered hands twisted in his lap.

Pepin's stomach churned. Once they gave the crown to a Merovingian, he and Carloman might as well proclaim to one and all that none of their own line was fit to wear it.

The weight of the prophecy bore heavily on him. He wished he could talk to Egar. Find out more about the magician's vision.

The quest to become the king of all Franks burned like a glowing coal in Pepin's gut. He felt the prophecy once again piercing his heart like a well-aimed lance. Nothing short of leading the Franks in battle with the crown on his head would satisfy his longing—to own the near mystical power of king in combination with the military power of mayor of the palace.

The crowd grew still, all eyes on Childeric.

Carloman cleared his throat and raised his hand. "Since the death of Theodoric, the throne has remained empty. My brother and I, mayors of the palace, choose Childeric, son of Chilperic II, to be king of all Franks. How say you to this?"

"I say 'yea' and well done!" exclaimed a nobleman. He struck the handle of his hunting knife on the wooden table.

"Childeric II, King of All Franks," cried another adding his knife handle to the pounding.

Soon all the men seated at the table were banging their knives in assent. A crown was handed to Carloman. He placed it on Childeric's head.

"Show us our king!" a captain's voice rang out.

Four soldiers brought forth Childeric's battle shield. Willing hands lifted the king from his throne to sit on the shield. Childeric smiled uncertainly as he hung on with both hands, his knuckles showing white.

The soldiers roared their approval as the king was carried ceremoniously around the table, held aloft on his shield. The din of banging hunting knives grew deafening.

Pepin wanted to shout for silence and cover his ears against the noise.

As Childeric was returned to his throne, the ear-shattering banging ceased.

With almost superstitious zeal common men and nobles alike slapped each other's backs.

"Now we have a Merovingian king on the throne, all will be well with us."

"Merovingians keep us strong."

"Merovingians succeeded where Rome failed. Who can overcome us now?"

Carloman turned to Pepin. Under cover of the cacophony, his voice was quiet. "I know you do not approve this move, but we shall still rule. We are mayors of the palace. We still dispense justice, decide on war, and live in the royal palaces. There is nothing left for the king but to be content with his name and his flowing hair. To sit on his throne and play the ruler."

Pepin felt his face crack like a mask as he forced it into a smile.

Carloman grasped Pepin's arm. "Good. You smile. Remember, the Merovingian has nothing left he can call his own, except a single small estate. It will bring him but scant income. And we shall still make all the decisions."

Pepin pressed his temple where an ache had begun. True, the king had little to his name. *Nothing but the love of the people who would never accept one of our family as king.*

When Childeric was once again seated on his throne, the nobles lined up behind Carloman and Pepin to kneel in the mud at the king's feet and pledge fealty to the new monarch.

At the conclusion of his coronation, the crowds cheered as King Childeric II climbed into his small wooden ox-cart. With a cry and a crack of the whip, the ploughman who served as driver started the two oxen moving.

"Many a peasant travels as well as *this* king," Pepin muttered to no one in particular.

But, even so, how could either he or Carloman convince the populace to place the royal crown on the head of a descendent of Pepin de Vain? How could anyone possibly replace those who traced their line to Meroveus—according to song and legend, son of a sea beast, a mighty serpent?

Chapter Eight

During the first years of Childeric II's reign, Carloman and Pepin invaded Saxony two years in a row. During the third year of Childeric's reign, Waifar took over the rule of Aquitaine from his father.

That year, Bertrada had another son. Pepin and the children went in to see the new arrival as soon as they were allowed. Four-year-old Rothaide immediately climbed up on the bed where Bertrada gently placed the baby in his big sister's lap. She sat absolutely still, a look of delighted wonder on her face.

Charles at three was far more interested in playing on the floor with his carved wooden horse. Meanwhile Pepin sat at the foot of the bed, holding two-year-old Giséle and doing his best to distract and keep her from scrambling over to touch the baby.

When Bertrada asked Pepin with what name this newest arrival should be christened, he responded, "Let us call him Carloman. That should please my elder brother."

"And remind him that since he is not married and has no children of his own, you, not he, has sired his namesake?"

A wave of irritation washed over Pepin, that she could so easily guess his innermost thoughts. But when she looked up, her brown eyes were filled with smiling love.

Pepin was at once disarmed. She knew him well —indeed, far *too* well—and loved him in spite of it.

She kissed the downy head. "Carloman he shall be."

In the fourth year of Childeric's reign, 746 AD, occurred an act so inglorious, so unforgivable, it changed forever the lives of both Carloman and Pepin.

Pepin first heard wild fragments of rumors as he returned with his personal guard from south of the Loire River. Although not pushing into Aquitaine, he felt it necessary to frequently inspect and bolster the Frankish holdings along that vulnerable border.

Spending the night in an estate between the Loire and the Seine, Pepin's host asked if he had heard.

"Heard what?" asked Pepin.

"About the battle in Swabia."

"What battle? Between whom?"

"Why, your brother and the Swabians, of course. Though I have heard conflicting reports as to the outcome." Anastasius looked pleased to be the first to impart such potentially calamitous news to his mayor of the palace.

As Pepin traveled toward Quierzy-sur-Oise he heard more bits and pieces.

"A slaughter..."

"Treachery..."

"The Swabians..."

"The Austrasians..."

When finally he arrived at home, Bertrada gave him what information she had been able to gather. Indeed the battle had been between the Swabians and Carloman's Austrasians. The Austrasians had won. And the victory was decisive.

She, too, had heard word of treachery, but did not know to whom to ascribe the foul deed. The pagan Swabians were held in such low esteem as to make treachery on their part fully believable.

Pepin decided to take his personal guard and leave immediately for Austrasia. Until he met with his brother, he could not credit anything he heard.

"Mea culpa! Mea maxima culpa!"

Pepin watched his older brother in astonished fascination. Carloman, always slender, was thin to the point of emaciation. His red-rimmed eyes had a disturbingly haunted quality.

Unsettling too, Pepin thought, to find Carloman here, in the bedchamber of the estate their mother had inherited from her uncle, Dodo, rather than the royal palace in nearby Metz.

In the dim light from the narrow wind openings, Pepin glanced at the well-remembered chamber where both he and Carloman had been born. The large bed dominated the small room.

Did his normally competent older brother seek to escape his demons by returning to the womb? Strange thought.

"Tell me again." Having heard a brief account of the story, Pepin was more perplexed than he had been before. "Start from the beginning. How did this *happen?*"

Carloman sighed. Made a visible effort to gather the details in his mind. "My major domo in the palace at Metz came to me and announced that a Swabian had arrived from the east."

"And this Swabian came alone?" Pepin could hardly believe it. Frisia, Saxony, Thuringia, Alemannia, Bavaria, and Swabia—all bordered Austrasia. Among them, one or another was always challenging Frankish right to rule. Constant vigilance on his part was the price Carloman paid to maintain control of the subjugated lands. But that a single representative would come alone to Austrasia was most unusual.

"Yes." Carloman was adamant on that point. "And in such weather! I remember looking out of the wind opening at the rain falling so heavily it obliterated all sight of even the nearest trees. I asked the major domo to see that the man was given dry clothing before being escorted to my chamber."

Carloman shook his head in misapprehension. "Following Father into battle was bliss. Fighting shoulder to shoulder with you, my brother, fills me with exhilaration. But to face such an unusual confrontation with no one to suggest a plan, left me feeling unnerved and inadequate."

Pepin shook his head. "I do not understand. But, never mind. Continue."

"His name was Recared. He was a nobleman. I recall that Recared was shorter than I by half a head or so. He had a broadly muscular body, and his round face and wide nose spoke of eastern tribal strains. Long dark hair, brown eyes and a swarthy complexion made him look even more foreign." Carloman shuddered at the memory.

"Recared knelt, extending his hands, palms together, in acknowledgment of my superiority. 'My Lord Carloman,' he said, 'I bring word of treachery planned against you.'

"I took Recared's hands between my own. Felt the cold fingers tremble. 'Recared of Swabia, sit you here—' I indicated the bench beside my table. '—and tell what you know.'

"Recared told me that Theobald, leader of the Swabians, although pledged in subservience to me, wanted to gain freedom for Swabia."

"By the light, the man would have been mad to try!" Pepin was as much puzzled as outraged. "Unless he joined forces with his neighboring realms, he could not hope to prevail against the might of your Austrasians."

"Theobald was not going to join forces," Carloman explained. "Nor did he plan to engage us in a fair fight. According to Recared, he was going to do it by subterfuge and cunning.

"I thought Theobald planned an ambush, but Recared said, 'I think, something even more sinister.'

"At that moment I had the uncomfortable feeling of an icy hand gripping my gut. 'But what?' I asked."

Carloman turned to Pepin. "If only you had been there to help me sort out the facts!"

Pepin shook his head in disbelief.

"Recared said he knew not what Theobald planned to do. 'Because I opposed,' he said, 'I am no longer privy to their planning. But I doubt not the result will be death to you and to the best of your army.'

"I tried to discern the Swabian's motives, but Recared's dark eyes gave no insight into his thoughts or feelings."

Carloman ran his fingers through his short-cropped hair. Unable to remain still, he strode to the bed and back. "I remember the rain continued to drum upon the earth. A gust of wind blew a curtain of water through the wind opening as I was looking out. It sprayed me with shocking cold."

He turned to Pepin. "By the bull! Why was I left to make the decision all by myself?"

Pepin shrugged. "Go on. Please."

"I asked what advice Recared had for me. 'No advice,' he said. 'Only to warn you to be aware. Should Theobald gather his army, let yourself not be caught with too few men. Turn the tables on him, if you can. Kill him first. By treachery, if need be.' And then Recared left."

"Surely he ate," Pepin said. "And stayed the night."

"Nay. He traded his tired horse for a fresh one, his sopping clothes for the dry ones we had given him, and a cold meal to take on his way."

"And what did you make of his strange tale?" asked Pepin.

"I had no idea what to make of it. All I could remember is what he said. *Turn the tables on him, if you can. Kill him first. By treachery, if need be."*

Shaking his head, Pepin sat on a bench by the table. "So you took your army into Swabia, planning on killing Theobald by treachery."

Carloman wrung his hands. "Only to preclude his doing the same to me."

"And tell me again, just how you accomplished this brave deed." How could his much loved and admired older brother have *done* such a thing?

"When we were in Swabia, I sent for my messenger. I told him, 'Go you to Theobald. Tell him he cannot prevail against the army of the Franks. He is to come, with his own army, here, to our camp to discuss terms of peace.'

"I agonized over what to do next. What if Theobald refused? I knew I would have to order my army to attack."

He looked at Pepin as if beseeching him to understand. "If only this were a normal battle, with lines drawn clearly on an open field. But I had no idea what treachery Theobald would use to kill me—and my men."

Carloman paused. "Just thinking about this makes my stomach churn! If I had waited, I might have found out—to my sorrow."

He ran his fingers through his hair. "If Theobald complied, could the Swabian not still plan deception? Place part of his army around the perimeter of the camp, the rest with him inside to parlay peace? In the still of night

Theobald's men could attack by stealth, slitting throats until I and all my men were dead."

Carloman shivered. "I do not fear death in battle. But to die at the hands of an *assassin!*

"The messenger returned. 'Theobald and his army come, my lord. They follow more slowly. Two days time at the most.'

"I was in a fever of indecision. But by the time Theobald and his men were sighted by the lookouts, I had, in desperation, made up my mind.

"A weak sun filtered through high thin clouds, illuminating the meadow where my army had set up our tents. By contrast, it made the surrounding forest appear even darker. I thought the enemy might be lurking in the shadows there. But, I knew that I had three men to every one of Theobald's who walked into our camp.

"The Swabian army laid their weapons on the ground. My men quickly surrounded them. At a signal, we grabbed each of the Swabian soldiers.

"Disadvantaged, the Swabians struggled with all their strength. Shouts rang out. Arms and legs thrashed. The skirmish ended when we took out leather straps. Soon the Swabians lay on the ground, firmly bound and gagged."

"What meant you by this?" demanded Pepin. "They came at your bidding. Peaceably laid down their arms—"

"They planned treachery!" cried Carloman. "But I would not give them the chance. I killed him first!

"With one swipe of my hunting knife, I slit Theobald's throat. His body jerked. His eyes were wide in shock. I was drenched in spurting blood. The captain holding Theobald for me was covered in its warm, sticky red flow. The entire deed took no longer than does a single *Pater Noster.*"

Pepin stood and faced Carloman. "I still do not understand why you killed Theobald in such a way."

"He would have killed me and my men if I had not!" Carloman protested.

"You *believe* this?"

"Yes." Carloman held out a hand as if beseeching Pepin to understand. "If I did not, I should go mad!"

"Why accept Recared's word?"

"Why should I not? What reason might he have to lie?"

"Reasons enough come to mind." Pepin tried to make order of his tumbled thoughts. "Perhaps he wanted Theobald out of the way so *he* could become leader of the Swabians. You fell for the plan and did the awful deed. Meanwhile Recared kept his own hands well out of it."

Pepin saw the plan so clearly, he wondered that Carloman had not thought of it, even as Recared had spoken. "By having Theobald become a martyr felled by a Frank, the Swabians will rally to him against all of us."

Carloman groaned, his look anguished.

Although Carloman had put them all at risk by his foolhardy deed, Pepin realized he must do nothing to further undermine his brother's fragile state of mind.

He strode across the room to clap a hand on his brother's shoulder. "What is done is done. Our best course is to continue as though your action was of no importance. We will gather our soldiers and reinforce our borders with the other tribes—Saxony or Alemannia. Perhaps Bavaria. It never hurts to make our presence known."

Carloman gave Pepin a sad smile as he shook his head. Regaining his composure, he walked to the wind opening and stood tall, his shoulders once more square and strong. Taking a deep breath, he turned to face Pepin. "I want no campaign this year. Give me this season for preparation. Show me your love and support, as I know you will."

Carloman's voice gained strength as he spoke. "I grow weary with fighting and the weight of leadership. I will retire from the world and live a monastic life."

Pepin could not believe his ears. "That seems a drastic solution to a problem that is temporary at best."

"A solution, not to *this* problem, but for the remainder of my life."

"A monk." The word felt strange on Pepin's tongue. He struggled to picture his brother in the somber robe of a penitent and could not. "Why?"

"I have sinned against the Lord," said Carloman. "I offer Him my life in exchange. If I serve Him, He will give me peace."

"But you were born to fight for the Franks, to be a leader of Gaul. Is that not also serving God?"

"*You* were born to fight and lead men, as was our father. I have never been comfortable in that role."

Pepin stared at a brother so changed, it was as though he had never seen him before. "What do you mean? You were always better than I in every contest. Strong in battle. Loved by the men who followed you."

"I am strong when I serve under someone else. I was confident only so long as I could be a captain in father's army, or go into battle shoulder to shoulder with *you*. But not when I have to make decisions alone—with no one to help me make sense of the situation."

"Have you sought counsel about your desire for the priesthood?"

Carloman crossed the room in three strides, a look of incredulity once again distorting his face. "Of course not! And neither will you!"

Pepin strove to make his own face reassuring, his voice placating. "I meant nothing by the question. I only thought asking someone else's view might help you make sense of your fear and remorse."

"A mayor of the palace cannot expect men to follow him if they think he doubts himself."

"I agree. I thought of someone who is not a soldier. Someone such as Archbishop Boniface. He is wise. And he has faced the pagan tribes, baptizing them for Christ. He would understand your apprehension."

Carloman paused, considering the idea, then shook his head. "Boniface is wise beyond anyone I know. But even *he* cannot fathom what is in my heart."

"He could ask questions to help *you* understand what lies there."

"No!"

"But why a monk? A hermit shut away from the entire world. Why not a priest, dedicating your life to God as part *of* the world?

Carloman turned his back on his brother. "No more! I will not discuss the matter further."

Pepin was surprised to feel tears gather and his throat tighten. *I am losing my brother. Carloman will be as gone from my life as if he had died.*

Chapter Nine

Pepin did, indeed, spend the better part of the following year with Carloman. Bertrada and their large brood of children settled into the estate near Metz. Meanwhile, Pepin and Carloman took long walks in the forest nearby.

"You seemed always underfoot," Carloman reminisced.

"I wanted nothing more than to be just like you," replied Pepin. "In every way."

"But you are nothing like me!" Carloman exclaimed. "You have a dogged perseverance that I will never have. Do you remember when we were in soldiers' training? I must have been ten or so and you perhaps seven."

"And you won every footrace, even against the older boys!" Pepin smiled and shook his head with admiration.

"But you," Carloman interrupted, "were determined to hit the tree trunk we used as a target with your ax, even if it killed you."

"And it nearly did!" Pepin laughed.

"I recall you stayed after everyone else had left. You started at a point close to the tree and threw the ax until you hit it three or four times in a row. Then you took a few paces back and started all over again, throwing from there."

"My arm felt as though it might fall off by the time I quit each evening."

"But soon, you were hitting the target nearly every time. You were far better than I. By far the best in the group!"

"Ah Carlo, you could have bested me, had you tried."

"But I had not your determination." Carloman shrugged. "I did *not* try."

"You were good at everything, even without trying."

"Things came easily enough," Carloman admitted. "As long as a skill was within my grasp, I never saw the need to strive for perfection. For you, perfection was the *only* acceptable goal. It still is."

Pepin looked at Carloman as if he had never seen him before. What did his brother mean? Did not *everyone* want to do his best? The fact that perfection was not attainable made it no less worthy a goal.

The succeeding year, Pepin and Carloman made the long journey to Rome. For the last time, the brothers rode shoulder to shoulder at the head of their armies. Oxen pulled wagons loaded with gifts Pepin had gathered to honor Carloman, and to pay for his pilgrimage and entrance into the religious life.

In talking with Carloman, Pepin had come to understand that his brother's blood no longer sang as he led his soldiers. Instead, he said he felt the gentle patience a father feels for a child who plays at grown-up games. "A king's crown or not," Carloman had said, "another tribe to pay homage, an estate pledging a share of its wealth—what would any of it matter?"

Unable to understand, Pepin welcomed the physical exertion of crossing the high mountains separating Gaul from Italy. Leading his horse as he climbed the steep path—his breath, chilled by the crisp cold air from the snow-covered peaks—helped him forget that at the end of the journey, he would part with Carloman. Perhaps forever.

As they descended onto the lower plains of Italy, his brother commented, "The sun's rays feel like a benediction."

Pepin stared at the alien, gently rolling landscape stretching out in shades of gold. Here and there, contrasting green fingers of Cyprus trees pierced the air. Look as hard as he could, he could not find one familiar dense forest of oak and towering pine.

As they approached Rome, Carloman pointed to a limestone ridge just below the summit of Mount Soratte. "I shall build a monastery in honor of St. Sylvester just over there. In a strange way, I feel as if I am returning home."

The basilica in Rome was filled to overflowing. It seemed everyone wanted to witness the ordination of the popular Frankish mayor of the palace, eldest son of the famed Charles Martel.

Pepin watched as Carloman followed Pope Zachary and the acolytes swinging censors up the long aisle of the nave. As Carloman passed, men reached out to touch his arm. Smiled their blessing. Made the sign of the cross.

Pepin merely watched without moving. He and Carloman had already said all there was to say.

At the foot of the altar, Carloman knelt before the pope. Zachary asked a blessing then began shaving the top of Carloman's head, leaving only a short fringe around the edges. Something, perhaps the feel of the cold, sharp blade on his head, must have startled Carloman. He flinched involuntarily, causing Zachary to nick his scalp. The small wound bled copiously and Carloman's face flamed.

As acolytes stanched the flow with cloths, Pepin was momentarily embarrassed for Carloman. But then the thought occurred to him that Carloman was not the first to bleed for his faith. Nor would he be the last.

Zachary and the acolytes led Carloman behind a screen in the sanctuary. There, Pepin understood, helping hands would strip him of his soft woolen mantle, fringed yellow tunic, linen breeches, and bright red stockings laced with bands of blue.

Pepin imagined what was happening. Carloman had told him that he would be wearing a hair shirt. It would prick his skin, stinging and uncomfortable. The pain would be bearable. But to wear it with humility, to let no one guess its constant irritation—*that* was the challenge. Pepin could only assume he wore it as penance for his sin in killing Theobald.

Carloman emerged, wearing a coarse linen robe, his bare feet shod in leather sandals.

Earlier, while the two of them walked in the quiet courtyard of the Roman basilica, Carloman had told Pepin he planned to pray from Psalm Fifty-one when he took the oath to become a monk.

"David, who wrote the Psalms and was the greatest of Israel's kings, sinned as grievously as did I," Carloman had said. "Remember you the story of David and Bathsheba?"

Pepin replied, "I remember she was married to one of his soldiers when they fell in love. But I do not recall the details of the story."

Carloman stopped walking. "David and Bathsheba slept together and she became pregnant. Meanwhile David's army, including Bathsheba's unsuspecting husband, Uriah, was out fighting the Ammonites.

"David sent for Uriah. His plan was to allow Uriah to sleep with Bathsheba so that no one would know he was actually the father of her baby. Uriah came, but refused to sleep in a bed with Bathsheba while his friends in the army were sleeping in open fields, far from home. Exasperated, David sent Uriah back to the battle along with a note to the commander to put Uriah in the front ranks where he would be killed."

Pepin struck his forehead with his palm. "I had forgotten David arranged for Bathsheba's husband to be *killed*!"

Carloman nodded. "Uriah was killed in battle. Bathsheba moved into David's house, became his wife and bore him a son. But David had committed an unforgivable sin."

Carloman looked at Pepin. "As a result of that terrible act, David wrote Psalm Fifty-one. If the Lord could forgive David *his* iniquities, perhaps He will forgive me mine."

Now Carloman knelt in front of the altar once more, and prayed from David's Psalm.

"Have mercy upon me, O God, according to thy loving kindness: according unto the multitude of thy tender mercies blot out my transgressions.

"For I acknowledge my transgressions: and my sin is ever before me."

As the choir of brothers sang the chants of Pope Gregory, Carloman lay, face down, arms outspread on the hard-packed dirt of the aisle.

Ah brother, Pepin thought, does the sharp sting of your hair shirt press into your chest? Do you smell the acrid scent of trodden ground? How could *you,* the once powerful mayor of the palace, have come to this?

Kneeling once again, Carloman prayed, "Purge me with hyssop, and I shall be clean. Create in me a clean heart, O God; and renew a right spirit within me."

Finally, Carloman rose, his face glowing. His smile seemed to encompass the entire universe. "Open thou my lips; and my mouth shall show forth thy praise."

"Amen" and "Hallelujah!" flowed from the choir.

Chapter Ten

Riding home from Rome, Pepin found himself short-tempered for no apparent reason.

Chlodomer rode beside him and innocently commented, "The religious service for Carloman was far more impressive than I had anticipated."

"It was disgusting!" Pepin exclaimed. "Seeing his head being shaved, made me almost physically ill."

He felt a stab of remorse at Chlodomer's shocked look of bewilderment, but was helpless to stop his outburst.

Chlodomer rode away, shaking his head.

A moment later, Pepin kicked his horse to follow his friend. "I meant not what I said," he apologized. "I have no reason to be angry with you."

Chlodomer slapped him on the back and smiled. "Methinks you are angry at Carloman, and are taking the force of it out on everyone else."

"Why would Carloman *do* such a thing?"

"The killing of Theobald, or becoming a monk?"

Pepin sighed. "Both. How could he have so thoroughly destroyed his life?"

Chlodomer shrugged. "It was *his* life. To destroy, or not."

The comment again enraged Pepin. He rode away before he said something else hateful to his best friend.

Thoughts of Carloman's denial of what his life could have been, all their father had expected, ate into Pepin. He chewed, like a dog on a bone, all the arguments he should have voiced the previous year. His anger grew with every step he took on that long return journey over the Alps.

He felt no pleasure in arriving in Dijon. Here he met Bertrada and their entourage to winter in Burgundy. But the end of travel brought with it no easing of tension.

He brushed away Bertrada's solicitousness. He found her expressions of love and gladness annoying. He could have kicked himself at the sudden look of hurt he saw well up in her eyes.

He hung his head. Sighed.

Even the children's exuberant shouts of joy made his temple throb.

"Shhh." Bertrada, gathering five-year-old Rothaide, four-year-old Charles, and three-year-old Giséle to herself like a mother hen gathering her brood. "Your father is tired from his long journey. Give him some peace."

That evening she brought him a steaming tankard of tea. "Drink this," she urged. "Saint John's Wort to ease anxiety. Valerian to help you sleep."

Pepin did as she asked, but to no avail. Wide-awake, he paced the gallery overlooking the great hall of Dijon. People slept on the floor below, inanimate lumps wrapped in their blankets. Tired guards watched him and yawned, barely able to keep their eyes open.

Pepin pulled his fur cape more tightly around him. In the fire pit below, the gigantic log smoldered, glowing red and sending a thin spiral of smoke toward the ceiling. Pepin felt none of its heat.

He rubbed his temple where the ache continued unabated. What was happening to him? He normally worked hard, played hard and slept more soundly than that great log below. Now he was too exhausted to work, too short-tempered to play, and yet could not still his body to remain the night in bed.

Ever since... Pepin forced his mind away from the sore subject. Refused to examine it too closely.

With a sigh, he turned and continued walking.

A few days later, the majordomo, almost cringing, quietly announced the arrival of Archbishop Boniface and his entourage.

Pepin managed not to snarl at the servant, and arranged his face in what he hoped was a pleasant expression.

"Father! Well come. You and those who travel with you."

"Pepin, my son." Boniface took Pepin's hand in his. Looked into his eyes as if to see into the depths of his soul.

Pepin broke eye contact, inexplicably uncomfortable with such scrutiny. "What brings you so far from home?"

"We travel from my archbishopric in Mainz to winter and see old friends in the cathedral of Saint Martin in Tours. As Dijon is on our way, with your permission, I look forward to spending a few days resting here. I am most anxious to hear an account of your brother's consecration in Rome."

Though Pepin's heart fell at the thought of talking about Carloman's becoming a monk, he managed to say, "Rest. Stay as long as you like. We shall visit. And Bertrada likes nothing better than a reason for a banquet."

In truth, he did felt his spirits begin to rise. As Egar the Magician had taught his brother and him languages, mathematics, history, and astronomy, Boniface had tutored them in theology and the tenants of the church when they were but youths. The archbishop had been one of his favorite people, ever since.

Late afternoon found Pepin and Bertrada on their high-backed chairs on the raised dais. Boniface sat in a place of honor next to Pepin.

Pepin pressed his temple with his fingers where the throbbing had returned. So far, nothing in Bertrada's pharmacopoeia had eased the ache for long, nor allowed him to sleep.

Pepin looked around. Servants stood behind the diners, holding torches to banish the winter darkness. The adults and older children sat on benches along several trestle tables while the younger children, most of them Pepin's, rolled and tussled with each other and a litter of puppies on the straw-covered floor. Five-year-old Rothaide wandered from the melee to sit on Bertrada's lap and nibble from the trencher she shared with Pepin.

Four-year-old Charles was in the thick of things with three-year-old Giséle doing her best to keep up on her short, fat legs. The baby, Carloman, sat on his nursemaid's lap, energetically banging the table with a wooden spoon. He would soon be on the floor with the puppies.

After eight or nine courses, Pepin had long since lost count, came the *piece de résistance*—an immense pie, so large as to require four grown men to carry it. In the middle, three plucked partridges, large and fat, glowed golden and crisp. Around them, six fat quail, surrounded by twelve skylarks, all added their rich juices to the culinary creation. The entire dish was garnished with thrushes and other small birds, all baked to a turn. Bacon cut into pieces the size of dominoes and sour grapes completed the bountiful dish, all cradled within an egg-rich crust.

Pepin, who usually relished his share of the dozen or so courses that made up a ceremonial meal, paused as his stomach clenched in a painful cramp.

Following crabapples, puddings with sweet sauce, and fruit pies topped with honey and spices, the pages offered pitchers of water, basins, and napkins so the diners could wash their sticky fingers.

* * *

Late that night, Pepin sat at a small table in his chamber, staring into the flame dancing in the brazier. Save for the guards stationed outside the doors, Pepin thought himself the only one in the entire compound still awake.

"Tell me, pray, what brings you such suffering?"

Pepin looked past the brightness of the flame. The rest of the room remained cloaked in darkness. But across the table from him stood Archbishop Boniface, dressed in the simple garb of a priest.

"Boniface?"

"What is it that bothers you? "

"What makes you..." Pepin began.

"Feel you have a problem? I am a priest." His voice resonated with compassion. "You ate but a bite or two of the sumptuous feast. You look as though you have not slept for a fortnight. Your temper is short. Your awareness of what is going on around you nonexistent."

Although the words sounded stern, Pepin saw mercy in Boniface's eyes.

"I would ease the burden you carry, if I can. Often sharing your concerns with another lightens the load." The priest smiled. "We call it confession."

Pepin shook his head and returned the smile in spite of himself. "You have named my symptoms, one by one. But I know not the cause." He began to look into his own heart, but shied away from what he might find there.

"How long have you felt this way?"

"Ever since... since Carloman took his vows."

The words, once out, had the effect of breaking a dam. Pepin was helpless to stop the flood that followed.

"Carloman killed the Swabian, Theobald. Killed him by treachery and deceit. I have no idea why he would do such a thing. It was so unlike him. He could easily have vanquished Theobald in open warfare as befits a Frank."

"You were not there."

Pepin put his head in his hands. "Had I been, none of this would have happened. But I was not." He sighed. "And then Carloman took vows. Became a monk. Withdrew from life. As good as died to me."

Boniface's voice expressed puzzlement. "You feel you are responsible—because you were not with Carloman?"

"Yes."

"But how can you bear the blame for Carloman's actions? Only *he* can answer for what he did. And, he is making restitution to God in his own way."

Pepin could only shake his head. A lump as large and loathsome as a rat lodged in his throat.

"Why do you feel *you* must answer for *his* deed?"

A heavy silence filled the alcove. It pressed on Pepin until he felt crushed by its weight. "Because I *prayed* to be rid of him!" He shuddered. "I did not want him dead, mind you. I love Carloman. But his becoming a monk seems to be a direct answer to my prayer. How can I *not* be held accountable for that?

Watch what you say, Pepin told himself. *Even though Boniface is a priest and cannot repeat what he hears in confession, he must not learn of the prophecy—and that I covet the crown.*

The archbishop broke the ensuing silence. "Carloman, as mayor of Austrasia and Burgundy, conflicted with your ambition to be mayor for all Franks, not just those in Neustria. Is that at least part of the problem?"

Pepin's head snapped up. "How do you...?"

"Know about ambition?" Boniface smiled, looking wise. "One does not become an archbishop without ambition. My life has been one of conflict, trying to know which of my desires are selfishly my own, and which are of God, given to me to carry out in His name."

"I never thought of you as anything other than a man of God. A priest. An archbishop. Serving the church without conflict or doubt."

Pepin looked at Boniface in an entirely new way. In the flickering light of the brazier, he saw a wrinkled face. Gray hair circling a bald head. "What were you before? How did you learn God's plan for your life?"

"You have heard of my youth?"

"Only that you came from Greater Britain across the Narrow Sea."

Boniface smiled and nodded. "Named Winfrith, I was born among the gently rolling green hills of a place called Devon. But even then, God called me. I felt myself pulled by His gentle but unrelenting hand. Running wild among the sheep, I would be startled to find myself kneeling, overcome by wonder at the beauty surrounding me. On saint's days, in a small stone chapel in the village, the priest read stories from the Bible."

Boniface laid a hand on Pepin's arm. "The same stories I read to you and your brother when you were young."

Pepin smiled at the recollection. He felt himself beginning to relax, enjoying hearing this beloved churchman tell of his childhood. Felt accepted by Boniface as a friend. Not merely a student or a supplicant at confession.

Boniface continued. "I longed with all my heart, to be as gentle yet strong in faith as Saint Peter. As Jesus.

"A small Anglo-Saxon monastery near my home allowed me to perform tasks—watch the sheep, gather wood. In exchange the monks taught me to read the Bible. At a time in life when my friends were mating and carving out sharecropped lands for themselves, I became a monk in the same monastery. Living a life separate from the world. Much as your brother, Carloman, has chosen."

"I cannot believe you—you of all people—were a monk. A hermit! And yet, you became an archbishop." Hope for Carloman niggled at Pepin's heart.

The archbishop smiled and continued, "At thirty, I was ordained a priest and left the monastery to minister to others. The King of Wesses, himself, appointed me envoy to the Archbishop of Canterbury. My career within the church seemed assured. From monk, to priest, to bishop, if all went well. Perhaps, at some point, even Archbishop of Canterbury! So you see, I do know about ambition."

Amazed, Pepin realized he could talk to Boniface, man to man, not just as a priest. "But how did you end up here?"

"At forty, I felt a call to change, and left what others saw as a promising career to become a missionary here, among the heathens across the Narrow Sea. Most Franks were already Christian. But Frisians, Saxons, and Thuringians—pagan tribes all—surrounded you here.

"After a while, the pope summoned me to Rome. There I received the name Boniface, and earned the title, Apostle to the Germanii. Your father was mayor of the palace when I returned here to my missionary duties."

Pepin stirred. "I cannot imagine leaving a position of prestige and power to sail off into the unknown. To arrive in a foreign country and minister to strangers."

"Those years—spent spreading the Good News to the heathens, destroying idols, baptizing pagans by the thousands, organizing the church in Bavaria, founding monasteries—were the *best* of my entire life."

The two men sat, the silence broken only by the sputtering of the flame and creaking of the wooden walls.

Finally Pepin stirred. "But God called you at an early age. And while you began as a monk, you became a priest and are now archbishop. How can your experience be compared to Carloman's? Martel's son. My brother. After a cowardly, treacherous act, he has turned in service to God as a monk, not because he was called, but out of penance.

"How can I not feel that Carlo's actions were in direct response to my prayers?" Pepin cradled his head in his arms. "I *asked* God to eliminate my brother from conflict with my ambition for sole leadership over the Franks."

Pepin paused. Sighed. "And He did."

"I cannot begin to speak for God." Boniface placed his hand on Pepin's arm. "But you might consider the possibility that Carloman was *always* called by God. But because he was Martel's son—and your brother—he felt compelled to deny his desire to serve God, and follow the life of warrior-leader expected of him. Perhaps, God *allowed* Carloman to commit this act of *cowardly treachery,* as you call it, to break that bond. To free him to follow his heart. To become a monk."

Pepin raised his head to look at Boniface. Could it be true? He began to pace the small chamber. Such an idea would *never* have occurred to him. Yet the plausibility of it was staggering.

"And," continued the archbishop, "perhaps God allowed Carloman's actions to compel your attention. As a warning."

Pepin stopped in mid-stride. Ice cold sweat broke out. Smothered by fear of God's warning, he could hardly breathe.

"Never underestimate the power of prayer. And *never,* my friend, try to diminish God to your own, human understanding. Have a care. The answer to your prayers may come in ways you never thought nor intended. But they *will* come in ways intended by God.

"You are now Mayor of the Palace for All Franks, and your brother is a monk. You are two entirely different men. That does not make either of you any more nor less precious in God's eyes."

Boniface stood next to Pepin, his hand on Pepin's shoulder. "Most men pray to bend God's will to their desires.

Better far, to pray for the insight to bend your own will to *God's* desires.

"Pray that God will bless this opportunity for leadership. But know that to place yourself in a position of power over men, is to put yourself at risk. Risk of envy. Of challenge.

"Pray that your call is truly from God—and not just your own ambitions."

With a new view of his life and the mandate of the prophecy, Pepin bowed his head. If the crown was *God's* will for him, he would face those dangers. If not, well, he would face that eventuality instead. With God's help.

Pepin fell to his knees at the archbishop's feet, placing his hands between those of Boniface.

Chapter Eleven

As mayor of the palace for *all* Franks, Pepin's domain now extended to Austrasia and Burgundy as well as Neustria. While the weather remained favorable, he and his men were constantly on the move from one area to another, making their presence known, solving problems, assessing men now sworn to follow him instead of his brother.

On this day, Pepin rode with his entourage, north and east from Soissons, into the Ardennes Mountains. The summer sun beat down on him, sweat making mud of the dust kicked up by horses' hooves. He brought the wineskin to his dry lips. Diluted sour wine slaked his thirst and felt wonderfully cool sliding down his parched throat.

The band, a half dozen on horseback and perhaps three times that on foot, proceeded without talking, each man lost in his own thoughts. They had first seen the distant walls and tower keep of Neufchâteau perched on a ridge of the foothills some while ago. The sun gradually started to slip from its noon height, the flat plains dropped away behind them and yet, the huddle of buildings surrounding the wooden great hall grew no nearer.

Pepin swiped at the sweat running down his face. How he missed Carloman, he thought for perhaps the thousandth time. His brother's absence felt like the gaping hole left by a missing tooth—far greater than the size of the tooth should warrant.

Pepin had written to Carloman. Notes telling of family occurrences. Reports on areas of the kingdom needing attention and what he had done about them. Of course writing was not the same as riding side by side, sharing the same experiences, but it was better than nothing.

Carloman never wrote back.

Carloman, do you think of me? Miss me?

Thanks to Boniface's comforting words, Pepin no longer felt responsible for Carloman's rash act and the penance that followed it. Pepin remembered the archbishop's comment that God answered prayers in ways the supplicant never wished for nor intended. Since that night, Pepin had been far more careful in what he prayed for. Tried to keep in mind to ask God for the wisdom to pray for that which *He* found worthy.

At last the group began climbing the foothills. The path grew steeper and rockier. The horses snorted and huffed with effort. Shadows of pine trees created welcome bands of shade across the path. Neufchâteau momentarily dropped out of sight behind a shoulder of the hill.

Chlodomer rode up to take a place next to Pepin. "What will you do about your brother?"

Pepin looked into the questioning brown eyes of his closest friend.

"What *should* I do?" Pepin asked.

Carloman was gone; he was far beyond Pepin's ability to *do* anything, either to or for him. Indeed, word had it his brother had already found his private monastery at Mount Soratte too popular with sightseers. People came from near and far to gape at the celebrated former Frankish mayor of the palace. They waited for him to leave the hut in which he lived alone—to cultivate his field, chop wood for the fire, draw water from the spring. Once outside, perfect strangers bombarded him with questions.

Some even had the temerity to knock on his door when he was inside meditating and praying. They somehow felt it was their right to begin meaningless conversations with him!

Pepin received word the past spring that Carloman had given up and gone to the Benedictine foundation at Monte Cassino. There he traded his austere garb for the dark habit of a Benedictine monk.

"What do you mean, 'do about my brother'?"

"He has been prisoner here for what, four, five years now? Are you going to leave him to rot or what?"

"God's death! *Grifo!* I forgot all about him!"

Strange, he never thought of Grifo as 'brother', though he was. A half brother at least.

Carloman had imprisoned Grifo at Neufchâteau following his abortive attempt to divide and conquer them early on. When they were first mayors of the palace for Neustria and Austrasia. Pepin had not given his half brother a thought since.

"I have no idea." Pepin laughed and shrugged. "What would you do if you were me?"

"I am not sure. What he attempted was treasonous, though thanks be to God, he did not succeed." Chlodomer rode in silence, looking to be in serious thought. "However, he *is* Martel's son. I would not want him for an enemy."

"Spoken like a true Neustrian!" Pepin held up his hand in mock surrender. "Tell me what I already know and give no hint of a solution."

Chlodomer grasped Pepin's hand briefly. "I cannot tell you what to do. Only think on it."

The road curved and Neufchâteau was suddenly before them. Small orchards and fields were planted in wheat with thatch-roofed hovels scattered higgledy-piggledy about. Vegetable gardens and chicken coops, pig sties and cesspits.

As Pepin and his men rode by, little boys ran to the side of the track to stare open-mouthed. As they crossed a bridge over the stream, a young girl handed Pepin a daisy plucked from the meadow, then turned shyly away.

"Many thanks to you, my lady," Pepin said, taking the proffered flower.

"She brings to mind my Rothaide," he commented to Chlodomer. "Looks to be about the same age."

The great stone grinding wheels of the mill made such a thundering racket, all conversation had, perforce, to stop.

Further up the hill, the party at last entered through the open gate and into the palace bailey.

Guards and pages took their horses and unloaded saddlebags. Delicious odors of roasting meats and baking breads assailed Pepin as they walked past the kitchen buildings to the great hall. They reminded him how long it had been since they broke their fast at daybreak.

"Well come, Pepin," said the majordomo of Neufchâteau. "What brings the mayor of the palace to our corner of Frankish Gaul? Came you to check up on your half brother?"

"That—though he can wait until the morrow—and to see that all is well. How fare you?"

"Well. Very well, m'lord. You arrive in time for the main meal of the day. Think you and your men can manage to eat sommat?" The majordomo's eyes twinkled.

"An entire animal fresh off the roasting spit and several loaves of bread each, I would warrant!"

Early the next morning, Pepin climbed the slight rise to the keep. The large, round tower, position of last defense, was built of stone with a wooden structure on top. Outside stairs led to an easily defended door. A platform offered a position from which defenders could cast stones on the enemy below.

As son of the great Martel, Grifo was imprisoned in a room in the wooden section on top, rather than the stone dungeon below.

At the foot of the stairs Pepin paused and looked up. From this angle the keep towered into a cerulean sky. What *was* he going to do about Grifo? As someone who led an intended invasion, he deserved death. But as Martel's son, killing him would serve only to make him a martyr and a focus for further treachery. Should he ever be allowed to go free? "Over my dead body!" Pepin muttered.

The guard outside Grifo's chamber saluted Pepin.

The cubicle inside was nearly dark. Little of the summer sun filtered in through the narrow slit opening. Pepin heard a rustle but could barely make out the figure as Grifo rose from the stool in the corner.

Coming together, Pepin was shocked. He had expected the same defiant, cocky youngster he had last seen at Laon. Grifo had aged far more than the six years that had passed since then. At twenty-one, he was thin and haggard. His unkempt hair lay greasy and lank on a head that looked too large for the rest of his body. Grifo's cheeks were sunken beneath a scraggly beard. Haunted eyes peered out from darkened sockets.

"My lord, Pepin!" The greeting carried Grifo's unwanted edge of sarcasm. "To what do I owe the pleasure?"

Pepin acknowledged his half brother with a curt nod of the head.

"Do I take it your visit portends some change in my condition?"

"It might," Pepin conceded. But what?

They stared at each other, eyes locked in combat. Grifo broke contact first. Pepin felt a glow of victory. Yes!

"We might begin by reviewing the options," Pepin ventured. "What do you see they are?"

"I can remain here or go free."

Pepin considered. "Oh, I think there are a few more. You could remain here, in this cubicle, until you die of old age."

Pepin walked over to the narrow slit. From it he could see but a sliver of the bailey, dry and dusty in the sunlight. No movement, no person, no sprig of greenery. "Or you could be moved to the dungeon below. Enclosed in the total darkness of cold, damp rock, you would die of old age much sooner."

Pepin sauntered back to look Grifo in the eyes. "Of course, I have every right, as mayor of the palace, to sentence you to death for treason. Death quickly. Or slowly. One piece at a time."

The quick intake of breath he heard filled Pepin with pleasure. He caught a flash of fear in Grifo's eyes before they turned blank.

By Mithras! Pepin thought. The boy has already died. The antagonism of his greeting was but habit. He has no fight left in him.

"I could let you go. Free. Disinherited. Banished.

"Or... free with estates to call your own. Income from their products. Villeins to work for you. Soldiers to follow you. Recognition as a nobleman. Charles Martel's son."

Grifo's head snapped up, his eyes wide in wonder. In their depths, wariness. A search for the trap.

Pepin was as amazed at the words he had just heard come from his mouth as was Grifo. By Mithras! What could I be thinking?

"You would do that? Give me my freedom and return of my estates?" Doubt edged with a thin line of hope filled Grifo's voice.

"I have no idea." Pepin heard the astonishment in his own voice. "I suppose it depends on you." He could not imagine allowing his upstart, hated, treacherous half brother to walk free. Nay rewarded with return of his own estates.

Pepin glared at Grifo. "I could as easily have you killed."

Grifo's chin lifted. "But you will not," the voice soft.

"What makes you so sure?"

"I have been here six years. Were you going to kill me, I would be dead long since."

Pepin pondered the truth of Grifo's words. He actually had but two choices. Walk away and let him rot or free him and give him a nobleman's title and estates. If he but banished Grifo he would have let loose a dangerous enemy on his borders. Many would follow Martel's son for their own gain.

He found himself once more looking out the narrow slit at the empty patch of dirt. He had no memory of walking from the center of the chamber. Could he as mindlessly walk away from Grifo?

Pepin turned. "Pledge me your service and I will release you from here. You may return to your own estates."

Grifo went at once to his knees before Pepin. He held up his hands, palms together in supplication. Pepin placed his own hands over his brother's as Grifo said the time-honored words, "I pledge..."

Pepin helped Grifo to his feet. "Go home." He could not bring himself to call the young man 'brother'.

Grifo gripped Pepin's shoulder for a moment, then turned and walked out the door.

Pepin stood at the top of the stairs and watched Grifo stride towards the great hall. Would he live to regret this decision, or would it put right a strained relationship?

Chapter Twelve

Chlodomer's parting words to Pepin as they returned from Carloman's former domain were, "Forget you not to come in a fortnight's time to help celebrate my wedding."

Pepin laughed. "How could I? You have talked of little else this entire campaign!"

"You will bring Bertrada and the children? Your Charles and Adele's son, Justin, are of an age to be friends."

"Worry not. I shall bring both Charles and Rothaide to liven up the festivities." Pepin slapped his good friend on the back. "Just be sure you change not your mind and decide to send Adele and her boy packing!"

"No chance of that!" Chlodomer's laughter joined that of his friend Pepin's.

Pepin and Bertrada, along with six-year-old Rothaide and Charles, five, traveled on horseback to Chlodomer's estate near Sels. Bertrada had the baby, Adélaide, bundled in a quilt that wound around them both. The two females appeared perfectly content as the babe suckled. Once sated, the gate of the placid horse rocked her to sleep.

Only four-year-old Giséle and Carloman, two, had been left at home in Quierzy-sur-Oise, where the entire staff would care for and spoil them. The travelers would be gone but a month at most.

The party traveled on horseback with servants leading pack animals loaded with supplies.

Pepin breathed deeply in contentment as he looked over their group. Beside him, Bertrada tilted her face to the gentle sunlight. Falling oak leaves carpeted the path, muffling the sounds of horse and mule hooves. The Oise River burbled along beside them. The honking of a flock of geese flying south in a "V" formation drew his attention.

"I am pleased that Chlodomer is marrying again," Bertrada said. "But tell me, why have we never stopped at his estate before? Sels is not so far from Quierzy-sur-Oise."

"For many years, Chlodomer's estate has been a sad place. He wanted not for friends to see it so."

Pepin paused, musing. "Not since the Battle of Poitiers, when we were but seventeen and nineteen, have I seen him so happy as he is now."

"Tell me," Bertrada encouraged.

"Where to start?" Pepin pondered, then began. "Chlodomer's father, Amalaric, was one of the first Neustrian noblemen to pledge his army to follow Martel's. I know he and my father became friends. Amalaric was a good soldier, his followers well trained and equipped. But..."

Bertrada looked at him quizzically. "But?"

"He was, at best, an indifferent householder. He cared nothing for nurturing the land that grew their food. Nor, it seems, for his family. Chlodomer's mother was aware that her husband slept with any winsome lass that would have him. And many would." Pepin shook his head.

"Until he became a soldier himself, Chlodomer saw little of his father."

Pepin turned in his saddle to check on the rest of their group. He heard childish voices as Rothaide and Charles visited, each sharing a horse with a servant.

"Chlodomer and I saw little of each other during the long journey leading up to the Battle of Poitiers. But I know that he gloried in being a member of his father's army. Of earning Amalaric's praise and attention.

"When we met the Muslims, the fighting went on for seven long days. During the last day's horrific battle, Amalaric was slain. And with his father's death, Chlodomer's fragile world shattered."

Bertrada reached out to take Pepin's hand. They rode for some time that way in silence.

At last Pepin roused himself. "Chlodomer told me, when he returned home with the news of his father's death, his mother took to her chamber, shrieking and tearing her hair. She refused food. Would talk to no one.

"His mother had, up to that time, been a beautiful woman, but inconsistent."

"How so?" asked Bertrada.

"For a while she would pay attention to the servants, get everyone on the estate working well together, then she seemingly lost interest. She would spend endless hours with her chambermaid, trying on clothes, having her hair combed. Meanwhile all work in the house ground to a stop. Chlodomer and his younger sister were left to take care of themselves. Even food preparation became haphazard.

"Fortunately, their majordomo managed to keep the villeins working in the fields, but even that was not as productive as it should have been."

"It surprises me Chlodomer remains so cheerful, after the childhood he suffered," murmured Bertrada.

""With Amalaric's death, things became even worse. His mother was so bad, he had no option but to commit her to a convent for safekeeping. His sister became a nun there as well. Chlodomer, perforce, pledged the convent a larger share of his treasure and output of his fields and craftsmen than he could afford, to support the two of them."

The Oise River joined the Seine at that point and the party turned east toward Paris. As mayor of the palace, Pepin and Bertrada often stayed in the royal palace on Paris' Île de la Cité. Nevertheless, Pepin found the clamor and bustle of the city overwhelming.

The children had never seen Paris before and nearly fell off their horses as they twisted and turned, trying to see everything at once.

After one night at the palace, Pepin was happy to leave the city as they continued southeast along the Seine.

"Yesterday you started telling me Chlodomer's story," Bertrada prompted. "What happened after his mother and sister went to the convent?"

"His estate was falling into disrepair when Chlodomer met and married Kriemhild. She, the daughter of a wealthy nobleman, brought a dowry that promised to save his holdings. Rumor has it, Kriemhild's family is directly descended from King Chilperic I and Queen Fredegund. Though I do not know that to be a *fact.*

"All was well for a while. But then Kriemhild died in childbirth, and the babe with her."

"How awful for Chlodomer!" Bertrada's look of compassion tore at Pepin's heart.

"The next I saw of him, he brought his soldiers to pledge their fealty to me when I became mayor of the palace. We resumed our friendship as though the years since the Battle of Poitiers had never interrupted.

"Fortunately, our campaigns have been successful and Chlodomer has shared in the bounty. His estate is once more on firm footing."

"And his betrothed, Adele?" asked Bertrada.

"From what Chlodomer tells me, she is a young widow. Her husband, an innkeeper and brewer in Sels, drowned in a boating accident on the nearby Yonne River some two years past. She has a five-year-old son by him, named Justin. Chlodomer is most anxious for Charles and her son to become friends."

Bertrada smiled and nodded.

* * *

Paris being the last town before Sels, the party made camp for the night along the Seine. The next day they followed the Yonne River where it branched off from the Seine and arrived by mid-afternoon at Chlodomer's estate.

Dogs barked. Horses neighed. Servants shouted. Pepin's children called out and ran around, getting in everyone's way. Through it all, Chlodomer stood, a foolish grin across his face, obviously happy they had come.

By the time the wedding day dawned, Bertrada had, without seeming to take control, turned the chaotic household into one of quiet efficiency.

Pepin accompanied Chlodomer, his friends, soldiers, and villeins to the Church of Saint Étienne in Sels for the wedding ceremony. Bertrada promised them all a wedding feast on their return.

When the wedding party—Chlodomer and Adele sharing a ribbon-bedecked horse, her son Justin riding with Pepin next to them, and their guests—arrived back at the estate, the mingled odors of roasting meat and freshly baked breads made their mouths water.

Servants had set up trestle tables in the flower-strewn meadow just outside the bailey. Pages turned spits upon which whole pigs and a deer roasted over red, glowing coals. Serving tables groaned under their load of fruits and vegetables, breads, pies and puddings.

Pepin could not remember when he had enjoyed a meal more. He rejoiced for Chlodomer and his pretty, plump bride, her soft brown hair adorned with flowers.

Young Charles and Justin ran from one table to another. Everyone handed them morsels of food, and soon their smiling faces were as grubby as their hands and knees.

The sound of pipes, drums, and a tambourine made Pepin's feet tap. As the dancers began moving to an open space, he asked Bertrada, "My lovely lady wife, would you honor me with a dance?"

"You are kind, sir. But I fear I have forgotten the steps. And I never was the most graceful of ladies—" she smiled, "—what with my big feet and all."

Pepin laughed. "You will know the steps far better than I. And you will never be anything but the most graceful of damsels to me."

He held out his hand, and she took it. Like young newlyweds, Pepin and Bertrada ran to their place in line for the dance. With the music to guide them, they dipped and bowed, swung and circled, changing partners again and again until ending up together at the end.

Flushed and laughing, Pepin brought a tankard of new wine to where Bertrada had collapsed on a bench. The cooling wine tasted both sweet and tart as he swallowed.

"Tell me, my sweet," he asked, "remember you when last we danced and laughed?"

"On our own wedding day?" she guessed.

"Mayhap you are right. And Rothaide is six years of age. Where did the time go? And why have we not laughed more —and danced?"

Bertrada fanned her crimson cheeks and took another sip of wine. "Your father died. You were made mayor of the palace. You had more important things to do."

"Mea culpa." Pepin admitted. "But *nothing* should be more important than enjoying each other, good food, wine and ale, laughing and dancing. Let us not forget to have fun along the way."

"Well said, my lord!" answered Bertrada, sealing their promise with a kiss.

Chapter Thirteen

Pepin decided to winter in Austrasia. Shaking his head, he remembered his encounters with Grifo.

His half-brother had no sooner pledged his fealty to Pepin than he fled, not to his own estates, but to Saxony. There he sought support against the very man to whom he had just sworn loyalty.

Immediately after Chlodomer's wedding, Pepin was forced to again gather his army and march eastward through Thuringia and into Saxony. At the sight of Pepin's army Grifo's supporters made a treaty, pledging their subservience to Pepin.

He knew their promises would last only until they felt stronger against the Franks. And wherever dissension was ripe to foment, Grifo would be there.

Nevertheless, for now they would spend winter in the estate near Metz that his mother had inherited from her uncle Dodo.

* * *

Midwinter came and went, as did Christmas and Pepin's thirty-third birthday. In spite of his pledge to enjoy laughter made at Chlodomer's wedding, the ensuing dark, humdrum days brought overwhelming restlessness. The great hall smelled much as any other great hall would at that time of year—vile. Pepin felt he had been cooped up since the beginning of time.

Girding himself in an additional, thick vest and his heaviest winter cloak of deep forest green, he let himself out of the door of the hall. Cold air assaulted his face, immediately banishing his lethargy. The empty bailey slumbered, a snowy scene in shades of grays and blacks.

Beyond the palisade, the forest beckoned. Without thought, Pepin waved to the guards, walked through the gate, and entered the trees.

He stood for a moment savoring the clean scent of pine trees and snow. Nothing stirred. He heard no sound, save a brook nearby, dancing and chuckling over stones on its way to meet the Moselle River.

Someone had recently come this way. Enjoying the unaccustomed solitude, Pepin followed the footprints in the snow as they led deeper into the thickening forest.

A scream broke his reverie.

Struggling through the drifts, Pepin ran toward the source of the sound. Fortunately for him, the footprints had packed the snow somewhat.

Another scream. Then a woman's high keening wail.

Cold air stabbed Pepin's throat and chest. Panting, he wished for longer legs.

Crashing through the trees he found himself at the edge of a small spring-fed lake. In a glance Pepin took in the scene. A woman, a villein from the estate, had been gathering deadwood for her fire. A pile of branches lay in a pile at her feet. She stood; her entire attention fixed on the middle of the lake where someone had broken through the cold gray surface of the ice.

"Oh, master!" she beseeched Pepin, "My son. Save him. I *implore* you!"

Pepin stripped off his cloak and thick vest. Struggled as he pulled off his heavy boots. Without a second thought or backward glance, he ran in stockinged feet into the marshy area surrounding the lake.

A black open space loomed near the center of the lake. Slipping and sliding across the ice toward the jagged edge, Pepin's weight caused another chunk of ice to break off. Shocking cold took his breath away. Dark water closed over his head.

Where was the boy? He could see nothing in the murky water. Frantically, he kicked and pushed his hands this way and that. Hoping against hope, to feel a solid body.

Nothing.

He came to the surface. Gulped in cold air. Went down a second time.

There! Something brushed against his leg. Reaching down he grabbed a handful of hair.

Pepin was almost out of breath. Lethargy from the cold sapped his strength. Kicking, he pulled the boy by his hair.

An explosion of blinding red flashed inside his eyelids. Was he dying?

He could not! He had too much to do. Too much to live for. His future as king, God willing. The boy's future as well.

Angry now, Pepin kicked harder. Battled the freezing cold and air-robbing water as though bludgeoning an enemy. Every stroke an enormous effort.

At last his head broke the surface. As he gasped, cold air seared his starved lungs, producing an agony of pain. He pulled the boy above water.

As though from a great distance, the mother's voice cried, *"You found him!* Is he alive?"

Disoriented, vision blurred, Pepin wondered if he had the strength to push his way through the thin ice. Could he do that *and* drag the boy with him? He had no choice. He *must.*

Turning toward the sound of the mother's voice he called out, "Put the longest branch you have, across the ice toward me."

Shuddering with cold, Pepin thrashed his way toward the branch the boy's mother had pushed out on the ice. "Hold fast to your end. Let not that I pull you, and it, out to the thin ice."

The woman grabbed the branch. Hanging on desperately, she dug her boots into the mud. Pepin took hold of the other end. Panting, he heaved himself out of the water, dragging the boy behind him.

The ice cracked.

Hurry! Hurry!

He pulled harder. Scrambled one leg, then the other up onto the fragile rim of ice.

Coughing water, he closed his eyes. Concentrated. Moved forward. Clutching the lifesaving branch, he crossed an endless stretch of ice. Towed the child.

Forward.

His body cried out for him to stop. Rest.

No! He could not.

Forward.

Pepin felt the woman grab his hand. Somehow he had made it to shore. *God be praised!*

Teeth chattering, Pepin hauled the boy, who looked to be three or four, off the ice. Held him upside down by his ankles. Water poured out of the lad's mouth.

Laying him on the snow, Pepin breathed into his mouth. Rolled him over. Thumped his back. Rolled him over. Breathed into his mouth again. More water rushed out from the blue lips. The boy coughed.

"Sweet cherubim!" Tears streaming down her face, his mother took the sodden boy to her breast.

"Wrap him in my vest. Hold him inside your cloak."

Pepin wrapped his own cloak over his dripping clothes. Taking off his wet socks, he shoved his bare feet into cold, stiff boots.

Grabbing the boy from his mother's arms he put him inside his cloak and—knees shaking—staggered toward the great hall. "Hurry! We both need dry clothing. A warm fire. A hot draught."

* * *

Bertrada stood, hands on hips, eyes snapping. "*Whatever* were you *thinking?*"

Pepin lay in bed under a mountain of quilts, a warm stone at his feet, sipping hot spiced wine.

Meanwhile the lad, Euric, was himself bundled in quilts, on a pallet near the log that burned in the center of the great hall. As the early winter dusk crept over the land, Euric had the warmest spot in the entire estate.

His mother sat watching him. Tenderly she brushed a lock of hair from his forehead. Once he had opened his eyes. Called her 'mama'. Said he was sorry for scampering away. He slept, eyelashes brushing once blue-white cheeks now turning rosy.

Unlike her two other babes who had died too soon, it seemed Euric had the will to live.

"Sweet Saint Ethelburga! What *were* you thinking?" Bertrada, upstairs in their chamber, demanded again.

Pepin thought back to the moment when he had plunged out of the forest onto the lakeshore. "I thought it could have been one of *our* children in the icy lake. That it could have been you, crying on the shore, begging me to help."

Bertrada's face softened into a gentle smile. Slowly, she shook her head. Sank to her knees, resting her hand on his chest. "You could have died."

Pepin felt once again, the shocking cold. The black water closing over his head. "Yes... I could."

Sleep, induced by warmth, his earlier exertions, and the wine, lured him. Thank heaven, this time he could surrender without danger.

"Would that have been such a bad thing?" he mumbled. "To die, saving the life of a child?"

As spring neared, Pepin pondered which of the recalcitrant border tribes to invade, and with that decision, where to hold the *Champs de Mars*. He sat in the chair of authority in the same great hall his father had come to as a boy in service to Dodo. His closest advisors occupied benches at the trestle tables.

"With the Saxons convinced of our superiority, think you it safe to turn our attention to the south?"

"Aye," several said at once.

"We have naught to fear from the Saxons for a while yet," agreed a nobleman.

"Confront Duke Waifar of Aquitaine," added another.

"By Mithras! He grows too cocksure of himself. Claiming lands in his name alone!"

The others tapped knife handles on the table in a gesture of agreement.

Pepin nodded. "We will call the *Champs de Mars* to meet in Tours on the first day of spring. From there it is an easy march to Aquitaine. Agreed?"

"Agreed!"

Knife handles hit the table with more resonance!

* * *

Less than a fortnight later, one of Pepin's most trusted messengers brought word of Grifo's latest skullduggery.

Forced yet again, to change his plans, Pepin gathered the local noblemen in the great hall.

"Go you to all my noblemen in Neustria, Austrasia and Burgundy," he ordered the assembled messengers. "Tell them to bring their armies. We meet in Strasbourg, not Tours. We fight this season in Bavaria."

"Bavaria?" questioned his noblemen. "Why not Aquitaine, as planned?"

"That whelp of a Saxon princess in Bavaria!" Pepin paced the great hall, kicking the winter's crushed and soiled straw covering the dirt floor.

"My sweet, young half sister, Chiltrudis, is a widow." Pepin made no effort to keep the sarcasm from his voice. "She rules Bavaria as regent to her son, Tassilo, who is but a small child."

"Surely, Aquitaine under Waifar poses greater threat than Bavaria under Chiltrudis." The Bishop of Metz expressed what all were thinking.

They agreed with "ayes" and knife tapping.

"If it were only that, we would now be preparing to march to Aquitaine." Pepin felt his anger rising. He turned his back on the assembly, fighting for control.

"God's death!" he swore, turning back. "My lying, scheming half brother has run roughshod over his sister and claimed rule of the duchy. The Bavarian chieftains support Grifo. Sudiger has brought his Swabians as allies. Even Lantfrid, Duke of Alemannia, is on his side.

"By the bull! When I get my hands on him...." Pepin felt his face heat and knew it was dark red. "His head will yet decorate a pike on the city gate!"

"Hear! Hear!" A deafening banging of knife handles on tables filled the hall.

Chapter Fourteen

Pepin's army, made up of noblemen and their soldiers from throughout the entire Frankish realm, crossed the Rhine at Strasbourg and marched, unopposed, eastward through Swabia. Contingents had reluctantly joined them from Frisia, Saxony and Thuringia. Every man of them knew their lives were pledged to guarantee no attack would come to Pepin from those quarters. Two noblemen and their armies had even come from faraway Aquitaine, as a guarantee of peace along Francia's southern border. Pepin was not alone in hoping their lives would not be forfeit.

The giant army crossed the Danube and turned southward toward Bavaria. For days they walked, following a tributary of the great river, across flat plains and through thick forests.

Ahead, the tributary split into two streams. Augsburg stood in the center of the Y, the snow-capped Bavarian Alps showing jagged in the distance against the pale spring sky. Crossing the stream, Pepin noted the huge grinding stones were still, silent—not in itself unusual for early spring. But his curiosity was piqued when he saw no one fishing. The nearby forest loomed dark and still. No sound of men chopping fallen trees into lengths for the fire. Nothing but the gentle chuckling of the brook. Where *was* everyone?

The army walked onward toward Augsburg, their footsteps muffled on the dusty lane. In the apple orchard, a gentle breeze loosened petals from the blossom-laden branches. They fell quietly to earth like warm, sweet-scented snow. Here the droning of bees nearly drowned out the birds, chirping as they carried bits of twigs to their nests in the branches.

Pepin's curiosity turned to apprehension as they marched past empty fields. How was it that no one tilled the moist black earth for planting? The ominous silence weighed heavily on his ears.

Pepin signaled his army to halt. Rank by rank the men stopped walking. Looked about. Anxiety filled their eyes. The horses snorted, then began munching at tender grasses growing along the track. Oxen, pulling the supply wagons, stood like inanimate objects in the middle of the lane.

"Pass the word along," Pepin called. "I know not where the people of Augsburg might have gathered. We may be walking into a trap. Have your axes in your best hand, ready for defense." Enemies rightly feared the fast-flying casting axes, which the Franks threw with deadly accuracy. "Loosen your lances. We may yet be called upon to fight!"

"Axes and lances—we be ready to fight the Bavarians!" cried a captain near the front of the army.

"Axes and lances for Pepin!" answered the soldiers.

"Victory to the Franks!"

Warily the army moved, horses' hooves and shuffling feet echoing in the empty town. No inhabitants walked the lanes. Nor weeded vegetable gardens. Nor brought water from the stream. No little boys ran to stare, mouths agape, at the mighty Frankish army.

Pepin turned and addressed his followers. "All must have heard of our coming. I wager those who are able have left in search of Grifo's aid."

"Good riddance!" came the response.

Little remained of the original Roman colony founded by Augustus, successor to Julius Caesar. To Pepin it looked a typically Frankish hamlet of thatch-roofed huts surrounding a large wooden building. Only the church was built of stone and had a protective wall surrounding its outbuildings.

Pepin sent a priest accompanying his army to the church to see who might have sought its shelter. The priest returned confirming Pepin's assumptions. The only remaining inhabitants of Augsburg were the elderly and the sick. And one old priest. All else had gone to find Grifo.

Pepin claimed the great hall, musty with lack of use. Neither Chiltrudis nor Grifo had wintered here. He walked from the large central room into an adjoining alcove. Over twenty years ago his father and Swanahild wintered here—conceiving Grifo. Because of Grifo's birth, Charles returned from that fateful campaign with a second wife and their infant son.

He felt a quiver of anticipation at the impending confrontation between himself and Grifo. What did Fate have in mind for them? Would Grifo be killed in battle? Would Pepin, himself? The death of either would clarify who should take the throne—if Egar's prophecy were to come to pass in their lifetime.

"There is nothing here worth pillaging," complained a captain. "They took even their candle sticks and wall hangings when they left."

"Mayhap the church be having better to offer," said a foot soldier.

"Hear me!" bellowed Pepin. "Whatever is in the church is in God's hands. Whether it be silver or the elderly, as long as they remain inside and try no treachery upon us, they remain safe. Do you understand?"

"Aye," mumbled the foot soldiers.

"But," asked a nobleman, "what if they come outside the wall? What then?"

"They forfeit treasure—or lives!" Pepin strode toward the dusty great wooden chair of authority and pounded the high back with his fist. "I will deliver our message to the priest myself, so there is no misunderstanding."

"Do we camp here, then?" asked a nobleman.

"Aye," Pepin answered. "The battle must come to us. The Romans knew where to establish a colony. The streams on either side of Augsburg give it natural fortification."

"How do we know Grifo and his men will come?"

"We are here. They will come."

Once again, the Frank's awesome reputation forced the enemy into submission without a fight. One by one the Bavarian chieftains arrived and laid down their arms, readily pledging fealty to Pepin.

Lantfrid of Alemannia, with his army, followed them.

Chiltrudis with her court came next—five-year-old Tassilo held firmly in hand.

Grifo arrived last. Pepin's half brother looked much improved over when Pepin had last seen him. His hair was trimmed, eyes clear, face fleshed out and full of color. Clearly neither of them would die in battle this day.

Pepin sat in the chair of authority in the great hall. The noblemen stood or sat on benches pushed back against the walls, murmuring quietly among themselves. Captains strode in and out, delivering messages to their patrons.

Pepin rubbed his temple. What should he do with Grifo? Had his half-brother died in battle, it would have been his ill luck. But with no battle, that opportunity would not arise. At least on *this* occasion

He thought, once again, of Archbishop Boniface's advice. *Pray not to bend God's will to your desires, but rather pray for insight to bend your will to God's desire.*

At last, Pepin summoned Grifo, Lantfrid, Chiltrudis, and Tassilo to stand before him.

"Grifo, why can you not be content with your portion?" Pepin asked, knowing the answer.

Grifo shrugged his shoulders. Held his hands outward. "I am a true son of Charles Martel. He and my mother were married, and I want my full share of his inheritance."

Although Grifo had yet again committed treason, Pepin knew he would not punish him. The same prophecy goaded Grifo and Chiltrudis that made him covet the crown.

"Grifo, this is your last opportunity. I will grant you full pardon and rule of Le Mans. You will be duke of twelve counties in Neustria. I *cannot* give you more."

"Will I *still* owe allegiance to you, my lord?"

"Of course." Pepin experienced a flush of impatience. "Nothing can alter that. Martel ordered it. Long dead, no one can ask him now to change his mind."

Grifo stood, unmoving.

Jupiter's balls! Get on with it. Pepin's head felt ready to burst. If Grifo did not accept the offer, Pepin would have no choice but to order the man put to death.

At last, Grifo knelt before Pepin and once more pledged his fealty.

Both knew it would not last.

The hall, which had grown quiet during the exchange, broke out into muttered conversation.

Grifo walked nonchalantly across the room and out the door. Free once more.

Pepin looked hard at Lantfrid. The man's reddish-blond hair, though evenly cut, grew past his shoulders. Hazel eyes reflected flecks of gold. The Duke of Alemannia stared back in defiance.

"You and your closest guard shall return to Francia with me and my army," Pepin decreed. "You may send the rest of your army home."

"Am I to be your prisoner?"

"Only if you insist." Pepin tried to judge this stranger's character. "I would know you better. You can follow me of your own accord—or in chains."

"Of course, my lord. My guard and I will follow you—" Lantfrid paused, assessing Pepin. "—willingly."

Chiltrudis stood next before Pepin. She held Tassilo by the hand. The years had not been kind to his half sister. The precocious thirteen-year-old at the time of Charles' death had turned into a careworn matron of twenty.

Pepin gazed at her, pondering. Had Odillo been good to her? Had she received the love and attention she so desperately needed? Looking at her, Pepin thought not.

How had her husband died? Not that it made any difference. At least he gave her a son. Another person to seek the crown?

Chiltrudis stood, her chin raised, challenging him. Tentatively she raised one brow and licked her bottom lip. The motion was gone as quickly as it began. Pepin doubted anyone else in the hall had so much as seen her tongue.

"Chiltrudis," he acknowledged. He could no more call her 'sister' than he could call Grifo 'brother'. "I understand you are a widow?"

"Aye." Chiltrudis cocked her head, then as an afterthought, added, "my lord."

"And you rule Bavaria—or did until Grifo came—as regent to Tassilo?"

"Yes, my lord." Her compliant answer was negated by a look of triumph.

Pepin nodded, acknowledging her right to rule. He understood her desire to become mother of the great king to come—*if* that was her destiny.

"Very well. I shall confirm Tassilo Duke of Bavaria."

Pepin watched, his chin resting on steepled fingers, as Chiltrudis coached her young son to kneel before the mayor of the palace.

The child's hands seemed incredibly small between Pepin's much larger, callused ones.

Tasillo's thin voice repeated the oath of fealty, not understanding one word.

Each of them—Grifo, Tasillo with Chiltrudis' guidance, and Pepin, himself—remained free to seek the promised crown in his own way.

Chapter Fifteen

After leaving Bavaria, Pepin and his army marched through the neighboring lands, eliciting renewed pledges of loyalty from Alemanns, Swabians and Thuringians alike.

Traveling with Lantfrid of Alemania had proven beneficial as well. Each took the other's measure and found cause for grudging respect. Who could tell what bloodshed had been averted by Pepin's insistence that Lantfrid come with him?

On entering Austrasia, he dismissed the noblemen and their soldiers and traveled through his own realm, settling disputes and building ties with those who still knew him only as Martel's son.

Pepin felt a welcome sense of contentment and accomplishment. We shall plan a festivity once we arrive home, he decided, to celebrate a successful campaign, accomplished with no spilling of blood. Hopefully, we will celebrate a good harvest as well. All the villeins and my guard shall be invited to attend.

Bertrada will enjoy planning the food. We shall have musicians, of course. He recalled their laughter and joy in dancing together at Chlodomer's wedding feast. We shall invite Chlodomer and Adele as well. Bertrada was quite taken with Chlodomer's bride.

In late fall of 749, a message came from Archbishop Boniface, inviting Pepin along with his family and entourage, to winter in Mainz.

Bertrada would have much preferred to winter in the villa, but given the invitation, she responded as Pepin knew she would.

"If the archbishop has requested our presence in Mainz, then Mainz it will be." She shrugged. "I shall have an opportunity to learn about a place I have never seen before."

And so, Pepin's large entourage wended its way towards Mainz. In addition to Pepin and Bertrada, their five children, from eight-year-old Rothaide to baby Adélaide, required a bevy of nursemaids and attendants. Scribes, cooks, pages, chambermaids, and guards were needed to run the household over the long winter months. Each of these officials and servants had families of their own in tow. Most walked the entire way.

The trip took just over a month, during which time villeins harvested crops. In the forests golden leaves dropped to cover the ground in a rustling cover of brown.

At last the weary party sighted Mainz. The sun setting behind them, flamed towering clouds pink and gold against the deepening blue sky. Its glow burnished the wooden structures and the myriad colors of the sky could be seen reflected in the deep, swiftly-moving Rhine River beyond.

The great hall had been readied for their arrival. Fresh straw covered the floor. Dancing flames licked at a giant log, promising welcome warmth from the evening chill.

Women of the town bustled from kitchen building to hall carrying round loaves of crusty bread. When the travelers were ready, they would fill the hollowed-out bread bowls with nourishing stew. The delicious fragrance made stomachs rumble and mouths water.

Adults sank gratefully to benches around the trestle tables. Pepin watched in wry amusement as his children reacted to the end of the journey, each in typical fashion.

Seven-year-old Charles and four-year-old Carloman shouted and chased each other around the tables, their keepers too tired to restrain them.

Pepin peeked under his table where Rothaide and her six-year-old sister Giséle huddled as they ate their supper. "I want to go h...home," he heard Giséle whisper, tears glistening on her eyelashes.

"Home, where?" Rothaide asked.

"H...home to the v...villa," Giséle hiccuped.

Pepin saw Rothaide give her little sister a hug and pat her cheek.

Meanwhile, the baby, two-year-old Adélaide, howled her displeasure at the food, the building, the journey, and the people trying to comfort her.

Pepin observed in amazement as Bertrada quietly brought order out of chaos. Within a week, Cook and her helpers were preparing meals in a well-stocked kitchen building. The contents of wagons and carts—clothes, bedding, pots and pans, chests, baskets, and bundles of possessions—put neatly where they belonged.

Mornings, Charles studied in the monastery classroom. Afternoons, he participated, for the first time, in soldier's training held in the yard under the tutelage of a member of Pepin's army. At four, Carloman, much too young for either activity, had daily tantrums when forbidden to do everything his older brother did.

Pepin waited but no message came for him to present himself at the residence of Archbishop Boniface.

With little to do, Pepin's feet often took him, unguided by thought, to observe his oldest son's training. The other lads in his group—sons of noblemen and soldiers—were all from eight to twelve years of age. Surprisingly, Charles was not the smallest among them.

Pepin cheered as the boys raced, ten laps from the starting line to a tree trunk and back. They began in a group, all eight boys together. By the time they had jostled to touch the tree trunk and begun the return trip for the first lap, the twelve-year-olds with their longer legs showed their advantage, sprinting out in front. Charles was in the middle of the pack. Two boys who were smaller, and one pudgy lad, struggled valiantly at the rear. By laps eight and nine, some of the sprinters were loosing ground, while some from the middle group surged forward, Charles among them.

All the boys were red-faced and panting by the time they finally crossed the line for the tenth time. Charles ended third. He joined the others, lying on the ground, gasping for breath. The last boy to cross the line burst into tears. Pepin felt sorry for the youth, but fully supported the training soldier who insisted, tears or not, the loser had to take his hand-slaps. This was soldiers' training after all. Loss in battle could cost life or limb. The consequence for losing any contest had to be serious to be effective.

Each of the seven boys took turns slapping the loser's hand ten times, one for each lap run.

Though the boy cried harder with each hit, he stayed to take his licks. Pepin nodded. If he could translate his misery into determination to better his performance, he would make a good soldier.

Another afternoon, they competed in throwing a casting ax at the tree trunk. The group started close to the trunk. Each boy was allowed three tosses. The line was gradually moved back, farther and farther from the target. Three misses in a row eliminated a boy.

Pepin's heart sank as Charles was the first eliminated. Now his son had the rest of the competition to anticipate his hand slaps. Pepin watched Charles closely. He acted as though unaware of his impending fate, as he cheered on his friends, commiserating with them when, one by one, they were eliminated.

He congratulated the winner before manfully holding out his hand to take his slaps. Although biting his lips and flinching by the end of the penalty, he did not cry.

Win or lose, Pepin found it easy to hug his son at the end of each day's training. And win or lose, the others in his group cheered him on as well.

Rain turned to sleet. Finally, snow fell, and with it came winter. A few days later, Archbishop Boniface sent for Pepin.

"Pepin! Well met." Boniface greeted him at the door to the archbishop's residence within the monastery compound.

Pepin studied his mentor's face. He appeared older now, with lines engraved around the hazel eyes and smiling mouth. Notwithstanding, the man radiated a vitality that belied his years.

Boniface led Pepin through the hall with its high-backed chair and benches pushed against the walls. "I have been wanting to talk to you for some while now." Boniface smiled. "I give you thanks for honoring my summons. And trust Bertrada and your not inconsiderable household are well settled in?"

"Bertrada can make any hall a home, and the family is doing well, all thanks to God," replied Pepin nodding.

They entered a smaller study and took seats at the table. Pepin looked in awe at scrolls and precious books filling shelves on two walls. A crucifix and small altar took up a third. Leather curtains hung at the narrow wind openings, doing little to keep out the cold.

Pepin looked to Boniface, waiting for the archbishop to tell him what the summons was all about.

At last Boniface stirred and cleared his throat. "Who, now, is king of all Franks?"

"Childeric II," answered Pepin. Everyone knew this. "Why ask you?"

"And what qualifications does he bring to the throne?" continued Boniface, ignoring Pepin's question.

"Qualifications? He is a Merovingian."

"And..."

Pepin shrugged. "What else is there?" No word of Egar's prophecy would escape from *his* lips. If they were to discuss the possibility of Pepin challenging Childeric for the crown, Boniface must be the one to bring it up.

"Does he settle disputes?" Boniface continued. "Appoint noblemen? Distribute the wealth of the kingdom? Lead men to battle? Protect our borders? Bring peace to the realm?"

"No." Pepin paused. "But what king ever has?"

"Clovis, the first of the Merovingians, wrested the power from the Romans. His sons ruled the kingdom in *fact,* as well as title."

"But that was hundreds of years ago!"

Pepin felt confident he knew where the questions were heading. Had longed to be king with his entire being for many years. But, now that the issue was about to be discussed, he felt even less inclined to reveal the depth of his obsession to wear the crown.

"True." Boniface smiled. "But who, in our time, rules the Franks without sitting the throne and wearing the crown?"

"If you mean by leading men to battle, defending our borders, settling disputes, I do, of course. Like my father before me. As mayor of the palace."

The chamber was so still Pepin could hear the sizzle of torches in their brackets. The slight rustle of the leather curtains moving in the icy drafts.

Boniface's quiet voice barely broke the near silence. "Should not he who exercises power have the title as well?"

Pepin stopped breathing. The secret, zealously guarded for generations, was still safe with him. No one outside the family knew they had been gathering power—scheming to place themselves in position to claim the throne—for a hundred years and more. Nevertheless, he half expected a bolt of lightning to rip through the study, killing both him and Boniface in a single stroke, simply because the subject was about to be broached.

Boniface looked at Pepin, his face innocently blank.

Pepin drew a deep breath. "But… how could that be? I have no Merovingian blood in my veins." How could he ever hope to uproot the Merovingian myth from the superstitious Frankish soul?

Boniface looked unperturbed. When he spoke, his voice reminded Pepin of the religious mentor who had patiently explained catechism and the messages of the Bible to two brothers when they were boys. "I have asked myself what the Franks would prefer—a leader with proven ability or an idiot with Merovingian blood?"

Pepin smiled in spite of himself.

Boniface paused, as though weighing each word. "I have prayed for guidance. The Franks need a strong leader. The pope and church in Rome also need protection from King Aistulf and his Lombards who threaten them even now.

"Because of that, I think my leader, Pope Stephen II, who succeeded Pope Zachary should be consulted."

"But Pope Stephen lives in Rome. And *he* is chosen of God." Pepin was truly confused. "What has the pope, chosen by God, have to do with the king of all Franks?"

Boniface sat forward, leaning his arms on the table. "Do you agree, had we no tradition of Merovingian monarchy, *you* would make an ideal king?"

Pepin closed his eyes. *Take care in what you pray for.* "Possibly. But we *do* have a tradition of Merovingian monarchy. How can *that* be changed? And what does any of this have to do with me? Or the pope?"

Pepin paused. Careful to say nothing he would later regret. "Besides, the Frankish nobility chooses its own king. At a *Champs de Mars.* And that king must be agreeable to the soldiers who follow their overlords, as well."

"Exactly!" Boniface sat back, a pleased smile on his face. "Ridding ourselves of Chilperic II, who has nothing and does nothing is no problem. Supplanting him in the hearts of the noblemen and their soldiers—*that* is our problem.

"What is strong enough to combat the Merovingian myth?" murmured Boniface, as if searching for an answer. He looked directly at Pepin. "The church. *That* is what! The pope has great authority because God chooses the pope. *God* must choose the Frankish king."

"But who can speak for God?" Pepin asked.

"The pope!"

"Why would Pope Stephen, or *any* pope, care whether or not I was king of the Franks?"

"Because the Roman emperor, to whom the pope is pledged, has moved to Constantinople. He is far away. And the Lombards are sitting on Rome's doorstep. Because you lead a mighty army! One that others dare not challenge."

At once the pieces slipped into place in Pepin's mind. In exchange for being named King of All Franks, he would be expected to lead his army southward, over the jagged Alps in defense of Rome.

Elation bubbled. Pepin felt with certainty that he was born to be king of the Franks. Even Bishop Boniface had said so. But was this truly God's will? Or was he praying to bend God's will to fit his own ambitions?

"Why do *you* champion me to be king of all Franks?"

Boniface looked toward the crucifix hanging on his wall. "Because, I truly think God has sent you to protect His church, both here and in Rome."

"You do realize that to speak such words is treasonous? Even though you are archbishop, the Merovingians and those who support them could kill you—a slow death by torture—for less."

"There is no one to overhear us in this chamber. And I doubt *you* will give voice to the accusation." Boniface smiled and Pepin felt the power of his charisma.

Pepin allowed himself to think seriously about the possibility. He had coveted the crown since his father's death. But always as some far-off dream. Was the throne actually attainable?

Boniface got at once to the business at hand. "Who will speak to Pope Stephen?"

"Not me, certainly." Pepin saw the problem clearly. "I must be seen as playing no part in any of this. Nor should you, directly. However, as archbishop, you will know whom to send. Pick a leading clergyman from Austrasia and one from Neustria. But what will they say?"

"Just what I said to you." Boniface thought for a few moments, then pulled out a sheet of parchment. Dipping a quill into ink already prepared, he wrote, saying the words as he put them down. "Is it expedient that one who is possessed of no authority in the land should continue to retain the name of king, or should it be transferred to him who actually exercises the royal power?"

Pepin nodded to Boniface, filled with respect for his religious mentor. "And what think you the pope will reply?"

"If I were to advise my God-appointed leader, I would have him say, 'He who really governs should also bear the royal name.'" Boniface put the pen in its holder. "He who actually leads the men, should be called King of All Franks."

The two men stood, grasping forearms in agreement. Pepin, his mouth dry, did not know whether to feel exultant or very, very afraid.

Chapter Sixteen

Pepin and Bertrada talked well into the winter night. From the warmth and security of their curtained bed, they discussed the meeting with Archbishop Boniface.

"I did not break my vow of silence," Pepin insisted. "I never once said aught of Egar's prophecy, or that those of us descended from Pepin de Vain had coveted the crown for going on five generations. No, I let him think the idea was his—though should we be accused of treason, my head is as vulnerable as is his."

"But, I still do not understand why he involved himself at all," protested Bertrada. "What does a churchman, an archbishop no less, have to do with the king of all Franks?"

"He said he thought my becoming king was God's will, though how he obtained such divine inspiration, I could not tell you."

Bertrada stroked Pepin's temple as his head lay on her ample breasts. Her fingers broke the tension building there. "Perhaps, as archbishop, he has a clearer understanding of God's word than we worldly folk."

"Perhaps. Though bishops and popes can hold their own with any 'worldly' nobleman or king, when need be." Pepin recalled stormy meetings between Archbishop Boniface and his father over Charles' installation of illiterate, militaristic bishops, and the use of church treasure to fund his battles. "And he has the very worldly expectation that I will help defend the pope and Rome from the Lombards."

"Who will Boniface send to meet with Pope Stephen?"

"He sent messages to Bishop Burchard of Wurzburg and Fulrad, Abbot of Saint-Denis, before I left him."

Bertrada's fingers stilled. "And with the pope's blessing, God Himself will choose you king of all Franks?"

"So Boniface believes."

"And you?"

Pepin took a deep breath. "When I heard the prophecy, I felt a stirring in my soul, like nothing I have ever felt before. I believe I was born to be king of all Franks. Whether that is God's will, as well, I can only hope. And pray."

The entourage, including Bishop Burchard of Wurzburg and Abbot Fulrad of Saint-Denis arrived from Rome, mud-stained and travel-weary, but smiling. Pepin and Bertrada received them in the great hall in Mainz.

"His Holiness, the pope, agreed with all we said," beamed a triumphant Burchard.

"See here. We have it in writing!" Abbot Fulrad pulled the precious parchment from a pouch attached to his belt. "It names you his choice for king of all Franks. He says, 'He who really governs should also bear the royal name.'"

"This calls for a toast!" exclaimed Burchard, taking up one of the tankards of ale the pages had brought before being dismissed. "To Pepin, King of All Franks!"

"To Pepin, King of All Franks!" all repeated.

Feeling his heart soar, Pepin smiled at Bertrada, who returned his look with one of her own. Understanding her message, he cautioned, "Get you not ahead of yourselves. "This is but the first step. Any change in leadership must be voted on by the Frankish noblemen and priests."

"Call a convocation!" urged Abbot Fulrad. "To my mind, the men would vote you king even without the endorsement of the pope!"

"By the rood, I pray you are right." Pepin took a deep draught of ale to cover his tumbling emotions. "Nonetheless, until we call a *Champs de Mars,* we can count on nothing. And each of us must keep all word of this a most carefully guarded secret. Our lives depend on it!"

A moment of silence followed his pronouncement. A look reassured Pepin that all realized the seriousness of his caution. Word of their mission to Rome was safe among this carefully selected group.

"To the *Champs de Mars!"* declared an enthusiastic Bishop Burchard.

"To the *Champs de Mars!"* responded the others.

Pepin, sitting amidst the nobles at the convocation, felt a wave of emotion, a combination of anticipation and fear, boil up unbidden in his chest as he stared at the figure of King Childeric II. Resplendent in his royal purple tunic, the king's hair flowed down his back in a swirl of shining spun gold. He sat on the throne, the high-backed wooden chair of authority, on the raised dais at the head of the trestle table in the great hall of Soissons.

Pepin cocked his head, staring at the king. Did Childeric know what was about to happen? As at past *Champs de Mars,* the noblemen and priests sat at the tables ready to listen, argue, and finally, vote. Soldiers and villeins packed the hall and stairway, while more crowded at the door.

Although a chill, rain-laden breeze gusted in through the wind openings, Pepin felt sweat bead his forehead.

Soissons, in the Oise Valley, several leagues north-east of Paris, had been a royal capital for nearly two hundred and fifty years, but in all that time the thick fortified walls of the palace had never seen such a convocation as this.

Pepin ran his fingers through his short hair. By Mithras, he was glad he did not have to speak on his own behalf. No one stirred, as the delegates to Rome, Bishop Burchard of Wurzburg and Abbot Fulrad of St. Denis, made their report to the assembled populace. The pope had also asked the beloved Boniface, Archbishop of Mainz to come as his personal representative.

With fresh determination Pepin turned his attention to the orations of the delegation. When they finished, the assembled men would cast their fatal vote. Would the chieftains bend to the siren lure of old loyalties and superstitions? Or would they place their faith in a new, more vital order? By the end of the day he would either be king of the Franks, or he might well be dead.

Did it matter that the Merovingians had become so degenerate that they could barely dress themselves unassisted? No! They had been kings forever and anyone who forgot that fact paid dearly. They had a long history of killing anyone who tried to usurp the throne.

More than anything, Pepin wanted to be king and he willingly took that risk. But he fervently hoped that the prominence of those who supported his claim would offset any opposition.

"Look you," Fulrad exhorted the crowd, "at our 'noble' king. Is he not glorious? Is he not beautiful?"

A murmuring of assent rolled through the hall, along with the required tapping of swords to shields in affirmation. All eyes turned to Childeric. He sat motionless, blue eyes glazed and unswerving. He had no more idea what was being discussed than did the mighty log walls of the building in which they sat.

"But," Fulrad shouted, "whose father saved our world from the dread Muslim infidels who came as far as Tours?"

"Pepin's!" roared the full-throated response.

"Who led our soldiers in battle and glorious plunder against the Aquitanians?"

"Pepin!" The shout was, if anything, louder, and filled with tremendous energy.

"Who has the blessing of our most Holy Father, the pope in Rome?"

"Pepin!"

"Who leads us to greater glories, land, honor and booty?"

"Pepin!"

"Who would you have be king of the Franks?"

"Pepin! Pepin! Pepin!"

The enthusiastic shouting and clamor was carried on the din of swords beating on shields, the acknowledged means of voting since time immemorial. Pepin would be king!

A soaring rush of exultation lifted Pepin. But, without warning his mood froze and, with a stomach-wrenching sensation, plummeted to the ground.

There, amid the tumult, sat Villicus. He and those around him had not joined in the clamor. Pepin caught the nobleman's eye and felt the challenge there. The hazel eyes, which could change color in the snap of a finger, glowed menacingly dark and dangerous. Not everyone wished the newly elected king a long life and prosperous reign.

Within a fortnight, Pepin sat on the high wooden chair of honor in the basilica of Saint Médard, looking down on Archbishop Boniface going through the offices of this most unusual ecclesiastic ceremony.

The thick walls of the basilica had absorbed the cold of winter and would remain so until well into summer. The thin slits of wind openings let in precious little light and the candles did their feeble best to illuminate the gloom that threatened from corners of the huge open space and the top of the high vaulted ceiling.

Childeric II knelt in front of Boniface, his long golden hair flowing past his shoulders.

Pepin felt his own closely cropped head. Childeric was lucky not to have his head, with its long hair covered in blood, stuck on a pike on the city wall. Had the vote gone the other way, Pepin had no doubt that would have been *his* fate! But his supporters needed no Merovingian martyrs. Childeric was to be sheared and sent back to the monastery where, hopefully, he would disappear from all minds.

Pepin gazed at Childeric as he knelt, head in place, long hair temporarily intact, his fine features like a figure chiseled in stone. Even his blue eyes looked as cold and lifeless as a marble statue.

Pepin wondered how much of this the Merovingian understood. It was not without cause that he had been called Childeric the Stupid, nearly to his face. Pepin sighed. Carloman had felt the Franks needed a king, and Childeric was the only Merovingian they could find. They had found him in a monastery and now he was to be sent back. Perhaps, like Carloman, he would be happier there. Pepin could not wish Childeric ill. None of this was *his* doing.

An involuntary gasp escaped from the assembled crowd as large shears hacked away at the long royal hair. Everyone in the basilica strained to watch as though half-expecting some dire, long-forgotten curse from an ancient pagan god to strike everyone stone cold dead at such blasphemy.

When nothing happened and Boniface continued cutting as if it were the most natural thing in the world, a collective sigh of relief floated toward the arched clerestory openings above their heads. Roughly-dressed fighting men smiled weakly at one another as if to say, *I knew all along naught bad would happen. But you should have seen the look on* your *face!*

It seemed everyone in Soissons was packed into the huge basilica of Saint Médard. Pepin knew that those who could not push their way in, were standing outside to witness, even at a remove, history being made during their lifetime. In the murmuring and shuffling of feet that followed the fateful deed, Pepin expected Childeric to react. To struggle to keep his hair and the crown. Was his an act of stoic acceptance or did the man truly have no comprehension of what was happening?

To Pepin's amazement, a single tear gently slipped down Childeric's cheek. He *did* understand! Pepin felt disgust that a grown man should cry. But Childeric was not like most—a man, yet not quite a man.

As the golden hair continued to fall, the royal demeanor disappeared; in its place emerged a figure with spiky, cropped head. Gone was the last of the Merovingian kings, descendent of the great Clovis. Soon enough, Pepin hoped, songs in favor of his own lineage would replace the verses celebrating the heroism of the Merovingians.

As a rough homespun robe took the place of the long fur cape, and the soft leather boots were exchanged for sandals, Childeric II disappeared forever. Becoming just one more black-robed monk, he took his place in a line of identical monks to enter a monastery closed to the world.

"Be you safe and protected, but—" Pepin fervently prayed, "live not to haunt our reign in popular imagination.

"I do this for both of us, Carloman," he murmured, missing his brother with an almost physical pain. He missed the roughhousing of their youth. Missed tossing ideas back and forth, knowing he could say anything on his mind without it being misinterpreted and used against him. He missed riding off to battle, side by side, ready to fight and conquer, knowing they acted as one—as if each was one face on a Janus coin.

"Pray for my soul, Carloman, and I will reign for you as well as myself," he promised.

He looked at those in attendance. The nobles stood in front as was their due. The cavernous building was a crush of people—soldiers, servants, and peasants. Almost all of them male. A few women of lower rank had worked their way into the back of the church.

Pepin thought of Bertrada. The Merovingians had no ceremony for their queens. While some wives had ruled either behind the throne or as widows—regents for young children—none had been ceremonially recognized. He and his wife had discussed whether she should witness the coronation. Bertrada had been happy to stay well away and supervise the feast that would follow in the great hall. With all those men, and some still touchy about deposing a Merovingian, who knew what might happen?

He missed her presence, though. She would influence his reign as she had his tenure as mayor of the palace.

He looked again over the assemblage. Their closely packed bodies did what the thin sun of March could not accomplish, providing warmth, pungent with the odor of unwashed clothes.

At long last—yet seeming surprisingly soon—Boniface reached for the royal crown and held it high overhead. This was the moment for which Pepin had waited his entire adult life. But was he ready? Worthy? Heart beating, Pepin prayed for a sign of God's blessing.

Boniface knelt before Pepin. Imagine, an archbishop kneeling before *him!* Then with great reverence, Boniface stood, placing the heavy gold and jeweled crown on Pepin's head. The weight of it came as a shock.

"My lords," cried Boniface in his resonant voice, "it is enough, by Frankish tradition, that you have freely chosen Pepin, King of All Franks. It is enough, and yet, for us gathered here, there is more.

"Our great and gracious God is a God of history. We know that He places Himself into human events. This He has done before, and this day, He has come to us again. His most holy representative on earth, Pope Stephen II in Rome, sent the message that him whom you have chosen king, has God also chosen. Pepin reigns, *Gratia Dei rex Francorum,* King of the Franks by the grace of God."

At that moment a sound like that of tearing cloth came from the highest rafters. All eyes shifted, startled, as a hawk plummeted from the shadowy recesses straight at Pepin, its feathers rending the air in a seeming death dive. With breathtaking control it checked its flight and landed neatly on the back of the throne over Pepin's left shoulder.

For less than an instant it remained there. In the wavering candlelight the massive chair seemed alive. The golden lions that formed the legs seemed to move and breathe and throw off sparks of power. The small dark eyes of the hawk glared malevolently at the crowd.

With a collective gasp, men fell to their knees, crossing themselves as they did so. Not a few involuntarily gestured to older gods, signs to protect themselves from spirits not entirely consistent with this service and this place.

Just so long as it took to trace a cross in the air, the bird remained with Pepin. Then with a mighty leap, it set itself once more into motion and flew up and up to the top of the cathedral. From there, the bird swooped down over the heads of the throngs of gathered townsfolk. Once more it climbed up and out a clerestory opening. Out of sight.

At that moment, there was not a man among them but would have followed Pepin right to the gates of hell. Without conscious thought, Pepin sank to his knees. "Oh God," he prayed, "thank you for this asked-for sign. Help me to be worthy. Guide me in Your way."

For perhaps the length of a *Pater Noster*, no one else moved, much less spoke. Then, as though waking from a dream the murmuring began, growing in strength until it became a shout. "Pepin, King of All Franks. Chosen by God. Long live the king!"

As the religious ceremony concluded, willing hands reached out to help Pepin take a precarious seat on his own war shield. Strong soldiers lifted him, shield and all, to their shoulders as dictated by tradition.

For as long as he lived, Pepin would remember the tumultuous trip through the church and out the door where people from all over Frankish Gaul waited to cheer their newly-crowned king.

"Pepin! Pepin! King of All Franks!" roared the crowd as once, twice, thrice, he traveled on his shield around the entire city of Soissons.

On this day, the holy scrap of Saint Martin's cape —cherished talisman of the Merovingians—became Pepin's own symbol. And Saint Denis of the Merovingians became the patron saint of the new house of Pepin.

Chapter Seventeen

Late that night, Pepin lay in bed above the great hall, exhausted, but too wrought up for sleep. The moon shone through the wind opening in a narrow, silver stripe across the floor. Inside the cave-like bed, all was pitch black.

His arm cradling Bertrada, whose head lay on his chest, Pepin mused aloud. "Strange, I thought I would feel different. Once the crown touched my head, I expected to be granted wisdom. To know, deep down inside, I *am* the great king of Egar's prophecy. And yet, I have no more understanding now than I did before."

Bertrada stroked his face with a gentle hand. "Perhaps wisdom will grow with time, like your hair."

Pepin smiled in the dark. "Ah yes. The Franks will have a shorthaired king for some months yet. But, what if Egar's prophecy was wrong? What if it is *not* our family's destiny to be king?"

Pepin felt Bertrada's weight shift next to him. "He would not be wrong. It seems to me, he *knew* these things."

"He *was* wise. But did he speak for God?"

"What do you mean?" asked Bertrada.

"To be crowned in a church. With God's blessing, as it were. To depose the Merovingians, whom *everyone* knows, *do* have the right to rule. Could what I have done be blasphemy? If I anger God, His wrath will fall not just on me, but those whom I love—you and the children."

Pepin heard Bertrada's quick intake of breath, followed by a long silence. When at last she spoke, her voice was filled with conviction. "You have done no wrong. You acted upon the advice of the wisest and most holy people we know. Egar told of your family's fate. The pope himself blessed the coronation. Directed Boniface to give you the crown. And God sent the hawk. You told me so, yourself."

"I only wish I felt wiser, more kingly. In the cathedral, I felt God's presence. But here, now, I am filled with doubts. What should I do? When will I *know* this is my destiny?

"How do I replace the Merovingian myth in the hearts of my followers, if I feel unsure myself?"

"Perhaps... just... wait. In the meantime..." Bertrada's voice faded. "Act the wise and powerful king of Egar's prophecy. As if God chose you, as the pope promised. Do so and you may then find you have become the *great* king to those who follow you."

* * *

For two years Pepin followed Bertrada's advice. He allowed his hair to grow long and acted as though confident he had every right to be king.

Bertrada traveled with him into every nook and cranny of their kingdom. Pepin settled disputes and oversaw the production of goods and foodstuffs that supported his monarchy. Truth be known, Pepin did what he had always done as mayor of the palace. And truth be known, the people treated him no differently than they had before.

In the spring of 753, Pepin called his first *Champs de Mars* as king of all Franks. He had in mind to fight the Saxons who were always looking to exploit any sign of weakness in the Franks. The war camp would convene in Cologne. Pepin felt more confident launching his first major campaign from Austrasia. They, of all Franks, were his family's strongest supporters. Were, hopefully, less tied to the tradition of the Merovingians.

After setting up camp for the night some days west of Cologne, Pepin went into the forest to relieve himself.

As he sent his stream strongly against the trunk of an old oak, he heard two soldiers talking.

"Why can things be not as they always were?" complained the voice of an older man.

"What mean you?" asked the younger-sounding soldier.

The two men stopped just short of where Pepin stood.

"How can we be having a king with no royal blood?"

Pepin tried to stop his flow. Move away. Could not.

"What be wrong with Pepin as king?" asked the young man's voice.

"The Merovingians be born special. They be descended from a serpent. Or so I be told. The serpent never loses. Pepin be... ordinary." The old voice sounded garrulous.

Pepin heard the telltale sound of splashing as the men relieved themselves. He was finally finished, but afraid to move. Wanted to hear what was being said about him. Was afraid they would discover him. Listening.

"Pepin be a better leader than Childeric the Stupid!" exclaimed the young voice.

"Pepin be a right enough mayor of the palace. But he be no having the luck of the serpent on him. Ye be needing the backing o' the gods when ye go into battle. And *that* be for them what has a Merovingian king. Not we, with naught but Pepin wearing the crown."

The two soldiers left the forest to return to camp.

Pepin felt his knees tremble. What if the old man spoke for a large segment of his followers? Prowess in battle depended on many things. Skill. Training. Leadership. Superior numbers. But most of all, confidence. If the army lacked confidence in themselves, because *he* was king, they were lost before they started.

Noblemen and their armies arrived from all over the Frankish-dominated territories. Austrasia, Neustria and Burgundy, of course. Frisia, Swabia and Alemannia as well. They camped along the mighty Rhine, just outside Cologne.

Flapping banners denoted each nobleman's claim to the soldiers who followed him.

Pepin watched as strong men, grunting and straining, brought the chair of authority along with several trestle tables and benches from the great hall of Cologne to the open area in the center of the encampment.

He had no problem with sitting in high-backed chairs whether in great halls or meadows when he traveled with Bertrada. As mayor of the palace, he had done so for years. It merely represented his authority to act in the name of the king. Now he *was* the king—and felt less secure sitting in the very same chairs.

The hearty shouts and bantering grew silent as noblemen and church leaders gathered on benches around the tables. Their captains and soldiers drew close behind them, equally silent. Pepin smiled at Bishop Hildegar and was rewarded with a smile and a nod in return. Hildegar had been appointed Bishop of Cologne the same year Pepin received the crown. Because of that, they shared an extra sense of camaraderie.

All eyes followed as Pepin, crown on hair grown long, took the throne.

"My friends," he addressed the crowd, "we meet today to plan continued battle against the Saxons who threaten our eastern boundary. They refuse to pay their just tribute to Frankish sovereignty over them. How vote you?"

Silence quivered. Pepin could say nothing more until those sworn to follow him declared themselves.

"The Saxons are a fierce enemy," opined a noblemen.

"But not against our combined might," cried another.

"I would feel far better," said Villicus, "if we knew Pepin ruled with the weight of Merovingian blood in his veins. Then he would lead us to battle with victory guaranteed."

Several soldiers nodded their agreement with Pepin's nemesis. A few were so brave as to tap their shields tentatively with lance handles.

Villicus smiled.

"We have been through all that before," said Chlodomer. "The offspring of the Merovingian serpent have withered and died. Childeric the Stupid was no brave war leader like those who began his line. We have not had a capable Merovingian king since Dagobert, way back when King Pepin's great, great grandfather, Pepin the Vain, was mayor of the palace. And even Dagobert was crazy."

A titter of laughter met this remark.

"If not for Charles Martel," Chlodomer continued, "and his son, Pepin, the Franks would be speaking Arabic and worshipping Mohammed instead of Christ. You know I speak but truth!"

Pepin smiled in appreciation of his friend's support.

"Martel's son for us!" Though not a yell, the soldier's voice was loud enough to carry.

"I follow Pepin," cried another.

Soon most were chanting his name.

"Pepin! King Pepin!"

A few of the soldiers looked uneasy. Villicus leaned over and whispered something to a nobleman next to him.

Pepin had no doubt as to the gist of his message. Let me but falter once, lose but one skirmish, and *he* will see it as proof I have no right to rule!

Although both Saxons and Franks lost men in the battles and skirmishes they fought, Pepin's army held the upper hand. Little by little Pepin pushed the retreating Saxons as far as Rehme, near Minden on the Weser River.

Flushed with confidence, he slapped Chlodomer on the back. "Is this not like old times, when we rode side by side with Carloman?"

Chlodomer grinned and nodded agreement.

Pepin's exhilaration was cut short the very next day, when word reached him that the Saxons had killed a Frankish cleric in Castle Iburg, just outside of Osnabrück. The cleric's name—Bishop Hildegar.

Three days later the Franks won their final battle in Rehme. The conquest seemed anticlimactic compared to the death of Bishop Hildegar.

Pepin looked back at his army as they turned toward home. His men plodded along the path leading across the nearly flat plain between Rehme and Cologne. Each nobleman, gonfalon waving in the breeze, led his own contingent. Captains, some riding, others walking, led groups of ten to fifteen soldiers. The foot soldiers trudged, two by two, as Charles Martel had insisted they do. Behind each group rolled an ox-pulled wagon filled with foodstuffs and supplies.

Pepin thought, my first campaign as king and a cleric is slain. Is it my imagination or are the soldiers unusually subdued? I hear precious little of the bantering good cheer that victory should ensure.

He swiped at the sweat running down his face with his sleeve. Perhaps the heat had something to do with their lethargy. They *did* return with wagons filled with tribute and plunder. At least this endeavor paid for itself.

Pepin had no doubt Villicus would use Hildegar's death as proof he did not have God's blessing to be king. He pressed his fingers to his temple. Hildegar had been a good man. Why *would* God allow him to die? *Was* this a message against him?

Pepin heard Bertrada's voice. *You have done no wrong. Act as if God chose you. Do so and you may then find you have become the great king to those who follow you.*

Pepin wondered what his father would do. *He would ride among the entire army. Calling each man by name. Giving praise and a slap on the back to captains and soldiers alike. Making each one feel known and valued.*

Pepin wheeled his horse around.

Chapter Eighteen

"Sire, you have a visitor," announced the major domo of the villa at Quierzy sur Oise.

Even after three years as king, the title "sire" still startled Pepin. Annoyance washed through him, as well.

Shuffling through the stacks of scrolls littering the table, Pepin grumbled under his breath, "You know better than to interrupt me in my private chambers when I am busy with all these reports needing my attention."

His thoughts raced on. Who is it that has come? Some people should be met in the hall, rather than in my chamber. And why could you not take care of him yourself?

Pepin looked up, ready to give the errant servant a thorough dressing down when the doorway was filled with a tall, slender figure in the black robe of a Benedictine.

Annoyance dissolved into joy. "Carloman! Is that actually you? I can scarce believe my eyes!"

In a thrice, Pepin was on his feet and across the room where the two men grasped arms.

"How is it you have come here? Do you have permission? Is anything wrong?"

"I walked. I have not only permission, but have been requested by my abbot to speak with you. And no, nothing personal is wrong. It is a matter of—"

"Pepin, I heard voices. Who is it?" Bertrada emerged from the doorway to a connecting room containing their bed and personal belongings.

At the sight of Carloman, her face broke into a smile of pleasure. "Carloman! Well come!"

Carloman strode to where Bertrada stood and kissed her hand. "Bertrada! How delightful to see you. The years are kind to you. But where are the children? I cannot recall seeing you without two or three about your feet and at least one to the breast."

Bertrada glowed at his praise. "Those 'kind' years have seen the children grown. The girls are sewing with the ladies of the court. Rothaide at twelve, is embroidering her dowry.

"Ten-year-old Giséle feels called to become a nun."

Carloman smiled and nodded, clearly pleased.

"If she is still of that mind a year from now," Bertrada continued, "we shall allow her to take the vows of a novice. The nuns at the Convent of Chelles will be able to help her discern whether hers is a true call from God, or merely a girlish fantasy.

"Even our 'baby', Adelaide, is six and learning to spin, weave, and wield a needle," Bertrada concluded with a smile.

"And Charles served this summer past on the estate our mother inherited from her uncle Dodo." Pride filled Pepin's chest. "He is tall for eleven and a true grandson to Martel. Gives as well as he gets with the older lads in soldiers' games. He is home for the winter, and next year will serve the court as a member of the army from Metz."

A page arrived with tankards of ale. The three pushed the scrolls aside and arranged themselves on benches to each side of the table.

Pepin touched his cup to Carloman's.

"Your namesake, Carloman, is tutored here." Bertrada glowed with a mother's pride. "He takes to learning far beyond anything I would expect of an eight-year-old. And his fluency in languages is truly astounding."

Carloman raised his tankard in a salute to his namesake's accomplishments.

Bertrada then took a piece of material, a detail for an altar cloth, from her pocket and threaded her needle with gold. Embroidering fine stitches, she began decorating a cross of red much as a monk might illuminate a beginning letter on a precious parchment.

Pepin looked fondly at the brother he had not seen for so long. "We have not given you a chance to tell why you are here. You say your abbot sent you?"

Carloman put down his tankard and looked solemn. "Yes. The Lombards are at Rome's doorstep once again. King Aistulf is determined to have Rome under his sovereignty. Pope Stephen appealed to the emperor in Constantinople for help." Carloman shook his head. "No help will come from *that* quarter."

Pepin had known from the first that Pope Stephen's endorsement of him for king carried with it an obligation to defend Rome against the Lombards. "And so, your abbot wants me to cross the Alps with a full army of Franks to defend God's representative on earth."

Carloman squirmed and avoided Pepin's eye. "Actually, the abbot, who is my superior, requests that you not involve yourself in the question of sovereignty over Rome."

"But, why not?"

"King Aistulf is ruler of Lombardy from the foot of the Alps to the northern boundary of Rome, an area which includes the monastery at Monte Cassino. While the pope is God's *religious* representative, in *earthly* matters the abbot is honor-bound to support Aistulf, his sovereign."

"Aistulf is known to be a cruel king." Pepin felt his face heat. "He would crush the pope as a rival authority!"

Carloman took a sip of ale. Avoided looking directly at Pepin. "I know naught of the king's reputation, but—" he folded his hands "—the abbot says we must do all we can to assure peace and avoid bloodshed."

Pepin stared at his older brother in astonishment. Support cruel Aistulf and abandon the pope? Allow the Lombards to overrun Rome?

In the following silence, Bertrada quietly slipped out to oversee the preparations for honoring Carloman at dinner.

"What is *your* feeling in the matter?" Pepin asked.

Carloman finally returned Pepin's glance. "I support my abbot's decision. I have taken an oath of obedience."

Exasperation tinged Pepin's affection for his brother. Carloman, Carloman, he thought. When following, you serve with valor and distinction. But can you not be your own man? Arrive at your own conclusions? Have faith in your own judgment?

"I have heard the message you deliver from your abbot and will think on it." Pepin realized the words sounded stiff and overly formal, but what could he do? "By the by, have you heard about Grifo?"

Pepin knew the abbot of Monte Cassino filtered all word from the outside world. He allowed the monks to hear only that which he deemed necessary to their well being—that which would not distract them from their vows to work, pray, and praise God.

"The abbot told me you had pardoned him," Carloman answered, "and allowed him to keep his estates. You did well. I should have done it before I left. To be honest with you, I forgot all about him. I put him in prison, then walked away. It has weighed heavily on my conscience ever since."

Pepin could have admitted the same offense, but did not. "You have not heard of Grifo since?"

"No."

"After failing to foster dissension against me closer to home," said Pepin, "our esteemed brother fled to Gascony. He joined Duke Waifar, who welcomes any who oppose Frankish rule."

Pepin reached out. Placed a hand on Carloman's forearm. "Grifo is dead. Killed. I heard about it on my return from Saxony this fall. It seems he was on his way to garner support with your King Aistulf in Lombardy. A Frankish duke, loyal to me, took it upon himself to quell the threat, once and for all."

He stood and walked to the wind opening that looked out on a winter-desolate atrium. "I have thought much on Grifo. Had our positions been changed, would not I have done much as he to get a rightful share of my father's power, land, and wealth?

"Though to be honest, had Grifo been named mayor of his own domain, he would likely *still* be dissatisfied with his lot, and want ours as well."

Carloman touched the heavy cross hanging on his chest from a leather thong, and then made the sign of the cross.

Pepin, annoyed, said, "You can pray for his soul. Pray for mine as well. My duke did only what I wished for, on more than one occasion. Though, I would have wanted naught but an honorable death on the battlefield for our half brother."

Carloman's voice, when he spoke, was filled with quiet agony. "You have nothing for which to atone. *You* did not kill him, as I killed Theobald. That makes all the difference."

Pepin felt a shaft of remorse. The Swabian chieftain! Of course Carloman would compare the two, though Pepin never had.

He strode back to the table, tried to change the conversation once again. "So, we should expect word from the pope come summer?"

"Pope Stephen waits neither for good weather nor a messenger. He left Rome last October. The fourteenth, or so I heard. I traveled lightly, thus made better time. To talk to you before he arrived. But he should be no more than a few weeks behind me."

"He is crossing the Alps, an ecclesiastic, with winter at hand? What must the man be thinking? I remember when we went for your vows. Those mountains proved a difficult journey for soldiers in the best of weather. What was it like this time?"

"Every bit as steep a climb, and bitterly cold. Snow, of course near the top, but not yet dangerous."

"The longer it takes him, the worse the conditions will be." Pepin shuddered. "God help him!"

"I suppose the pope thinks He will."

Pepin sipped his ale, taking a moment to order his thoughts. "How do *you* feel? Does it bother you that King Aistulf will conquer Rome? Rule Pope Stephen?"

"The abbot says that temporal leaders should matter not to the pope. God will protect and guide him in matters of the church. That should be his only concern."

Pepin held his tongue. If Carloman had any thoughts of his own on the matter, he would not give them voice.

Shaking his head, Pepin said, "We shall go nearer the Alps to meet Pope Stephen. Move our winter court to the palace of Pontyon in Burgundy. Would you come with us?"

"No. I will let you see him alone. I have been given permission to visit Metz before I return to Monte Cassino."

At the main meal in mid-afternoon, Pepin sat between Bertrada, to his left, and Carloman on his right. As the pages came bearing platters of roasted meats and pies filled with every type of bird, Pepin basked in a feeling of love for his brother. In some ways sitting next to Carloman was just like boyhood times. But, dressed in the austere garb of a Benedictine, the man was all but unrecognizable.

Carloman stabbed a piece of meat with the tip of his hunting knife. "I do hope you will think on what my abbot has requested."

"He truly wishes King Aistulf to prevail over Rome?"

"It matters not who prevails over Rome, militarily. Remember Christ's advice, 'Render unto Caesar that which is Caesar's, and to God what is God's.' In earthly matters, Monte Cassino is part of Aistulf's realm, and we must serve his desires. He is our military protector."

"Perhaps your abbot is right. He is certainly closer to the situation. And his allegiance to Pope Stephen is every bit as binding as is his to King Aistulf," Pepin reasoned.

He sipped his wine. "I shall think on what you have told me," he finally said.

That night Pepin, remembering Boniface's advice, prayed for the wisdom to bend his own will to God's desire. Following the abbot's wishes would be by far the easier choice. King Aistulf had done nothing to threaten the Frankish realm. Convincing his noblemen to gather their armies and climb over the Alps to fight the Lombards would be no easy task.

Perhaps Carloman, bearing a message from the abbot of Monte Cassino, was God's messenger as well.

The entire household moved from the villa just north of Paris to the palace of Pontyon, south of Dijon near Chalon-sur-Saône.

On arriving, Pepin thought—not for the first time—with the exception of his villa, one palace was much like another. His eyes swept the large wooden great hall. Kitchen buildings nearby—but not so close as to threaten the hall in case of fire. A stable and soldiers' sleeping quarters. Blacksmith's shed. A scattering of thatch-roofed, wattle and daub huts. Storage buildings.

Pontyon differed from most in its pleasant situation with the Saône River flowing nearby. Shading his eyes with his hand, Pepin saw the hamlet of Chalon in the distance with the snow-capped Alps towering behind. Somewhere up there, the pope was struggling to cross in the dead of winter. "I wish you Godspeed," he prayed.

Winter solstice, then Pepin's thirty-eighth birthday, followed by Christmas passed in a blur of celebrations and feasts interspersed with solemn worship services in the church in Chalon. This winter, each event was overshadowed by the expected arrival of the pope.

At last, in early January of 754, word arrived. The pope and his party had crossed the Frankish border. A group of soldiers was to be sent as escort for a welcoming committee of ecclesiastical and lay dignitaries to greet the pope.

"Papa," begged Charles, "please let me go with the soldiers to meet Pope Stephen!"

Pepin gazed fondly at his son. The boy was sturdy and would not hamper the group. Dignitaries would surely be slower and more complaining. "You will serve the court as a soldier when spring comes. I see no reason why you should not be allowed to meet the pope as one now."

At Charles' shout of joy, Pepin cautioned, "Remember, as a soldier, you must follow directions and not get in the way of the adults."

"A soldier! I will remember, papa. And if anyone should attack the pope, I know how to fight and will defend him!" Charles ran to tell his mother the good news.

When Carloman heard that Charles was to be allowed to go with the party to meet the pope, he begged to be allowed to go as well.

"No," his father told him. "Charles goes as a soldier. You are but eight-years-old and just beginning your soldier's training. Your time will come. But not until you are older."

"Why must I always wait?" Carloman's face took on a thunderous look. "Charles is allowed to do *everything,* and I am always told to *wait.*"

"This outburst is one of the reasons you must wait," replied a stern Pepin. "You are acting like the child you still are, not like a soldier who accepts orders whether or not they are to his liking!"

A bustle of activity and barely suppressed excitement filled the palace. Once the greeting party had escorted the pope nearer, Pepin prepared to go out and meet the entourage and welcome the Holy Father to his realm.

"In what manner should I greet the pope?" Pepin asked his wife. "Should I go as a king with crown and fur-lined mantle clasped with gold, or as a soldier fit to protect him from Aistulf and his Lombards? What think you will most likely gain his favor?"

"I understand Pope Stephen is himself, humble. I think he would respect someone who greets him in humility rather than pride."

"I value your judgment. I shall go in the guise of the pope's marshal, rather than King of All Franks, which he has made me."

Pepin trudged through the snow—walking as if doing penance, rather than on horseback. He worried that just this once Bertrada might be wrong. Pope Stephen could well arrive in the splendor of Papal robes embroidered in threads of gold, a jeweled cross on a golden chain on his breast. And here I come, he thought, looking poor and downtrodden. It will seem as though I think so little of the pope that I have not bothered to don my best garments. Or worse still, that I manage my realm so poorly, I own no proper clothing.

Three miles from his palace, Pepin met the entourage. Soldiers halted their steeds. Dignitaries fell behind. The pope, wearing the simple dress of a pilgrim, rode forward to meet Pepin, King of All Franks.

"Thank you, Bertrada," Pepin whispered to himself as he knelt in the snow to receive the pontiff's blessing.

The pontiff was thin. Deep shadows of fatigue lined his eyes. But those same eyes radiated joy and warmth.

Stephen smiled. "We made it! The journey, no matter how long—how difficult—was indeed blessed by God."

Pepin rose, feeling washed clean by the touch of the pope's hand on his shoulder. Stephen's unwavering gaze warmed him down to his toes, even though he stood in cold, winter snow.

As Pepin walked back to the palace beside the pontiff's palfrey, he made up his mind. He would do whatever Pope Stephen required of him.

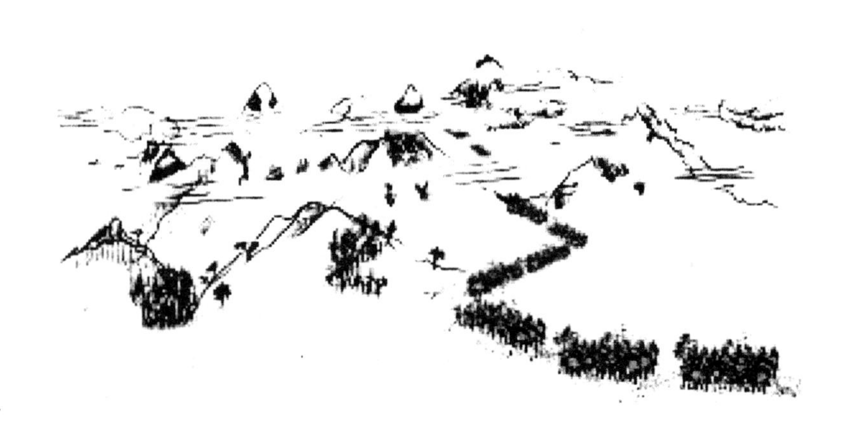

Chapter Nineteen

The winter at Pontyon seemed shorter than usual, no doubt due to the company of Pope Stephen. Having someone with the pope's stature to visit with made the normally cold, dull days seem to fly by.

"Knew you Pope Zacharias?" asked Pepin over the main meal within days of the pope's arrival.

Stephen swallowed a tender morsel of game bird. "Oh, yes. I own him much. He made me a deacon. And my brother Paul as well."

"Pope Zacharias conducted the ceremony consecrating my brother, Carloman, as a monk some few years back."

"I was there." The pope nodded to the young page offering to pour him a goblet of wine. "I hear he is now at Monte Cassino."

"Well, actually, he is now at Metz. My brother's abbot at Monte Cassino has given him permission to spend the winter at his old home."

Pepin shifted uncomfortably in his chair, not wanting to broach the subject of Carloman's journey to see him. Purposely steering the conversation away from Carloman and his abbot's request he asked, "So you succeeded Zacharias as pope?" asked Pepin,

Stephen sat back. Smiled. "No. But the reason for that is an interesting story."

Bertrada leaned forward from her place on the other side of the pope. "Do tell us."

"When Zacharias died, an elderly Roman priest was elected pope. He took the name Stephen II."

"But that is *your* name!" Pepin scratched his head. "I do not understand."

Stephen smiled, his brown eyes twinkling. Pepin felt the pope's warmth drawing him into the story.

"The priest was elected pope," Stephen continued. "He was installed in the Lateran Palace, home of the popes of Rome. But, he suffered a stroke three days later and died the following day. The problem was that he had been elected, but had not yet been properly consecrated, and so, according to canon law, he was *never* really a pope."

Pepin and Bertrada exchanged amazed glances. "And then *you* were elected?"

"Yes. I became the *second* Pope Stephen II." His chuckle warmed Pepin's heart.

As the days wore on, Pepin and Bertrada learned more about their esteemed houseguest.

"My younger brother, Paul, and I were born into a noble Roman family," he explained.

The three of them were sitting in Pepin and Bertrada's chamber above the main hall. A brazier glowed at their feet. Bertrada worked on a bit of embroidery.

"But we were quite young when we were orphaned," the pope continued. "We were taken into the Lateran. The monks and priests there, and indeed Pope Zacharias, himself, raised us. They became our family. And so, it was quite natural that both of us should regard the priesthood as our calling."

"I cannot imagine what it must have been like, growing up as young children in the residence of the pope of Rome," Pepin commented.

"Not really so different from being raised in any court in the land. We seldom came into contact with females, of course. But other than that, we were fed, nurtured, reprimanded, and encouraged, much as any other young children. And, I imagine, we were loved and protected far more that most."

Stephen held his hands out to the warmth of the brazier. When "Zacharias' successor died just four days after *his* election, I was elected pope.

"Rome and the papacy has been menaced by King Aistulf of Lombardy from nearly my first day as pope," Stephen told Pepin as they walked outside on a rare sunny but cold day. "He conquered Ravenna and seems to regard Rome as his fief. I have appealed to the Byzantines, but receive no answer to my pleas."

The pope sighed. "It was different when the Roman Emperor lived in Rome."

That spring, Pepin and his household returned to Quierzy. They took leave of Pope Stephen at the monastery of Saint-Denis near Paris.

As the heavy gate of the monastery swung open, Stephen laid his hand on Pepin's shoulder. "For your hospitality this winter and your promise of aid to Rome, I give you God's thanks as well as my own."

"The honor was ours." Pepin knelt at the pope's feet. "We could have no higher honor than to defend Rome for Christendom. How long will you remain at Saint-Denis?"

Stephen signaled Pepin to rise. "For a year. Then I must return to Rome. I trust God and you, His strong right arm, that by then it will be safe to do so."

"You will attend the General Assembly at Quierzy?" Pepin asked.

"Send word and I will come." The pope raised his hand in blessing. "God be with you."

When the General Assembly gathered, translucent, light green leaves crowded tree branches while white and yellow blossoms dotted the meadows.

Seated in his massive, high-backed chair in the middle of the meadow, Pepin knew he appeared impressive. The crown, jewels catching flashes of sunlight, weighed heavily on his head. His reddish-blond hair lay hot on his neck, and down his back. He wished he felt as powerful inside.

He looked over those seated at trestle tables radiating from in front of his chair like spokes from the hub of a wheel. Pope Stephen had place of honor nearest the throne, as was his right. The pope visited easily with Boniface who sat next to him, looking solemn but pleased.

Pepin caught Chlodomer's eye further down the bench. His friend gave him a smile and a tiny wink of encouragement. His ruddy complexion appeared even brighter under the spring sun.

Closer to the head, but at another table from Chlodomer sat Villicus. His close-set eyes stared intently at Pope Stephen. The nobleman's cropped gray hair glistened. Everything about him seemed thin and disapproving from his slender frame to his beaked nose and pursed lips.

Villicus must have felt Pepin's gaze on him, for he turned his way. Briefly, Pepin considered averting his head to avoid meeting him eye to eye. Just as quickly he shook off that thought and stared back at the Neustrian nobleman.

Villicus was wealthy and, perhaps because of that, popular among many of the noblemen from Pepin's domain. Villicus had, from the beginning, expressed open contempt for Austrasian Pepin, in *any* capacity, mayor *or* king.

The sound of drums followed by horn blasts brought the crowd to a stunned silence. Please, God, prayed Pepin, let the ceremony sway the men to my will. *Our* will, Pepin amended. Pope Stephen's. Mine. *And...* hopefully, Yours.

From the edge of the forest marched a group of musicians carrying banners in red and blue, playing stirring rhythms and fanfares. All men strained to see as the group proceeded at a stately pace to stop directly before Pepin's chair of authority.

A scribe emerged to stand before the musicians, facing the assemblage. An expectant hush followed. Unrolling a scroll, he read, his voice loud and clear. "Noblemen, churchmen, soldiers, all: Hear ye the words Pepin would pledge to God's representative on earth.

"Pope Stephen II! I, Pepin, King of All Franks, on this fourteenth day of April in the fourth year of my reign, the year of our Lord 754, do solemnly swear before all men present, to do my best to obey all orders given me by Pope Stephen. I do further promise to return to the pontiff the exarchate, the independent leadership of Ravenna, and the rights and places of the Republic. This I will do with God's aid and the backing of my most loyal armies—noblemen and villeins, soldiers, all."

The scribe turned to Pepin. "Do you so solemnly swear?"

Pepin felt trembling begin at his legs, move up through his stomach, and on to his heart which began pounding. Although the men present were not asked to vote, they could, if they wished, fail to endorse Pepin's actions.

He rose to stand next to the scribe.

Drums and horns played, causing men to pound on the tables or their shields, in spite of themselves. Never before had martial music played so dramatic a part in a *Conventus.*

The pope, resplendent in his embroidered robe and crown of Saint Peter, moved to take his place next to Pepin.

When the music stopped, Pepin knelt at Stephen's feet and placed his hands together between those of the pontiff's. Swallowing to clear his throat grown tight at the solemnity of the occasion, he declared, "I do so swear to obey, protect and defend Pope Stephen and Rome."

Pepin felt his hands being released. Reverently, Pepin took Stephen's fingers and kissed the offered papal ring to seal his promise.

With a flourish, Pepin rose. Took the scroll from the scribe. Laid it on the trestle table, and with a challenging glance at Villicus, signed his name with a quill dipped in ink.

"May God Almighty bless you, King Pepin," said the pope as he took the offered charter.

With that, drums beat and horns blared. Men cheered and kept time with swords on shields.

As he stood, Pepin took a deep breath. The deed was done and none had gainsaid him nay!

Soon afterward, Pepin and Pope Stephen sat with heads together, on a bench in the atrium of the villa at Quierzy, reading the message Pepin had just finished writing.

From Pepin, King of All Franks to Aistulf, King of Lombardy. May it be known by all in Lombardy that I do hearby pledge to Pope Stephen my aid and defense of Rome. Therefore, say I, return you and your armies to Lombardy and do not again violate Roman territory.

Spring sun warmed the protected central court. A gentle breeze stirred, causing the flowers in the formal gardens to bob their heads. Pepin breathed deeply of the sweet-smelling air. "The messenger awaits to take this to Aistulf. Think you words on parchment will be enough to deter him?"

"Not mere words on parchment," the pope replied, "but *your* reputation as leader of a fearsome army. You have secured borders on lands more widespread than any since the days of the Roman Empire. Who would dare challenge your might?"

"Every chieftain of every tribe to the east." Pepin rolled the parchment. "To say nothing of Duke Hunald of Aquitain. Why should Aistulf be different?"

"Send the messenger. I think Aistulf will not challenge you to battle over Rome."

"I pray you are right. Many Franks would not support such an endeavor." Pepin thought of Villicus and his cronies.

Stephen looked perplexed. "But you are king! You order men to come and they come. You order men to go and they go. If you order the armies to follow you over the Alps and into Lombardy, surely they must follow."

Pepin sighed. "I wish it were that simple. The armies are pledged not to me, personally, but to the noblemen who lead them. Those noblemen pledge themselves to me. But by tradition they vote whom to follow and where to fight. They may well look askance at crossing the Alps to fight for Rome when our own borders need strong defense."

"They will follow," the pope said. "Recall you how they beat their shields at the assembly?"

"That was in response to the drums and horns. I doubt they connected their actions with following *me* to war."

"They have followed you before. Why should they not continue to do so?"

Pepin searched deep within himself. Tried to be honest. Set aside his own ambitions. "At first they followed because I was mayor of the palace to a Merovingian king. And Charles Martel's son. Now I am king, and have less credibility than when I was mayor."

Pepin stood, restlessly pacing the atrium's pathways. He turned to Stephen. "When first the Franks became a force with which to reckon, before Clovis and the Merovingians, they met as a tribe each spring to vote on a leader and organize for battle."

The pope nodded, though he wore a puzzled look.

Pepin continued. "With the Merovingians grew legends. First from their prowess, then from fabled beginnings as descendants of a serpent.

"Now *I* am king. Duly voted by acclamation. But without the trappings of legend. A mere man wears the crown. Each nobleman thinks himself my equal, that he could be the next king. My orders come neither from a long revered bloodline nor the magic of legend."

Pepin returned to the bench.

Stephen placed a hand on his arm. "I think you underestimate yourself, my friend."

"I do *not* underestimate the power of noblemen like Villicus, who see themselves as possible future kings, over *my* dead body!"

The pope rested his chin on templed fingers, his expression one of deep thought. At last he looked into Pepin's eyes. "Send the message. Then wait and see. If you act with assurance, others will come to see you as king. The only possible King of All Franks."

"And if Aistulf challenges me to battle over Rome?"

"I have a plan that might strengthen your position. But for now, send the scroll. It may yet be enough."

Chapter Twenty

May 754

With his realm at peace and the messenger he sent to Lombardy still clambering over the Alps, Pepin received an unexpected summons from Archbishop Boniface. Gathering his personal guard, Pepin left immediately on horseback for Mainz on the Rhine.

Once there, the elderly priest greeted him with a smile and a handclasp. "I give thanks you were able to respond to my request so quickly. Come, the day is fair, let us sit here."

Pepin sank to the stone bench against a wall, grateful for the dappled shade of an old, fully leafed apple tree.

"Have you time to indulge an old man's request?"

Pepin leaned against the wall and looked at his favorite religious mentor. He could not deny that the archbishop had aged since the coronation. Fewer white hairs ringed his bald head. He observed a slight tremor in the gnarled hands. A stoop in the once ramrod-straight posture. How much longer would he have the pleasure of Boniface's company?

"For a certainty," he responded. "What better way could I spend a lovely spring afternoon?"

I have been thinking back on my life. Boniface sighed. "This must be what happens when you get old. Seventy-eight years! Who would have thought I should live so long?"

Pepin felt a rush of affection. "Reward for a life spent in service to God and man."

"I once told you the years spent spreading the Good News to the heathens, destroying idols, baptizing pagans, organizing the church, founding monasteries, were the *best* of my entire life."

"I remember," said Pepin, recalling how Boniface had come to him as though an angel sent by God, when he was in despair over his brother, Carloman.

Boniface sat straighter. His eyes snapped with new vigor. "And *that* is why I have called you here!"

Pepin beheld the change in his mentor with wonder and confusion. "Me? Why?"

"I wanted to talk to you—as sovereign *and* friend. To tell you that I plan to retire from the archbishopric of Mainz."

Pepin nodded. "At seventy-eight, you have certainly earned the right to retire. To lead a more restful life."

"No, no. That is *not* my intention. I am going back to my calling. Back to Frisia and the pagans that still live in darkness there. I must be about my Father's business. I will save souls, while yet there is time."

"Do you truly feel you have the stamina to travel? To exhort others to hear the Gospel? To change their lives and beliefs? And besides, who will replace you here?"

"Yes, I do. As for my replacement, come I will introduce you to Lullus, my disciple. I know you will like him."

Pepin smiled and shook his head in amazement as he watched Boniface, walking stick in hand, pull himself up from the bench and hurry off to the scriptorium to find Lullus. Bemusedly, the king followed.

Once there, Boniface took his disciple by the arm. "Lullus, my good man," he said. "Come with me. We have work to do, you and I. With my friend, King Pepin's approval, you are about to become Archbishop of Mainz!"

Fortunately, Pope Stephen was still visiting in Saint-Denis. Pepin and his guard accompanied a startled Lullus, and a newly energized Boniface, to meet with the pope.

Though perplexed, Stephen granted Boniface's request and ordained Lullus as the new Archbishop of Mainz.

"Are you certain you want to go to Frisia again?" the pope asked Boniface.

"Yes! I have but little time left. I must use it to baptize the heathens."

"At your age, I am amazed you feel the call. But go. With my blessing. And God's."

Pepin clasped the hand of newly appointed Archbishop Lullus. Then, turning to Boniface, said, "I can but echo Pope Stephen's words. I, too, am amazed you feel the call, but send you forth with my blessing."

* * *

Less than a month later, Pepin received an urgent summons to Saint-Denis. There, a somber pope met him at the door of his residence. "A novice, one of the group who accompanied Boniface to Frisia has been brought, badly injured, to the infirmary here."

Pope Stephen gazed at the ground, shaking his head. Then, with a visible effort, raised his eyes and straightened his shoulders. "I did not want you to hear his story as memorized by some messenger."

Foreboding filled Pepin. "What story? By the bull, what has happened?"

"Come with me," the pope urged. "The novice, Gontram, is still in the infirmary. I will take you there so you may hear what transpired from the lips of one who witnessed the whole event."

Pepin crossed the threshold into the infirmary with dread. The young man lay on a cot, badly bruised and with a great bandage around his head.

"Gontram," the pope spoke gently, touching the novice's shoulder, "feel you strong enough to tell King Pepin what happened in Frisia?"

The injured man nodded, grimacing as a brother assigned to work in the infirmary, helped him sit straighter and cushioned his back with pillows.

Gontram looked Pepin in the eye for a moment and then began. "Bernard and I were novices, sent to assist Archbishop Boniface and three other priests in converting the pagans. Twelve soldiers went with us into Frisia.

"Then on June fifth—"

"How do you know it happened exactly on June fifth?" Pepin interrupted.

"I grew up here in Saint-Denis. Learned to read and write in the monastery. As scribe, I was charged with keeping a day-to-day account of our journey."

"Because of what happened to Boniface and the others," Pope Stephen commented, "June fifth, 754 will be writ into history. But," he gently urged Gontram, "continue."

"It being my turn to assist him at mass, Boniface awakened me just before sunrise. Silencing me with a finger on my lips, he beckoned me to dress and follow him.

"The archbishop donned his homespun priest's robe, no different than what I wore." Gontram paused to smile fondly in reminiscence. "Boniface once told me..." Gontram paused as if gathering strength, "that this cloth felt finer, more honestly his, than had his embroidered archbishop's robe."

Gontram closed his eyes, his face nearly as white as the pillow on which it rested. Without opening his eyes, he continued. "Emerging from the tent Boniface took a deep breath of cool air. I heard him say softly, 'This is the day which the Lord has made. Be joyful and rejoice in it.'"

Gontram opened his eyes and looked directly at Pepin. "Looking back on it, I think he knew this was *the day*."

Pepin stared at Gontram, unable to speak.

Twisting, trying to find a more comfortable position, the novice continued, "I..." Gontram swallowed. "I helped Boniface spread a cloth upon the trestle table that did double-duty as our altar. With shaking hands he unwrapped the crucifix and reverently placed it in the center.

"He had told me his favorite passage in all the Bible was from Paul's letter to the Romans.

"That day, I heard him murmur, *'Recompense no man evil for evil. Live peaceably with all men. If thine enemy hunger, feed him; if he thirst, give him drink. Be not overcome by evil, but overcome evil with good.'"*

Pepin nodded in understanding. "I cannot count how many times Boniface quoted that passage to my brother Carloman and me."

Taking a deep breath, Gontram continued. "Boniface genuflected before the crucifix, and crossing himself said, 'Blessed Lord, make of me what You will. I am Yours.'

"Behind us, I heard the others stirring. Soldiers girded themselves with weapons, ready to defend us should the pagan Frisians attack. Boniface sniffed, seeming to savor the sharp scent of wood smoke as my fellow novice, Bernard, stirred the fire. We would soon smell potage simmering in the large black kettle. My stomach rumbled in anticipation, though I knew it would be some time before we celebrated mass and could break our fast."

Gontram paused, licked his cracked lips. The brother who hovered nearby like a guardian angel held a cup of water to Gontram's lips. After a few swallows he waved the cup aside.

Pepin felt his heart constrict in sympathy for the injured young man. "Rest now, if you are too tired to continue. I can return later."

"No." Gontram shook his head, wincing in the pain the movement caused. "I want to tell all that happened—now.

"Boniface blessed the bread, which would become the body of Christ, slain for us all, in remission of our sins. As he poured the wine into the chalice, a ray of sunlight caught the deep red liquid, making it sparkle like a jewel.

"With this act, I *knew*, in a way much stronger than I had ever felt before, that *this* wine would indeed become *the* blood of Christ, spilled for us.

"I heard Boniface murmur, 'Christ, you gave your life for me, I dedicate my life, anew, for you.'

"At that very moment, pandemonium broke out. From the darkness of the forest came unearthly, bone-chilling screams." The novice's voice grew stronger. "Heathen Frisians, score upon score of them, crashed through the tree branches and bushes, shrieking and brandishing lances.

"They outnumbered us, countless scores to one. The soldiers fought gallantly to protect us. Threw hand axes. Grabbed lances with one hand. Swords with the other."

Gontram shuddered at the horrible memory. "Long hair thick with rancid grease. Clothes of flapping animal skins. Frisians poured across the short distance separating us from them. A few of the barbarians fell. Screamed in pain where casting axes hit home. But for each Frisian that fell, ten more took his place.

"Startled at the sudden chaos we could not move. Frozen! Those on the perimeter fell where they stood. Blood spurted from fatal wounds inflicted by Frisian swords." Gontram gripped Pepin's arm.

"Then, as we surrounded him in defense, Boniface called out, 'Hold, hold my children. *We cannot kill the very men we came to save!* Scripture biddeth us return good for evil. This is the day I have long desired, and the hour of our deliverance is at hand. Be strong in the Lord; hope in Him, and he will save your souls.'

"For an instant, hand-axes stopped in mid-flight. Soldiers became statues. Frisians ceased their awful shrieking.

"A club smashed into my skull." Gontram's eyes bulged. "My teeth slammed into each other. I felt a crushing pain. Brilliant colors blossomed behind my eyes.

"And then, the most amazing thing happened."

Gontram turned his gaze to Pope Stephen, as if seeking benediction. With the pope's nod, the novice continued. "I seemed to hover above the scene. Dozens of others floated with me. I saw the entire battlefield spread out below. The bodies of the slain lay twisted on the ground. The surviving Frisians charged Archbishop Boniface. He, alone, stood upright. Around the archbishop lay the priests who had followed him, a tangle of corpses. My body and Bernard's among them.

"Helpless, I watched a Frisian's ax bite into the Archbishop's skull, slicing it in two!

"I remember no more."

Gontram paused. Took another sip of water. Then continued, "Some while later, I am told, Frisian Christians arrived to recover Boniface's body and give it proper burial. They said he held a book containing several works of the fathers, stained and covered with his blood. It was open to a writing of St. Ambrose on "The Blessing of Death".

"The next I knew, I was here, on this cot, in this room at Saint-Denis. I know not how I survived when everyone else died. I only know that God gave me the grace to live. I am more convinced than ever before, that my life is His."

With his narrative finished, Gontram sighed and closed his eyes in exhaustion.

Pope Stephen made the sign of the cross over the novice. "Following the martyrdom of Boniface," he said, as if to continue Gontram's tale, "thousands of Frisians converted to Christianity. By this unselfish act of love, Archbishop Boniface achieved far more than his most fervent wish."

Pepin, overwhelmed at the strange tale of his mentor's martyrdom, had forgotten to breathe. Now he seemed to have forgotten how. He was suffocating, and could not force air into and out of his lungs.

He gripped Gontram's shoulder. "I... I thank you for telling me," he whispered.

Pepin turned to Pope Stephen, unable to say more. The pope nodded in compassion. His hand on Pepin's arm, Stephen said, "Boniface was a close friend. With this knowledge, you have suffered a grievous blow. Take some time for yourself while you come to terms with the archbishop's death."

Grateful, Pepin twisted his mouth in a sad smile. Stumbling on legs that felt like potage, he left the infirmary. Without plan, he moved through the monastery grounds of Saint-Denis like a dead man.

His first awareness came as he pulled open the heavy wooden doors leading into the church. Inside all was dusky grays and blacks, the air scented with dust and remnants of incense. A tiny flame glowed red inside its holder under the crucifix at the far end of the building. In the silence, the great door closing resounded like a battering ram.

The flame drew Pepin. His footfalls soft on the dirt floor, he walked the length of the cavernous building. At the railing to the sanctuary, Pepin knelt.

"Why?" he asked. "Heavenly Father, why take Boniface in such a cruel way? Boniface did naught but good in this world. He loved You. Desired naught but to do Your will. If pain was to be suffered, that pain should have been mine."

The king laid his head on the railing. "Boniface gave me the crown, saying that act was Your will. I was more than ready to believe him. I, not he, longed for the throne with every fiber of my body. If the coronation was blasphemy, the blame is mine, not his.

Without thought, Pepin's body slipped to the floor where he lay, arms outstretched, a living replica of the Crucifix hanging high overhead.

"Oh God! *Mea culpa.* The guilt is mine. Heavenly Father, *mea culpa.*"

As Pepin lay there, he saw Boniface—not on the ground, bloody, his skull hacked in two—but on a cross. He heard a deep voice say, *"This is my son in whom I am well pleased."*

In that instant, Pepin understood the death of Boniface was an appropriate result of a righteous and virtuous life.

Boniface died achieving his heart's desire—converting pagans to Christianity.

"It had *nothing* to do with me. Any more than Carloman's decision to become a monk.

I am not the center of the universe. *God* is."

Chapter Twenty-One

Pepin had barely returned home and begun mourning the death of his religious advisor and patron when a messenger arrived in Quierzy with word from Pope Stephen.

"His Eminence, the pope, requests your presence at Saint-Denis. He has received a message from King Aistulf ."

Wondering whether his threat of intervention had been enough to cause the Lombard king to withdraw from Rome, Pepin left for Saint-Denis on horseback with a small contingent of guards early the next morning.

Pepin experienced a feeling of benediction the moment he entered the gate in the monastery wall. His student days at Saint-Denis had, by and large, been pleasant ones. Added to that, the religious community itself exuded a sense of quiet purpose.

A choir of monks rehearsed in the church. The haunting melody of a chant by Pope Gregory wafted out through the open door, further lifting Pepin's spirits.

A teaching brother had brought his class outdoors on this mild summer afternoon. They sat at his feet in the shade, practicing both reading and Latin with the Beatitudes.

"Blessed are the meek," piped a young boy's voice.

"For they shall inherit the earth," responded the class.

Pepin paused, momentarily reliving his own time spent studying here as a youth. The memory made him smile.

"Blessed are they which do hunger and thirst after righteousness," read another lad.

"For they shall be filled," answered the others.

Pepin strode on. Near the infirmary, a brother knelt on hands and knees working in the herb garden. He weeded neat plots of rosemary, chamomile, feverfew and boneset.

Farther on, next to the kitchen building, two black-robed brothers worked in the vegetable garden. One tied bean vines to a pole while the other hoed between rows of young cabbage heads.

Pepin entered the bishop's residence, which had been made available to Pope Stephen during his sojourn at Saint-Denis. He blinked in the sudden cool darkness. As his eyes adjusted, he saw the pope seated at a table reading a scroll.

Pepin crossed the room to kneel and kiss the papal ring.

"Pepin! Well come," greeted Stephen.

"You have news of Aistulf?"

"Yes. Though not what we had wished." The pope sighed. "Aistulf will not give up his claim on Rome. With the awesome wall of the Alps to protect him, he apparently feels safe from Frankish intervention."

Pepin's heart plunged to the pit of his stomach. "And well he might. I have grave doubts my noblemen will choose to follow me over those forbidding mountains to wage battle with an enemy who threatens not their own lands."

"Not even to save Rome for Christ's church?"

Pepin smiled. "They might consider fighting for *your* safety—were you to dwell here at Saint-Denis. Or Soissons. Or Tours. But Rome is a long way off." Pepin shook his head. "To follow me into a battle unlike any the Franks have ever fought... and I who sit the throne without benefit of a serpent as progenitor."

The pope reached across the table to lay a hand on Pepin's arm. "I have a plan to strengthen your claim to the Frankish crown."

"So you mentioned before. What have you in mind?"

"A second coronation."

For an instant, Pepin wondered if he had heard the pope correctly. "Boniface crowned me once. In a church. What difference would a second crowning make?"

"The difference is that Boniface performed the ceremony in my name. This time I would do it *myself*."

"Well, if you think a second coronation would help sway popular opinion in favor of my reign..." Pepin heard the doubt in his own voice.

"Not just *your* reign, Pepin. This time, Bertrada will sit on a high-backed chair next to yours. To symbolize her authority to give birth to royal infants. Charles and

Carloman will stand next to you, showing their right to inherit the crown.

"You will rule," Stephen said, "not just as one man from a crowd of equally likely men. With this ceremony, the house of Pepin will be declared to have royal blood. And you will be its first royal king."

Pepin stared at the pope, thunderstruck. The idea that the pope's authority could change his blood like communion wine, into something new, took his breath away.

The day before the ceremony, Pepin and Bertrada walked together. In the meadow behind them, Franks from near and far camped cheek to jowl in hundreds of tents.

A festive mood reigned over the crowd. Banners flew from noblemen's tents. Villeins had bedecked theirs with bright ribbons and boughs of flowers and greenery.

Musicians gathered in impromptu groups from which the skirl of pipes and cadences of drums mingled with the shouts and laughter of men, women and children.

Pepin turned to survey the scene and smiled at the joviality he saw and heard.

Leaving the noise and confusion to enter the forest, the huge oaks and dense greenery created a muted and calming atmosphere. "So you and I both, are to become royal?" Bertrada mused. "Our children, and their children's children will be hereditary kings of the Franks?"

"So Pope Stephen assures me," Pepin answered.

Bertrada stopped to pick a few stems of Saint John's wort with their yellow flowers in bloom, and put them carefully in her pocket for future use. "So the long-ago vision that has guided your family for a hundred years and more, has led to this. But what, exactly, does having the pope bless the coronation mean?"

"I will try to explain it to you, as he explained it to me." Pepin seated himself on a log, patting a place for Bertrada to sit beside him. "In ancient times the Romans worshipped many gods. They thought of their kings, their Caesars, as gods and worshipped them as well.

"Meanwhile the Franks chose their leaders annually, by vote of the noblemen. With the first Clovis, who descended from the legendary birth of Meroveus, sired by a sea-beast, so *their* story says, the office became hereditary to the Merovingians. When a king died, the noblemen still voted their approval of a successor, but were limited to men who had royal Merovingian blood."

Pepin took Bertrada's hand in both of his. "When the pope celebrates our coronation, he will tell the Frankish noblemen they now must vote for men who have *our* royal blood. Instead of a legendary sea serpent as proof of our royalty, we have God's blessing, bestowed upon us by Pope Stephen. I, and our children, and their children's children will rule by divine right! Our line will be royal because *God* chose us."

Pepin looked up through the tree branches to the sky beyond. "I wonder, will our blood—yours, mine, Charles, Carloman's—be different, after the coronation?"

He shrugged and looked back at Bertrada. "I know not *how* our blood will change to become royal. But, having Pope

Stephen declare it, will certainly help win over the die-hard followers of the Merovingians."

"We can but hope." Bertrada smiled and patted his hand.

The twenty-eighth day of July in the year of Our Lord, 754 dawned bright and warm. The church at Saint-Denis was packed with excited, sweating people. Not just noblemen and soldiers, but highborn women among them. They murmured in anticipation as the sun glinted off gold-trimmed crimson and cobalt paintings of apostles and saints on the ceiling above the clerestory openings.

Pepin sat next to the altar, Bertrada to his left. He breathed in the scent of flowers that always seemed to float about her. She wore her finest violet linen mantle, its wide, flowing sleeves ending at the elbow. Her brooch, a cluster of garnets and pearls set in gold, returned sparks of light, reflecting the nearby altar candles. Twelve-year-old Charles and his eight-year-old brother Carloman stood behind their parents, fidgeting with excitement.

Pope Stephen appeared, dressed in his ceremonial cassock encrusted with embroidery and jewels, tall, pointed hat perched imperiously on his head. In his right hand he held a staff topped with one large, brightly-colored stone. He began the long procession from the back of the church toward the altar, following a youth who swung the censer from which streamed clouds of sweet-smelling incense.

Mass, with its liturgy and chants from the choir of brothers, transported Pepin to another realm. Here, where his father was buried alongside older Merovingian kings, Pepin felt surrounded by his people's history. And by God.

Behind him, Charles and Carloman grew weary of standing and began slyly poking each other. A silent, reproving look from the pope reminded them of the solemnity of the occasion and they immediately stood tall and still.

Following the mass, Pepin knelt before the pope, who anointed him with holy water, tracing the shape of the cross on his forehead.

"Boniface consecrated you King of All Franks in my name. Now I reconfirm you in that role. You have been chosen by God to rule all Gaul."

Pepin returned to the throne, while Stephen anointed first Charles and then Carloman as kings to be, in their own right. At the touch of the pope's hand on their foreheads, the boys stared at him, eyes wide, a look of awed terror on their faces.

Taking the Frankish crown from its place on the altar, Stephen reverently placed it on Pepin's head. After wearing this same crown on ceremonial occasions for three years and more, its weight felt familiar. And yet the crown seemed to have gained new importance.

"I proclaim you, Pepin, King of All Franks, and more. No longer shall the city where Saint Paul was crucified look to the emperor of Constantinople for guidance and protection. For now I declare that you, Pepin, King of All Franks are now *Patricius* of Rome as well."

One by one, first Pepin, then Bertrada, followed by Charles and Carloman, knelt before Pope Stephen, felt his hand upon their heads and reverently kissed his ring.

The pope turned to the multitudes cramming the church. His voice rang with conviction. "Turn you not from whom God has made royal. As the Merovingians looked to Clovis and those who could trace their lineage directly to him, so now God directs you to accept *only* Pepin. His bloodline is royal and worthy to wear the Frankish crown."

Pope Stephen's voice rose to thunder, "Under pain of excommunication from Mother Church, choose you not for king any man from other than this family, henceforth and for all time!"

The entire church fell silent.

Pepin felt himself grow warm with a burning desire to fulfill this promise of greatness, all but guaranteed by the pope. Please God, he prayed, let me live up to all that has been pledged here this day.

During the long ceremony a ray of sunlight had been moving across the floor of the church. It now came to rest on Pepin, like a benediction from God. The light reflected on the golden crown, sending shafts of brilliance from the large jewels set therein.

A ripple of awe spread through the congregation.

"Amen. Amen. Hallelujah and Amen," sang the choir.

Pepin took Bertrada's hand in his; felt it tremble as he held it close. She sent him a look of love and pride.

"Amen," she whispered.

"Amen," he responded.

Chapter Twenty-Two

That summer, twice-crowned King Pepin and Queen Bertrada accompanied their daughter, Giséle, to the convent of Chelles. She had never once wavered on her conviction God had chosen her, and she wished nothing more of life than to be a bride of Christ.

"You will be a novice for two years," said the Abbess of Chelles as they sat on hard benches in her austere outer chamber. "Your parents," she looked first at Pepin, then Bertrada, "may visit you once each year.

"If at the end of your novitiate, you still desire to be a nun, you will take your vows and be accepted into our order. If you find in your heart that this is not what God desires for your life, you will be allowed to leave and return into the world. No one in the convent will think any the less of you."

At the end of their interview, Giséle clung briefly to her mother and father. Pepin felt her quiver and he consciously strove to imprint the feel of her body in his arms.

"You know that you can send for me to come get you, if ever you should so desire." His voice sounded husky even to his own ears.

"I know, papa. But I am sure I will not." She paused, looking into her father's eyes. "Thank you."

Pepin would for the rest of his life, treasure the memory of her gentle touch on his cheek.

If it had not been for Giséle's delighted smile and the anticipation dancing in her green and hazel eyes, Pepin would have been heartbroken when the heavy gate of the nunnery clanged closed behind them. But he had prayed as earnestly to God as had Giséle, and now surrendered her to His keeping. If hers was, indeed, a true calling, he would support her and the Convent of Chelles with his continued prayers and treasure.

"Who knows," he commented, his arm around Bertrada, "one day she may become the Abbess of Chelles."

Pepin spent the remainder of the summer and fall in negotiations with King Aistulf of Lombardy. He sent a letter by messenger. In it he demanded the towns and lands captured by Aistulf, including Byzantine Ravenna, be restored. But not to the emperor in Constantinople—rather to the Church of Saint Peter in Rome. He signed himself, "By Divine appointment, Defender of the Holy Roman Church."

"I, Aistulf, King of Lombardy," came the reply, "will enforce my borders any way I see fit. Rome sits to my south like a plum, ripe with treasure. Ready for plucking. If it falls into my hands, so much the better."

Aistulf's reply continued. "I do not tell you where you may go within Frisia, Saxony or Aquitaine. Dare you not tell me leave Rome or return Ravenna! I grant Pope Stephen safe passage back to Rome. No more!"

Pepin felt his hopes for a peaceful solution to the problem of Rome plunge. Nothing would stop Aistulf but defeat in battle.

Worst of all, he could see Aistulf's point. Let the Lombards try to meddle in Frankish affairs and see where it would get them! Why should Pepin meddle in theirs?

Filled with foreboding, Pepin traveled to Saint-Denis to confer with the pope.

Pope Stephen waited for him in the bishop's residence. After relaying King Aistulf's latest rebuff, Pepin asked, "Why can you not be content to live and direct all churches from here? Why must it be Rome?"

Stephen looked startled at the question. "The city of Rome is key to the entire papacy!"

"But why?" asked Pepin.

Stephen strode the length of the room. Turned to face Pepin. "Because the pope's authority comes directly from Saint Peter. Christ said to him, 'You are Peter, and on this rock I will build my church.' From that charge, Peter became Bishop of Rome. Since then each pope has been anointed the successor to Peter.

"Of all the honorifics that go with the papacy, the most precious title is that of Bishop of Rome. That title gives the pope—those who preceded me and those to follow—authority over all churches."

The Pontiff spread his arms palms raised. "How could a pope be Bishop of Rome from any place other than Rome?"

With a sigh, Pepin realized he had no choice. "I will convene a *Champs de Mars* and do my best to convince the noblemen and their armies to climb the Alps and take the battle to Lombardy on your behalf."

The noblemen met in the royal palace of Braisne. Outside a steady rain fell. The atmosphere inside the great hall was equally chill and dark. The straw cuttings on the floor were crushed and filthy from a winter's hard use and mud from many boots. The mutinously angry feelings among the men were as disturbing as the overwhelmingly offensive odors.

"*I* will not order my men to climb those fearsome mountains to fight against the Lombards, with whom I have no quarrel!" declared Stilicho, a nobleman from Neustria.

Villicus smiled.

Pepin's gut twisted in discomfort. "But we are called by God to be Defenders of Rome! We cannot turn our backs on Pope Stephen. On Rome. On God!"

"God and the pope may have declared *you* Defender of Rome," cried Totila, a nobleman from Burgundy. "But He spoke not to *me* on the matter. You go. Fight God's fight against the Lombards. As for me, I will take my army and return home!"

"Hear! Hear!" shouted several others.

Pepin noted with bitterness that Villicus was loudest among them.

He had tried to warn the Pontiff that this might be their reaction. But Stephen had been unable to conceive of such an idea.

Pepin's supporters and detractors, nearly at blows with one another, demanded he take action. Shouts and fists might well lead to unsheathed knives and swords.

He *had* to get their attention. His own shout in the din would matter little. Taking advantage of an opening on a bench that had been vacated, Pepin climbed onto the table. Stood there. His face contorted with rage.

This rash act by their king caught all men by surprise. In silence they stared at him. Amazed.

"Yes, Stilicho," he thundered. "Take your armies back to your estates in Nuestria. Go you, Totila, home to Burgundy!

Pepin's voice grew dangerously quiet as he faced his archenemy. "Even you, Villicus."

With a sweeping gesture, Pepin included the entire gathering. "All you who hold God so lightly, go to your homes. Think God has need of you? Think you to discredit me?" Pepin sneered. *"No!* So leave. All of you. *Now!*

Pepin took a deep breath and looked heavenward. "Those who remain fight on the Lord's side. We shall prevail, even if it be one man to five hundred of Aistulf's. We are glad to see you go. We who remain have God's blessing. You who go have naught but your own."

So saying, Pepin turned and deliberately stepped down. Regained his seat in the ornate, high-backed chair.

His eyes swept across the gathering. Men who minutes ago had been giving vent to their anger, stood silent. Eyes downcast. Feet shuffling the fetid straw of the floor. Slowly, they returned to their seats on the benches.

Onlookers who had crowded the hall—captains and even a few soldiers standing pressed against the walls—stopped their shouting. Looked questioningly at their leaders. Tried to gauge which way the wind blew.

Not one nobleman picked up hunting knife and shield. Nor signaled soldiers to follow. Nor made move to leave.

Chapter Twenty-Three

Rain, which had fallen during the *Conventus,* continued unabated. Pepin delayed two days, hoping for better weather. At best it dwindled to drizzle, but soon renewed its force in windy squalls. The sound droned in Pepin's ears with mind-numbing effect. It soaked into the ground and floated in pools, a sea of mud.

At last, fearing the men would grow weary of the wait and begin leaving for their homes, Pepin and his armies loaded soaking-wet supplies on the ox-pulled wagons. With the Pope in attendance, they began slogging their way toward the Alps.

As had his father before him, Pepin made it a point to talk personally with the men who followed him to battle. By now he knew all of the noblemen by name. Knew who supported him with whole heart. Who wavered. And those who would take pleasure in his failures—still hoping to climb over his back on their way to leadership themselves.

Rain dripped off the hood of his warm travel cloak, creating a pungent smell of wet wool. Pepin turned his horse to ride awhile with Chlodomer. His friend's army followed Pepin's own personal guard.

Chlodomer greeted him with a smile and strong handclasp. "Nice weather for fish and ducks."

"Methinks we should issue webbed feet and gills to all soldiers who go to war in spring." Pepin's heart warmed that his friend could still smile and joke with him.

They rode companionably, side by side. Their horses snorted and touched flanks as if content with each other's company as well.

"Recall you our first campaign?" asked Chlodomer.

"With my father against Duke Eudo in Aquitaine?"

"The very same." Chlodomer grinned, his brown eyes twinkling. "We practiced throwing our axes against stumps and logs in camp every evening along the way. We threw so many times my arm felt as if it might leave my shoulder and fly to the stump along with the ax."

"And sharpened our swords until they could have split a hair in two." Pepin felt once again the sense of urgent activity that had covered their excitement and trepidation at being part of a grown-up company.

"And then, Eudo's men surrendered without a fight!"

"How disappointed we were!"

Chlodomer looked at Pepin, his eyes suddenly serious. "With battles under our belts, we would be less upset if King Aistulf were to do the same."

"To fight and win is glorious," Pepin replied. "But to win without a fight—without bloodshed or loss of comrades—is better yet. I pray Aistulf will change his mind and give in."

"Fight or no, we *will* vanquish the enemy, for God is on *our* side!"

Pepin gave Chlodomer a salute. "Aye, we shall return victorious." He felt much heartened by his friend's support.

Wheeling his horse about, he sought out Villicus. He must give equal attention to his enemies.

Villicus wiped the rain from his face with a flourish. "The very skies weep, that we seek a fight so far from home, with one who has done us no wrong."

"The skies weep because it is *spring*." Pepin's sense of well-being disappeared. "They care not one whit whom we fight—or where."

"Mayhap the skies care not—" Villicus' smile came nowhere near reaching his eyes, "—but God who creates all things in heaven and on earth, may well be trying to send you a message."

"The pope speaks more clearly of God's will than either you or I. Forget you not, we seek this battle on *his* behalf."

With difficulty, Pepin suppressed a smile and kept a straight face when Villicus failed to find a ready retort. However, the man's pursed lips and taunting look bode poorly for Pepin's peace of mind. Villicus would not hesitate to press any advantage against him.

Pepin continued working his way along the line of men, offering encouragement alike to boys on this, the first adventure of their lives, and seasoned soldiers, plodding through the mud. All seemed pleased to have the king speak with them personally. None voiced doubts about his right to wage war on the Lombards. At least not to his face.

He spoke briefly with Pope Stephen who traveled with his personal entourage between two armies from Neustria. "How feels it to be returning home after a year and more in Frankish Gaul?"

The pope smiled. "I look forward to Rome. My toes have not felt warm since they began climbing the Alps two winters ago."

"A fine way to talk about our warm Frankish hospitality!" Pepin gave Pope Stephen a look of mock dismay.

"I did not say my heart was not warm—just my toes."

Pepin saluted. "To a successful trip—*and* warm toes." He turned his horse and cantered off, hooves splashing in the wet and mud.

"God's greeting," Pepin said to a skinny, wizened old man, driving an ox cart loaded with foodstuffs wrapped tightly against the rain.

"And to you, sire," the man replied.

The oxen pulled their heavy feet through the muck with a sucking sound. Wooden wheels screeched their protest against axles swollen with water.

"By what name are you called?" asked Pepin.

"Hugo, sire. And I be knowin' ye since ye be but a small twig. I were a footsoldier what followed your father."

"You fought with Charles Martel?"

The old man sat straighter with pride. "Saxony, Bavaria, Aquitaine. I fought 'em all. Even stood against them heathen Moslems in the great Battle of Poitier. How Martel rode his horse, seein' we be standin' shoulder to shoulder, chest near touchin' the back o' the man to the front o' us. Again and again, them murderin' madmen rode they horses faster'n the wind, curved blades flashin' like lightning. But we held, by Mithras! Charles Martel backed us, an' we held.

"He been a good man, your father. Now it be up to you to do him proud."

Pepin felt a momentary tug of sadness at the memory of his father—so beloved by the men who would have fought through hell for him. Pepin wondered fleetingly how the soldiers would remember *him* when he was old. Or dead. With all his heart he hoped it would be with the respect and pride that rang so clearly in Hugo's voice as he spoke of the renowned Charles Martel.

Taking leave of Hugo, Pepin peered into the steady rain. His father had been the greatest leader of all time. Why had he not been king? The soldiers offered him the crown after the Battle of Poitier. But Martel turned it down. Said the throne was not his destiny.

In his heart, Pepin knew he could not begin to measure up to his father, yet *he* had the title and the long hair. How could he possibly be king when his father had felt unequal to the task?

Pepin sat straighter and squared his shoulders. He was king because his father fought hard to be able to hand him unparalled leadership over the Franks. *And* because God, through Pope Stephen, had chosen him.

Days passed in a blur of rain and mud. The whole world appeared gray and chill. As the land tilted towards the Alps, placid wide rivers narrowed to raging torrents, spewing white water, carrying logs and whole trees tumbling and churning in their wake.

The men climbed from the foothills into the mountains, leaving behind them the last small hamlet offering a dry place to sleep, albeit cheek to jowl on the floor. They ate their last belly-warming pottage simmered over a kitchen building's fire.

As the track wound higher, they knew they would have to sleep where nightfall found them, be it wet or dry. If all they could find were rain-soaked logs, their hunger would have to be satisfied with cold biscuits, tough smoked meat and raw onions.

Following a track growing ever steeper, rain gave way to stinging sleet. Pepin was forced to dismount. Leading his horse by the halter, he panted for breath as his boots sank into thick mud.

Ox cart drivers urged the giant beasts onward while footsoldiers put their shoulders to the wagons, helping push the load up the slippery track.

Trees grew more stunted, then disappeared altogether, leaving boulders in their stead. Men shivered and coughed, their noses running red and raw with naught but a rough, wet sleeve to wipe them.

Young Gaiseric, who had learned something of the healing arts, was hard-pressed to help the men who suffered from chills one moment and burned with fever the next. With no way to heat water, he could offer no soothing teas of feverfew, sage or thyme.

The same remedies had little effect when floating in frigid water from barely melted ice and snow. They needed to be simmered carefully to release their healing properties.

More and more men fell ill with the ravages of grippe, bringing the army to a grinding halt. Soon flux of the bowels added to their miseries. Then, one by one, men began to die.

Pepin wept, his tears mixing with sleet upon his cheeks, as he carried the lifeless body of Hugo, and laid him gently with the others in a shallow grave, painstakingly pried from the rocks.

"He was a good man," he said to Pope Stephen.

The pope put a hand on Pepin's shoulder. "They were all good men. Now they will be heavenly soldiers for Christ." He peered out from exhausted, red-rimmed eyes. Offering comfort, confession and absolution of sins had kept him awake most of the night.

He turned to face the grave. Fifteen corpses, with others likely to follow. Making the sign of the cross over them he said, *"Requiem aeternam dona eis, Domine,* Eternal rest grant them, O Lord, *et lux perpetua luceat eis*, and let perpetual light shine upon them."

Those who had the strength piled stones over the grave to keep hungry beasts from desecrating the bodies.

Pepin slept fitfully that night, his clothes and blanket wet and cold. The deaths bothered him. He knew all who had died. Their names. Family stories. To die in the heat of battle was one thing, but to succumb to sickness was frightening. How could they fight an enemy they could not see?

At dawn something startled him awake. What was wrong? An ominous presence filled the silence of his tent. It seemed as if the entire world had disappeared, leaving him the sole survivor.

Grabbing his knife, he cautiously opened the flap. The silence outside was even more pronounced. At last comprehension dawned. The rain had stopped! In its place, a thick, dank fog shrouded everything. Shadowy figures drifted in and out of sight as wisps of clouds wafted by.

The camp had an eerie feel, men becoming little more than ghosts. The entire area seemed a foreign place of mists and shadows. Pepin's shiver had nothing to do with the cold. He banged his shin on an unseen rock and took two wrong turns before stumbling into Gaiseric's tent.

"Five died over the night." Gaiseric's shoulders sagged. "At least, that I know of. Perhaps others as well. There's naught I can do."

"What are their names?" Pepin did not truly want to know. However, hearing the worst, steeling himself before he saw the faces of dead friends, made it less difficult for him to bear.

Pepin stood again at the edge of a mass grave filled with the stiffening bodies of fighting comrades. The remainder of the army behind him was but indistinct forms huddled into cold, damp cloaks and blankets.

Pope Stephen raised his hand and opened his mouth to say the words of the requiem mass. No sound came forth. The pontiff closed his eyes, swaying slightly. Then with fresh resolve, he opened his eyes and silently mouthed the all too familiar words.

Trudging back to his tent in the murky fog following the brief service, Pepin's heart ached for Pope Stephen. The man looked less well than some who had died. If he should succumb to exhaustion and illness, Pepin would lose an admired friend and religious advisor. Another one.

Pepin stopped in his tracks. If Pope Stephen should die... there would be no point in continuing. Why fight against King Aistulf and his Lombard army if Stephen were not to be Bishop of Rome?

Villicus and others would read the pope's death as an undeniable sign from God that Pepin, in taking the battle to Rome, had chosen unwisely. Was—even though the pope had declared him chosen by God and of royal blood—no longer fit to lead the Franks. Be king.

A shadowy figure emerged from the swirling fog and clasped Pepin by the arm. Chlodomer's features came into focus. "We have a problem," he said.

My men are dying, thought Pepin. The pope looks soon to follow. The army is stopped in its tracks on the side of a wet, cold mountain. An unknown enemy waits on the other side. Known enemies on this.

"Tell me," Pepin ordered, bracing himself.

Chapter Twenty-Four

"Our numbers have dwindled further," Chlodomer said.

Alarm flooded Pepin. "More have died?"

"No. Left."

"Left?" Pepin asked. "Where? How?" No need ask *why.*

"Just packed their weapons, took food from the wagons and left. Turned around and started for home."

"And Villicus did nothing to stop them." Pepin gestured in disgust. "Probably encouraged their discontent."

"What will you *do?*"

Pepin forced himself to consider his options. "What *can* I do? Many of the men are too sick to walk. The oxen cannot pull more weight up this steep track. Even with healthy men pushing from behind, they can barely make the wagons move. The rain has stopped, but the fog makes us blind. In the wet and cold, more men will sicken and die."

"And those who can, return home," said Chlodomer.

The two friends stood silent in the mist. What would Father have done? Pepin wondered.

The answer came as clearly as if Charles Martel were standing next to him.

"Order the men to pack their weapons and belongings," Pepin said. "We move out immediately. Every able-bodied man shall walk. The most severely ill may ride my horse and those of the other nobles and captains. The weak may hold on to stirrups or wagons to help them up the mountain."

"How can you order sick men to climb this God-forsaken wasteland?"

"How can I not?"

By mid-day, Pepin and his army had staggered above the mountain-hugging cloud. The sun shone with a brilliance that stabbed their eyes. It had no warmth here at the top of the world. A brisk wind cut through Pepin's warmest cloak as if he were naked. He felt for the poor footsoldiers whose clothing was flimsy at best.

Holding his horse's rein in one hand, a walking stick in the other, Pepin gasped the cold air. It pierced his chest like a lance. He looked back at the rag-tag army following him. A sick man, Godegesil, rode his horse. The poor man looked to have lost consciousness, but held onto the horse's mane with both fists. The army stopped behind Pepin. Panting, they tried unsuccessfully to catch their breath.

Below, the cloud looked innocent and soft. Its white mounds gave no indication of the deaths, pain and suffering it had caused.

With a supreme effort, Pepin raised his hand to signal the army to begin walking again. His feet were as if made of stone. Numb with cold and too heavy to lift.

But Mont Cenis Pass was in view. Pepin wanted to show his men their suffering was nearly over. The way would be downhill from here on. He forced himself to lift one unfeeling foot and then the other. Tugged the rein. The horse, flanks heaving, followed.

An appalled silence surrounded Pepin as the men joined him in looking over the summit. A jumble of boulders now obliterated the way down the mountain paved by Roman Legions. Their stone slabs now tilted at impossible angles.

Avalanche?

Earthquake?

The hand of God had wiped out any hint of a path.

Jagged mountains rose steeply on each side of the rock-strewn track. They could scramble over the boulders or retreat back down to the foothills to struggle through an entirely different mountain pass!

At Pepin's gesture, two of his own guard began to climb gingerly down. They went carefully, testing each rocky step. If a boulder should roll after they put their full weight on it, a broken ankle would be the least of their injuries.

Rather than go straight down, they worked diagonally across the littered rocks. Pepin's heart stopped and the watching men gasped as Manaulf, younger of the two by a half dozen years, started a rockslide. They saw Manaulf fall, rocks tumble, and a puff of dust rise before they heard the low rumble.

Alcuin, stocky and strong, shouted, his words lost in the rumble of falling rocks. When the slide stopped, he began climbing down, slow but steady. Manaulf's body lay unmoving amid the boulders.

At last Alcuin reached the still form. Manaulf stirred. Shook his head. Reached for his leg.

Pepin watched as Alcuin spoke to Manaulf. Carefully felt his calf. Ankle. Foot.

The men cheered as Alcuin helped Manaulf to stand. The two men continued down the rocky slope even more slowly than before. Manaulf leaned heavily on Alcuin. Now and again the two went on all fours or sat and slid over the boulders. After what seemed a very long time, they reached safety below.

Pepin let out a breath. Wiped his brow. Thanked God. Two had managed to get down. But what about the rest of his army?

Taking their cue from Manaulf and Alcuin, the men began to pair up. Their chances of making it down were greater if they helped each other. Soon the steep slope was covered with men trying to find the best way down.

With a shout, one man fell. Started another rockslide. But this time the moving boulders and the man's body ran into those ahead of him. Knocked them down. Caused an even greater avalanche. The others stopped, watching in horror.

The air was filled with a cloud of dust. The roar and rumble of tumbling boulders. The screams of men. Some in terror. Others in pain.

At last the horrible thunder ceased. Slowly dust settled. A few men began to move gingerly. Testing for broken bones. Dislodging small rocks and pebbles to continue their mindless journey rolling downhill. Some men cried out in pain and panic. Others remained still. Arms and legs at strange angles. A stain of crimson spreading, covering the rocks beneath them.

Late that night Pepin went from man to man, comforting and encouraging the small remnant of his once strong army. What sickness had started, the rocky pass had finished.

Fortunately Chlodomer survived, though with a huge bruise on the side of his head. One eye was swollen completely shut.

Villicus survived. Unscathed. Of course. Pepin could not help but wonder why so many good men were killed while Villicus remained unharmed.

At least Pope Stephen was safe! The men had willingly helped him down the treacherous descent.

At last, Pepin succumbed to food. A warm fire. Sleep. Blessings all.

Pepin awoke to clear skies and bird songs. With a smile, he emerged from his tent. Not since before the *Conventus* at Braisne had there been such a morning!

The smile disappeared as he surveyed what remained of his army. Most of the men still slept. Many were ill. All but a pitiful few had ugly bruises and bloody bandages. Pepin shook his head.

He made his way to Chlodomer. One side of his friend's face was swollen beyond recognition. He was awake, though in obvious pain. Nonetheless he held out a hand to Pepin and managed a lopsided grin.

Pepin grasped the offered hand. "By Mithras, you are one ugly Neustrian!"

Chlodomer gave a small nod of agreement and winced. "What plan you now? March we on Aistulf as we are, a small mangy dog worrying a wild boar?"

Pepin looked over the encampment again. "No. We shall wait here for the Lombards."

"You think they will come?"

"Of course. If we go not to them, they must perforce come to us. And the longer we wait them, the better."

Chlodomer looked puzzled. "Why say you that?"

"Give us a fortnight to recover and we might yet prevail. Even if we are out-manned four to one."

"And if we have not the fortnight?"

"Then we shall pray God for help. And, as my father said on more than one occasion, use *our* weakness as strength and the enemy's strength as weakness."

Chlodomer looked puzzled. Tried to shake his head. Moaned and sank back into his blanket.

"Rest now, my friend." Pepin touched Chlodomer's shoulder briefly. "Soon enough I will have need of your strong arm."

As soon as the men had broken their fast, a subdued group gathered around Pepin. Well aware of their losses, they looked from one to the other. Apprehension about what King Aistulf and his Lombard army might do to them showed clearly on every face.

"This campaign has been doomed from the start," began Villicus. "It had neither the blessing of God, nor the support of those of us who argued against it. Folly led us here. Folly and your own…"

Something in Pepin snapped. "Jupiter's balls! Villicus, you sound like a mewling kitten. If you cannot fight like a man then—then just *shut up!*"

Their mouths open, eyes wide, the soldiers stared first at Villicus then turned to face Pepin.

"We shall pray God," said Pepin, regaining his composure, "for time to heal our wounds and strength against the enemy. In the meantime I have a plan…."

A rock bounced down the steep slope behind them. Then another. The signal. Their lookouts perched halfway up the dangerous slide area had spotted the Lombards off in the distance. The army approached, ready to fight.

Pepin looked about. Only half the few who had survived illness and the treacherous descent from 7,000 foot Mont Cenis Pass remained in the clearing.

Most of those were still wrapped in their blankets, apparently not yet recovered from their ordeal. The others were perched dispiritedly on boulders against which the camp nestled. A half dozen slumped on logs that had been pulled around the fire.

Pepin watched Pope Stephen go from man to man, hearing confessions and giving absolution for sins before the coming battle.

Pepin closed his eyes briefly and prayed for strength, for victory against all odds. Then he went from man to man himself. "Have you your knife? Lance? Throwing ax?"

At each affirmative nod, Pepin smiled. "Rest while you can. Move you not too soon. Trust God." He grasped a hand. Gripped a shoulder. Went on to the next.

At last he joined those sitting on the logs. He took a deep breath.

"When?" they asked him.

"Soon."

They heard footfalls sounding in the forest. Branches snapped. Aistulf's army emerged into the clearing.

Pepin and those sitting with him looked up in feigned surprise. The Lombards laughed. Began to reach for weapons in scabbards.

Without warning axes flew through the air, felling the first rank of Lombards. As the next rank entered camp, still loosening their weapons, the seemingly injured and ill Franks leapt from their beds, lances and knives in hand. Pepin and the others sprang from their logs, at the same time throwing their axes at the attackers.

Even with the advantage of surprise, the Franks were outnumbered four, five, six to one. They quickly formed a phalanx, facing the Lombards, their backs to the rocks.

Wielding a sword, Pepin fought side by side with his men. Thrust and parry. The Lombards kept coming. Using a two-handed hold, a man swung his sword at Pepin. Ducking, Pepin felt the blade graze the top of his helmet. With a kick, Pepin knocked the man, already off balance, to the ground. Finished him with a thrust of his sword. Turned to face the next one. And the next.

The Lombards curved around Pepin's footsoldiers and scrambled into the boulders, hoping to outflank the encamped Franks. Just then, rocks—loosened by the remainder of Pepin's men who had been hidden on the hillside—rumbled with a deafening roar down on them, quickly felling the hapless Lombards.

The men scrambled down the steep slope on paths prepared during the previous few days. Joined their comrades in the bloodbath.

The rout.

Those of the Lombard army who could, ran for their lives. Franks chased them into the forest and returned to their encampment with abandoned ox-pulled wagons filled with precious supplies.

That evening they sat around their campfire, flushed with success.

Chlodomer turned to Pope Stephen and asked, "If God intended us to be victors, why think you he allowed so many Franks, good men all, to perish before we even got here?"

Silence descended as each man thought of a comrade, brother, cousin who had died, either of illness or the terrible avalanche of rocks just behind them.

At length the pope said, "Recall any of you the story of Gideon?"

"Gideon?" asked Chlodomer.

"Who is *he?"* asked a voice in the darkness.

"Was, not *is,"* corrected the pope.

"What does someone who has already died have to do with *us?"*

"A great deal, if you would understand God's design," responded the pontiff. "Hear the story."

A quiet rustling ensued as men settled themselves, followed by silence broken only by the snapping of the fire.

The pope began, "Many hundreds of years before the birth of Our Lord, there lived a man in the land of Israel named Gideon. In those days the Israelites had fallen into evil ways so God allowed the Midianites, a ruthless and powerful eastern tribe, to prevail over them.

"The poor Israelites fled their homes, dwelling in caves on the hillsides for protection. When they planted crops, the Midianites invaded and set up camp in the middle of the fields, ruining the crops, killing the livestock. The Bible says they came with their livestock and tents in numbers beyond counting—like swarms of locusts.

"Although Gideon was the least likely son in the weakest tribe in Israel, the Lord chose *him* to lead his people against the powerful Midianites. Gideon asked God to give him signs that He had truly chosen a poor man such as himself to lead the fight.

"Finally convinced, Gideon and his men were ready to fight the Midianites. The Lord said, 'You have too many men. Tell anyone who is afraid to return home.' Twenty-two thousand men left while only ten thousand remained."

Pepin smiled at this. He recalled saying much the same thing at the last *Conventus.* But no one left when he gave them the option.

The pope continued. "The Lord said you still have too many men. Take them to the spring to drink. Gideon did as instructed. The Lord sent back all who kneeled to drink, lapping the water like dogs. He allowed Gideon to keep only the three hundred who drank from water scooped up in their hands.

"Only then, did God give victory to the three hundred Israelites against the hordes of Midianites."

The pope sat back. A satisfied look on his face.

"But," Chlodomer expressed the same confusion felt by Pepin and no doubt others. "Why did God send men away instead of letting them join the fight?"

"Because He wanted all to recognize the victory belonged to God, not man alone. If superior forces win, what is the miracle? But when outnumbered armies pray God for victory—and their cause is just—then God intervenes on their behalf.

"Just as God allowed you Franks to vanquish the Lombards, even though most of your men were killed before the battle even began." The pope stood and raised his hand in benediction. "To God the glory! To God the honor!"

The men sat straighter, proud to be chosen by God.

"We shall chase King Aistulf and his army until they beg for mercy. They shall know we fight on God's behalf!" declared Chlodomer.

"Hear! Hear!" cried a dozen voices.

Pepin felt his own blood stir.

A tapping of hunting knives on shields, on rocks, on the logs they sat upon signaled his army's agreement.

Villicus added his voice. "We shall plunder the hamlets, burn the crops and pillage the great halls. We will return to Gaul with goodly treasure as befits a Frankish campaign!"

The entire army let loose a mighty roar and banging of knives on shields.

"King Pepin over Aistulf!"

"Franks over all!"

Pepin swelled with pride. For the first time in my life, he thought, I agree with Villicus!

Chapter Twenty-Five

King Aistulf paced the grand hall in his capital city of Pavia like a caged bear. The brick-walled building had never closed in on him this way before... how strange.

He glared at a group of Lombard noblemen clustered against the wall. "I have been king of Lombardy for six years. And we have won *every* battle we have fought in all that time. Is this not so?"

"Yes, sire," the noblemen chorused.

Aistulf strode to the end of the hall. Turned. Shouted. "Who took Ravenna from the Byzantines?"

"You did, sire. It now belongs to Lombardy."

Aistulf smiled. "Yes. It belongs to me." He noted the relief on his noblemen's faces at his quiet voice.

"And so shall Rome!" he bellowed. The noblemen blanched. Aistulf felt marginally better.

The king sauntered to the messenger kneeling just inside the entrance. Stood over the cowering man. Resisted the impulse to kick him.

"Tell us once again. Where is Pope Stephen?"

Aistulf's voice turned quiet once again. Enunciated each word carefully. "And that runt, Pepin, with his miserable Frankish rabble? What have they been doing?"

"They follow the Po River out of the Valley of Susa. While the Lombard army came swiftly to Pavia, the Franks move slowly. They raid every hamlet and town. Kill those who oppose them. Disperse the rest to forage for themselves in the forests. Pillage everything of value. Take any crops ripe enough to eat. Burn the huts. Add our people's livestock to their entourage."

Aistulf turned on his heel and began pacing again. At last he stopped in front of his noblemen. Turned his back on them to face the messenger and shouted, "Get *up!* Get *out!* The very sight of you makes me want to puke!"

The king turned to his supporters. Took a deep breath. Regained control. "There must be some way of stopping those damnable Franks. Assemble our army. The Franks will have no time to prepare a defensive position. Take the battle to them. This time we will," Aistulf examined a hangnail, bit it off and spat it out, "approach them differently. We now know that puny as they seem, they are a force with which to be reckoned."

"Sire," interjected a nobleman, "the men will not leave Pavia to engage the Franks. They fear the enemy's casting axes, which fly through the air faster than falcons. And with equal accuracy."

Aistulf glared at the man who had spoken with such candor. Unfortunately, he spoke but truth.

"Shall we stay here and allow those misbegotten barbarians to ravage Pavia? Is that what you want?"

"We could negotiate with Pepin," suggested a timid voice.

"Negotiate? With a madman who kills, burns and pillages? By all that is holy, how do you propose we make him pause long enough to negotiate?"

"We could ask his brother Carloman to come. Pepin would listen to him," offered the same timid nobleman.

Aistulf felt a stillness wash over him. For the first time since their ignoble defeat in the Valley of Susa, hope glimmered. "Yes.... He would listen to Monk Carloman."

The king smiled. "We will *negotiate*. Promise the moon. The stars. Anything to get him back on *his* side of the Alps."

Aistulf pushed his face close to that of the timid nobleman. The man blanched but dared not move as the king's spittle showered his face. *"Then* we will take what we want! And *Rome* will be *first!"*

King Aistulf turned to the rest of his cowering noblemen and snarled, "Where is this monk? Beloved brother of that runt, Pepin?"

"He is still in Frankish Gaul. I believe he has permission from his Abbott to visit Metz," answered a tall count standing toward the back.

"Still in Gaul? What in the name of all that is holy, is he doing in Gaul? We need him *here*. Now. This very day!"

When no one moved, Aistulf stamped his foot in frustration. "Do *not* just stand there like a bunch of sheep. Move! Go! Order him to return. Now!"

"Yes, sire," a chorus of voices replied. The men nearly trampled one another in their rush to leave.

Pepin pushed his army on toward Pavia and King Aistulf. Good weather and fresh food taken from the hamlets they leveled had done much to restore the men to fighting shape. Morale had never been higher.

"With God's aid, we shall surely prevail over the Lombards," Chlodomer enthused. He and Pepin rode side by side, following the Po River. A warm breeze rustled new leaves in the trees overhead. The sun-dappled shade made travel pleasant.

"Perhaps." Pepin felt nagging doubt. Not that God could lead them to victory, but that God would intercede for them in every battle. "In a fair fight the Lombards will outnumber us. And if they refuse to engage us on an open field, army to army, but stay within the city of Pavia..." he grimaced. "The defenders always have the advantage."

The two men continued in silence, each contemplating the conflict to come. At last Pepin said, "I wish we could force him to negotiate, but I know not how."

Pepin gazed at Pavia on the Ticine River near its confluence with the Po. The forest shielded his army from view. Before them stretched cleared fields with summer crops sprouting green and tender. Closer in, orchards blossomed and vineyards sent out new tendrils. A scattering of small huts clustered about two large brick buildings—a church and the great hall. Both somberly impressive, with buttresses reinforcing the heavy plain walls which supported wooden roofs.

He considered his options. Where would they want the battle to take place, if there was to be one? And if they besieged the town, where was the enemy's greatest vulnerability? Food and water. River and fields. But how could they protect themselves from the army within and at the same time guard their backs from reinforcements likely to come from the rest of Lombardy?

Pepin placed his largest contingent along the river. The Ticine would protect their backs. The rest of his soldiers set up camp under the fruit trees. Cleared fields would at least give them a view of anyone trying to come to the aid of Pavia from out of the forest. And the Franks had full advantage of food as it ripened while denying the Lombards access to their own crops.

The town appeared empty of inhabitants. Pepin reasoned they were most likely sheltered in either the church or the great hall.

Once the tents were set up and the camp functioning well, he ordered his Franks to systematically level one unoccupied hut at a time—after removing all food, tools, clothing and anything else of value.

Pepin was surprised, but pleased, that King Aistulf did not bring his army out to fight the Franks face to face. The longer the Lombards waited, the stronger his men became.

Some weeks later, a small delegation emerged from Pavia. They approached the Frank's encampment without weapons, carrying a white banner.

"King Aistulf would negotiate with Pepin, King of All Franks," they cried.

"Let Aistulf and his noblemen come outside the town, hands empty of weapons," replied Pepin. "I, with Pope Stephen and my noblemen, will meet him."

The Franks set up a trestle table between the vineyards and the ruins of the huts nearby. Pepin and Pope Stephen sat on a bench on one side. King Aistulf and his priest sat across from them. Behind each side stood a handful of noblemen. The Lombard army remained out of sight in the hall. Pepin's army stood, fully armed, within the confines of their camp—well out of earshot.

"You must respect Pope Stephen's rights which he inherited from Saint Peter," Pepin began. "He must be allowed to rule Rome."

Aistulf glowered at Pepin—the pope—the Frankish noblemen and the army beyond them. He looked to his own priest who nodded infinitesimally. "I will agree, Pope Stephen may have Rome."

The pontiff smiled, his relief evident.

Until next time, Pepin mentally finished for Aistulf.

When at last the sun set on the negotiations, Aistulf had agreed to return Ravenna as well, and pay permanent tribute to Pepin as overlord. He would send forty hostages back with the Frankish army as guaranty of his promises.

In return, Aistulf was allowed to keep both his life and his crown.

Pepin turned to face Pope Stephen. “Tomorrow our army will accompany you to Rome.”

The pontiff looked alarmed. “You need not come with your entire army! You will want to return with your treasure and hostages to your own lands. Now, while the weather is good. I am safe with but token Frankish emissaries to accompany me to Rome.”

Pepin looked at the pope. I like him. Respect him, he thought ruefully. But now we have shown him our strength, he wants us back. Far back. Way on the other side of the Alps. Pepin smiled and shrugged. If our positions were reversed, I would want the same.

“As you wish. I will send Chaplain Fulrad and enough soldiers to guarantee your safety with you to Rome.”

As the Frankish army prepared to return home with their treasure and forty hostages, word came that Pepin’s brother, Monk Carloman, had died on his journey from Metz to Pavia to plead with Pepin to negotiate a settlement with King Aistulf. Carloman had gotten no farther than the city of Vienne when he took ill. He languished for several days before dying peacefully.

A mournful Pepin ordered Carloman’s body buried at the monastery of Saint Benedict. Carloman belonged to the Benedictines more than ever he had to the Franks—Charles Martel’s son or no.

Chapter Twenty-Six

Pepin's homecoming at the villa in Querzy was all he could have asked for. The grand building offered everything he had lacked during the campaign. Sunlight filtered through wind openings. Flowers of every hue filled the gardens in the atrium. At the villa Pepin found warmth. Plentiful food. Compliant servants. A doting wife.

In autumn Pepin received a letter from Pope Stephen. He read it to Bertrada as they walked hand in hand in the apple orchard. He reached up, plucked a shiny red apple and handed it to her. Then took one for himself. He crunched into the apple. Tasted its tart-sweet meat. Felt the juice run down his chin.

"The letter says, 'King Aistulf has not permitted one handful of earth to be restored to blessed Peter and to the Holy Church of God.'"

Pepin looked up. Smiled, his eyebrows raised. "Why am I not surprised?"

"Why did you negotiate with him, if you had no trust he would keep his word?" Bertrada asked.

Pepin sighed. Shrugged. "Slim though it seemed, there was a *slight* chance he might honor his pledge. He sent forty hostages as guarantee. How could I not at least try to settle the matter without further bloodshed?

"Besides we had already killed so many. Outnumbered, weak with injuries and illness—we wanted nothing so much as to believe him and come home."

"So, you will return with overwhelming numbers, fresh and whole to fight again?" she asked.

"I hope not. We may start with overwhelming numbers, fresh and eager to fight, but climbing the Alps will only leave us decimated once again. Perhaps the pope will find others nearer at hand to give him aid against the Lombards.

"I would like, at least the *chance* to become the great king of Egar's prophecy. But to do that, I must do what kings do. Defend and extend our *own* borders. Settle disputes within *my* realm. Assure the people they have my ear and best intents."

Bertrada licked apple juice from her fingers and looked at him. "The people have no complaints on that account."

"Thanks to you. While I fought battles on Pope Stephen's behalf, you toured my domain and did what I should have been doing myself."

Pepin took her hand. Kissed the fingertips. Then the base of her throat before moving his lips to hers.

Reluctantly he pulled away and continued. "Meanwhile the Saxons are as contentious as ever. My *sweet* half-sister Chiltrudis and her son Tassilo thumb their noses at me from their duchy in Bavaria."

"Yes. I know," Bertrada interrupted. "And the Aquitanians no longer put up even the slightest pretense of swearing fealty to the Franks. And the Muslims! They are still a burr in our side in Septimania from the Pyrenees to the Middle Sea."

Pepin smiled and gave her a hug. "Of course. *You* already know all this even more clearly than I. Jupiter's balls! I have no *time* for Aistulf and his whoring Lombards."

Word came on the first of January. Aistulf was *again* marauding the area of Rome, burning houses around the basilica of Saint John of Lateran, the pope's church.

Pepin heaved himself up from the bench by the table in his chamber. "God's death, I shall have to gather an army and fight him all over again!"

"Why not let Pope Stephen fight his own battles?" asked Bertrada, perplexed. "Or lose and be subject to King Aistulf? Why must *you* rush to his aid each time he calls?"

Pepin cocked one eyebrow. "Because I am king of all Franks by *his* order and blessing. *And* protector of Rome by his decree." He smiled. Shrugged. "And because I *like* the man and want to do whatever I can to help him."

Once again, Pepin found himself on the brink of Mont Cenis Pass. On this campaign the weather had been kinder.

Far fewer had died. Except for the noblemen and some of the captains, most of his army was new. They had not yet experienced the arduous journey to carry the fight to the Lombards. But all had heard of the disastrous descent down the boulder-strewn mountainside the previous year.

One look—and to a man—they were ready to return home. Let Pope Stephen take his chances with King Aistulf.

One look and Pepin felt ready to return home with them. How could he convince men to follow him down that dangerous slope when his own knees turned to jelly and his guts clenched in fear at the sight of it?

He looked at his army and had no idea what to say. Should he shout imprecations at them? Call them cowards? Get on his knees and plead with them?

He sat on his horse, trying to take charge of his emotions. "You have heard how the rocks and boulders will tumble at the slightest misstep."

Pepin was surprised that his voice sounded firm and natural. He had half expected it to quaver and break. "The resulting avalanche will kill any who happen to be in its path. What you have heard is true. Like you, I want not to tempt my fate on this pass.

"But good Pope Stephen depends on our strong arm to defend him against the evil Aistulf." Pepin paused, letting his words sink in. "King Aistulf, who forfeited his hostages. Who swore an oath, with no intention of keeping his word.

"We *must* carry the fight to the Lombards on Pope Stephen's behalf. Face Mont Cenis with courage. Respect what it can do to us. Step carefully. Work together. Help each other. If we can conquer our fear of the mountain, *nothing* stands in our way.

"Remember, God blesses our campaign. We will overcome the boulders. We *will* vanquish the Lombards!"

The men began to smile. Punch neighbor's arms. Tap shields with hunting knives.

"We can do it!"

"Franks over Aistulf!"

"Neustrians over the mountain!"

"Austrasians over Mont Cenis!"

"King Pepin over all!"

With that they started gingerly climbing around the boulders of the treacherous pass. Their courage filled Pepin with wonder, as he led the way.

Pepin surveyed his army with pride. What a difference between this force and the decimated straggle of men he had led last year!

They built their camp in the same location, at the foot of the boulders in the Valley of Susa. Within days, the lookout sent word. King Aistulf's army had been spotted entering the forest leading to the Frankish camp.

At a quiet command the army formed a traditional phalanx of fighting men. They stood, shoulder to shoulder in ranks eight, ten, twelve men deep. Shields held in readiness, they looked like one huge scaly beast bristling with lance tips.

The Lombards crashed through the forest. They pulled to a sudden stop at the sight of the Frankish army.

"Stop you not now!" King Aistulf's voice carried loud and clear in the ensuing silence. "Move! Unbuckle your weapons. Hold up your shields. Form lines." The king waved his arms, his hands flapping helplessly. "God's body! Where is your fighting spirit? You worthless, spineless, misbegotten sons of whores. Must I do *everything* myself?"

The Lombard king swore, kicked and prodded his army out of the forest. The men unsheathed their weapons and cowered behind their shields.

Pepin noticed smiles playing on the lips of his men. "Forward, one!" he shouted.

With well-disciplined precision, his army moved as one body a single step forward. Though still out of range for their casting axes, they had narrowed the open space between the two fighting forces.

One of Aistulf's footsoldiers turned tail and unluckily ran headlong into his king. Without hesitation, the maddened monarch lowered his lance, gutting the poor man.

"Must I kill you, one by one myself, or will you stand up like men and fight the Franks?"

With renewed vigor the Lombard army formed ranks and faced Pepin's men. They moved far enough forward that all of their men, including the noblemen mounted on horseback were clear of the forest.

Even the feared flying axes of the Franks, though they felled a goodly number, were not sufficient to stop the Lombard army. It moved forward as much on mind-numbing fear of its king as on courage in the face of battle.

Pepin cheered as his front line of men threw their barbed javelins. The iron-headed weapons imbedded themselves in the Lombard's shields. Franks rushed forward and stomped on the trailing wooden handles, jerking the shields down, forcing them out of the enemy's hands.

With swords, they stabbed and hacked the unprotected bodies of the front rank of Lombard footsoldiers. The bloodbath that followed overcame the Lombard's fear of Aistulf. To a man, they quit the fight and ran.

Once again King Aistulf sued for peace. Pepin granted him life and continued rule of Lombardy, taking as his victor's share the city-states of Ravenna, Rimini, Pesaro, the Duchy of Urbino and a portion of the Marches of Ancona.

"But why did you allow Aistulf his throne, let alone his life?" asked Chlodomer. "He will only play you false again."

The night was late as he and Pepin sat in front of their campfire. With the exception of sentries posted along the edges of their camp, the army slept.

"I know he means nothing by his oaths and hostages. But for now, he is of no importance. We must first go to every town and duchy we have won. Each nobleman must give us hostages along with the keys to his city gates in homage to our victory. *These* we will take to Rome."

Chlodomer's eyes gleamed in the light of the fire. He smiled at the picture of conquering hero Pepin painted.

Chapter Twenty-Seven

Pepin looked over his shoulder at the string of armies behind him. The thought occurred that they had come full circle. The road that led the Roman Legions to conquer Francia, now brought the Franks back to Rome!

Immediately behind him came his own personal guard, all on horseback and headed by a gonfalonier holding the pole from which flew the banner of Pepin, King of All Franks, depicting the holy remnant of Saint Martin's cape.

The rest of the armies stretched in a serpentine as far as his eye could see. Noblemen and their captains rode on horseback. Footsoldiers walked two by two, following the colorful banners of the family to whom they were pledged.

The highest ranked noblemen carried, along with their own gonfalons, the banner of one of the cities captured from the Lombards. They were charged with protecting not only the keys to the city, but hostages from there as well.

Huge ox-pulled wagons, piled high with provisions and plunder of war rolled slowly after each army. The rumble and screech of wooden wheels nearly drowned out the crunch of heavy boots on the cobblestones. Some footsoldiers sang lusty songs. Others walked in rhythm to tattoos played on drums of different sizes.

Around them the countryside had turned the golden color of honey. Here and there vineyards basked in the sun. Tight clusters of small green grapes waited for its warmth to turn them into sweet, juicy, purple orbs.

Chlodomer joined Pepin. "Look! Rome!"

Pepin followed the line of Chlodomer's pointing hand. "I do believe you are right. There, on the hill, the Temple of Jupiter. How fine it looks with its stone pillars all around."

"Yes, I remember it from when we brought Carloman to Rome," Chlodomer said. "The white marble buildings of the city are nothing like our wooden Frankish towns."

Pepin's throat constricted at the memory of his previous journey to Rome. With Carloman. Moisture gathered unbidden in his eyes.

Chlodomer, ever sensitive to his friend's feelings, grasped Pepin's arm. "You miss him still. Your brother."

Pepin nodded, not trusting his voice.

"See there," Chlodomer pointed to the right. "Is that not the pope's residence and church, San Giovanni of Lateran?"

"Yes!" Pepin's heart raced at the thought of meeting Pope Stephen. To be the hero, who had, once again saved Rome from the ravages of King Aistulf and his Lombards, gave him great pleasure.

They passed outlying farms, some of them naught but burned-out shells. They stood forlornly, mute evidence of the Lombard's threat to Rome.

A small contingent of Roman centurions approached on horseback. "Pepin, King of All Franks?" asked the leader.

"I am King Pepin."

"Pope Stephen requests we lead you and your army to a place to camp beside the Tiber River. His Eminence asks your presence and that of your noblemen at a special mass to be celebrated on the morrow in the Basilica of Saint Peter. Afterwards, he looks forward to hearing of your exploits over the Lombards."

White tunics trimmed in red, legs bared except for sandal straps, the Roman soldiers seemed unaffected by the heat. Pepin felt as though he were riding through an oven. Sweat dripped down his face and onto his chest. His clothing was suited to a northern early spring, *not* a Roman summer!

He envied the Romans their close-cropped hair. His own symbol of Frankish monarchy created an additional blanket on his neck and down his back.

The next morning Pepin and his noblemen entered the basilica filled with immaculately clean and exquisitely coifed and clothed Roman citizens. Senators, consuls and patricians wore silken tunics and togas striped with threads of gold and silver.

Pepin breathed a prayer of thankfulness he had allowed himself to be taken to a Roman bath the evening before. He had been soaked, oiled, massaged, and then washed again until even Bertrada would not have recognized him.

People shifted to allow the Franks to walk between them to the front of the church. A low murmuring and open stares followed Pepin. He knew what they were saying.

"Is *that* the king?"

"That short one with the long hair?"

"He looks not at all formidable!"

"How could *his* army have defeated the Lombards?"

The looks on the Romans' faces told of their concern as well. They had traded a known enemy—King Aistulf and the Lombards—for one unknown.

What would Pepin and his Franks demand of Rome?

How long would he and his army remain?

When the Franks finally reached their places of honor at the foot of the high altar, Pepin was startled to see a Byzantine contingent from Constantinople already there, just across the aisle.

"What are *they* doing here?" he quietly asked Chlodomer.

Chlodomer shrugged.

"They came not when Pope Stephen begged their help against the Lombards," Pepin murmured. "Nor came they in defense of the towns Aistulf took from them. Why *now* are they here?"

Pope Stephen entered, following an altar boy swinging the censer. The familiar fragrance of incense and the sound of the choir singing chants drove any concern about the Byzantines from Pepin's mind.

He was pleased to see the elderly pope looking fully recovered from his ordeal of climbing the Alps the previous year. Pepin had been terrified the pontiff would not survive the journey.

Kneeling. Standing. Praying. Listening. Pepin allowed himself to be fully immersed in the service. When Pope Stephen finally said, "Itta missa est," the Frankish king had to pull himself back to the present.

As the congregation left for home to break their fast, a trestle table and benches were brought to the front of the sanctuary. The Byzantines sat on one side, the Franks on the other. Pope Stephen occupied the chair of authority at the head of the table.

"So, my friend," Pope Stephen turned to Pepin. "What have you won as your victor's share?"

Pepin returned the pope's smile, pride filling his chest to nearly bursting. The most revered man in the world had become a friend. To be able to help him, made the trials of the campaign shrink to insignificance.

He nodded at Chlodomer who rose and bowed to Pope Stephen. "Your Grace."

The pope held up his hand in blessing. A warm twinkle in his brown eyes belied the formality of his gesture.

Chlodomer turned and gave the emissaries from the Byzantine emperor a brief glance. "M'lords."

They nodded in return.

Chlodomer turned once again to Pope Stephen. "After our victory over the Lombards, we traveled first to Ravenna, which Pepin won as part of his spoils of war.

"When we arrived, the gates were flung open in welcome to King Pepin and our army of Franks. Citizens of the area—noblemen, craftsmen, soldiers, and farmers—all met us in the open center of the town.

"Then the noblemen knelt before Pepin in submission to his authority over them. They held their hands between his and pledged their fealty to his rule. Thus did also the officials of the town and the captains of the armies.

"All pledged themselves to Pepin." Chlodomer gestured with pride to the king.

"A document," he continued, "writ upon parchment proclaims Pepin's right to tribute, one day's work in seven—whether it be crops of the field or products of the craftsmen's hands—all to go to Pepin, their king."

With this, Chlodomer pulled a scroll from the bag tied to his waist. He showed it to Pope Stephen and then placed it on the table in front of Pepin.

"And as symbol of his ownership of the city of Ravenna," Chlodomer continued, "gave they him this key to the gates of their city."

With a flourish, Chlodomer pulled from his bag a huge iron key with filigree work decorating its handle. This, too, he laid on the table in front of Pepin.

Although he felt like raising his fist in victory, Pepin merely smiled at his friend before nodding seriously to acknowledge the ceremonial receipt of the symbolic gifts from Ravenna.

He then turned to Villicus who rose and followed Chlodomer's speech with one of his own relating the peaceful transfer of Rimini to Pepin's throne. This was followed by similar presentations by three more Frankish noblemen. After which they each placed scrolls and keys to the city gates from Pesaro, Urbino and Ancona on the table in front of Pepin.

"What will you do with these towns?" asked Pope Stephen. "Plan you to keep them or return them to the Byzantine Empire from which they were taken by King Aistulf and his Lombards?"

Silence engulfed the sanctuary. Pepin felt the eyes of the Byzantine ambassadors boring into him.

Would those be his *only* choices? To keep the cities for himself would mean having to defend them from further attack by the Lombards. Rather than fortifying Rome, they increased his burdens south of the Alps. When would he ever be free to rule his own kingdom? Become the great *Frankish* king of Egar's vision?

On the other hand, to return the five towns to Byzantium solved nothing. Those from Constantinople had shown little concern for their holdings here in the past—neither to defend the towns *nor* Rome. Pepin would lose that which was his by right of victory and still have need to defend Rome against the Lombards.

"I thought to give them to Pope Stephen," Pepin said. "So he could use the armies and tributes in defense of Rome from the Lombards."

The Byzantines scowled.

Pope Stephen looked surprised, then confused. "But I cannot own towns and peoples and armies! I am a vassal to the Emperor of Rome who lives in Constantinople. All earthly things I have are his by right."

The Byzantine contingent smiled, their relief evident.

The leader of the ambassadors stood and faced Pepin. "The Roman Emperor has empowered us to be generous to you, Pepin, King of All Franks. He is prepared to reward you for your service in winning back the towns that had been lost. You will receive treasure in gold. In silver. In valuable gems. Horses from the Berbers, too. All these gifts are yours to use in rule and defense of your kingdom to the north of the Alps."

Not only the Byzantines, but Pope Stephen as well, looked expectantly at Pepin. He could see by their expressions that all viewed this as an entirely acceptable solution. They would thank Pepin and pay him well to stay far away. On *his* side of the mountain barrier.

Nothing was working out as he had planned! What could he do?

Pepin tried to think of an alternative solution. What would his father have done? What would Egar have advised? He sat for some while in silence, searching deep within himself for an answer.

He thought back to what Pope Stephen told him. That he inherited the office of pope from those who stretched all the way back to Saint Peter. He whom Christ had called 'The Rock'. Upon whom the church was built.

With *this* thought, Pepin had his solution!

He turned to Pope Stephen. "The towns are mine, won in battle, to do with as I wish." Pepin tossed his head. "I have decided I shall not keep them."

Pope Stephen nodded and smiled, his relief evident when he realized the Frankish army would not be forever camped on his doorstep.

The Byzantine ambassadors started whispering happily among themselves.

"Nor shall I give them to Pope Stephen."

The pope shrugged.

The ambassadors smiled to each other.

"Nor to the Emperor of Byzantium."

The ambassadors froze.

"I shall give them to Saint Peter!"

"But..." protested Pope Stephen.

"But... but..." sputtered the Byzantines.

"But—" Chlodomer stood, "—Saint Peter has been dead for seven hundred years and more!"

Pepin, the weight of decision lifted from his shoulders, felt as though he were rising above the delegations. Floating high near the painted ceiling of the basilica of Saint Peter. Looking down on the scene from above. "I took Ravenna, Rimini, Pesaro, the Duchy of Urbino and the Marches of Ancona for the sake of the Roman chair and under the aegis of Rome shall they remain. I give them, not to Pope Stephen, who is vassal of Byzantium, but to Saint Peter, Bishop of Rome and his descendants—the popes, the bishops of Rome —in perpetuity!"

Pepin gathered the five keys in his arms. "As token of my donation to Saint Peter, I bring these keys to his tomb."

A smile of understanding slowly transformed Pope Stephen's face.

Chlodomer sat with a thud. "But, I do not understand!"

Pepin could well understand his friend's confusion. "Pope Stephen, the man, cannot own or rule over lands and cities. All Stephen has, he owes as a vassal, to Byzantium—*in exchange for their protection.*" Pepin looked pointedly at the ambassadors, who squirmed, refusing to return his gaze.

"But if the cities belong, not to Stephen, but to Saint Peter, to be handed on to succeeding Bishops of Rome as part of the office, then the emperor of Byzantium has no claim on them.

"With the armies of five cities at his beck and call," Pepin continued, "and the produce and treasure of their tributes, any pope should be able to defend Rome against her enemies without having to beg help from either Byzantium or the Franks. As overlords of five cities—much as they are bishops over all churches—the popes will be equal to any king on earth!"

The pope sat straighter in his chair of authority. To Pepin it seemed his mitered hat resembled a crown.

The ambassadors glowered.

The Franks smiled. They would no longer be expected to clamber up and over the Alps whenever the Lombards harassed Rome.

"Come," said Pepin. "Let us break our fast."

He strode down the empty basilica, hearing the scraping benches and rustling clothing of men behind him hastily standing to follow.

Chapter Twenty-Eight

Retracing their steps over the Alps, Pepin actually welcomed the coolness of the high mountain air. Following the descent into his own domain, Pepin gratefully toured fields and orchards that were bursting with food to see his realm safely through another winter. He breathed deeply, air redolent of tart-sweet apples and sun-warmed grapes. He took comfort in the familiar scents of home and harvest.

Finally seated in the great hall of his winter court, Pepin watched the messenger who had just delivered a packet from Rome stride out the door. A log smoldered in the fire pit. Shadows gathered in the corners of the large room.

Guards stood at both doors and on the gallery above, as well. The major domo hurried into the hall from outside, a page scurrying at his heels.

Pepin pried open the missive. Walked to the wind opening, squinting against the faint light. Read the message. In a surge of emotion, he paced the length of the hall.

Looking about, he saw no one with whom to share the momentous news.

"Bertrada!" he called.

No answer.

Climbing the stairs as quickly as his legs allowed, Pepin called again, "Bertrada!"

A quick glance into the room he shared with his wife revealed a brazier burning on the table, illuminating chests, baskets and bundles stacked neatly against the walls. Showed the covering pulled over the large bed against the far wall. No Bertrada.

Pepin hurried along the gallery. "Bertrada!"

"What is it? What is wrong?" Bertrada called. She emerged from a storeroom, hastily locking the door with a huge iron key, one of many on a metal ring tied at her waist.

Pepin grabbed her hand. "Come. You *must* hear this!"

When she saw the grin he could not squelch, her expression changed from concern to one of curious bemusement. She allowed herself to be led to their chamber.

Grasping her shoulders, Pepin thrust her to a bench. Seating himself opposite, he smoothed the message on the table. "Listen to *this*," he commanded. Catching the fitful light from the brazier, he began to read.

Pope Stephen, Bishop of Rome, Overlord of the Pentapolis:

To Pepin, King of All Franks, Greetings,

> As you will no doubt recall, my major concern when you left Rome after making me overlord of all you had captured, was that King Aistulf still ruled Lombardy. He soon proved himself as faithless and devious as ever he was wont to be, fully prepared to break all oaths and desert his hostages.
>
> I prayed deliverance from Aistulf's threat. The Lord, Our God, heard my supplication. The Lord is still a God of history who acts for them who believe in Him.
>
> Soon after my prayer, King Aistulf went hunting, and was smitten by the judgment of God. He fell from his horse. The ailment that he contracted from this accident brought about an end to his life within a few days.
>
> The Lombards have taken heed of my advice and chosen Desiderius as their new king. He is a friend to Rome and poses no threat to God's holy city or to you, Pepin, my protector and benefactor.
>
> God be praised! Hallelujah and Amen.

Pepin sat straight, a weight lifted from his shoulders. "With King Aistulf dead, I can now turn my full attention to ruling the Franks. I shall fortify our borders. Subdue the Saxons. Bring Aquitaine once more firmly under our hand."

"That is good news, indeed." Bertrada took his hand, her eyes glowing in pleasure. "Forget you not Duke Tassilo of

Bavaria when making your plans. I think it might not be amiss if you were to reassert your preeminence over *that* domain as well."

"Pull tight the young man's tether?" Pepin smiled.

"Something like that."

"How old must my sweet half-sister's whelp be these days?" he mused. "He was five when I named him Duke of Bavaria with Chiltrudis as regent. That was what—" Pepin pondered, "—two years before my first coronation? Could it have been so long ago? Tassilo must be thirteen by now. Perhaps fourteen. Fully old enough to understand the oath he takes on his own behalf."

"Make the ceremony impressive," Bertrada warned. "That young man is surrounded by noblemen urging independence from the Franks. He is of an age when he will be only too ready to listen."

"Impressive... Yes. Indeed."

Pepin held his assembly at Compiégne on the Aisne River, a day's journey west of Soissons. Leaders arrived from all over the realm. Priests wore their most ornate vestments, the Franks their most colorful attire. Banners flew in the brisk spring breeze. Clouds scudded in an azure sky.

Tassilo arrived with his magnates, all adorned in their best jewels for this, his oath-taking as Duke of Bavaria. From this day forward he would rule his duchy on his own, without his mother's guidance.

Pepin, at forty-three, had never felt more kingly. He sat in the high-backed chair of authority, with its carved armrests and legs in the shape of lions' claws. The wind ruffled his long hair now streaked with gray. The weight of his gold, jewel-encrusted crown sat familiarly on his head. His bright blue mantle was clasped at the shoulder by a large silver and amethyst brooch.

When the playing of pipes and drums signaled the ceremony was about to begin, Pepin's sons, fifteen-year-old Charles and twelve-year-old Carloman took their places on either side of Pepin's chair. The crowd of noblemen, captains and footsoldiers parted to let through a procession of priests and bishops. Their raiment of purest white, encrusted with threads of gold and crimson, glistened in the spring sunshine.

The priests carried ornately gilded and jeweled reliquaries containing bits of bone from the saints. They parted to stand on either side of Pepin's chair.

Into the open space in front of Pepin, walked Tassilo followed by his magnates.

"I swear by all that is holy," Tassilo intoned, "to be a loyal and obedient vassal to Pepin, King of All Franks. To behave honestly and faithfully, in accordance with the law and as a vassal should to his lord."

Tassilo knelt in front of a bishop and reverently placed his hand on the offered reliquary. "I swear this on the body of Saint Dionysius—" he moved to the next reliquary and the next "—and Rusticus. By Eleutherius, and the bones of Saint Germanus. By the blessed cape of Saint Martin."

At last Tassilo came to kneel before Pepin. The king felt the Duke of Bavaria's strong young hands, warm and vibrant between his own hardened palms.

"I, Tassilo, Duke of Bavaria, swear to remain faithful all my life long, to Pepin, King of All Franks, and to his sons, Carloman and Charles after him.

"I shall serve them. Pay tribute to them. Lead armies to their aid. This I promise by my oaths on the bones and relics of the saints."

As Tassilo rose and walked proudly away, his magnates came, one after the other, to repeat the oaths of fealty to Pepin and the Franks.

Once the last of Tassilo's men had completed his pledge of fealty, all eyes turned to Pepin. He could read the one question on every face. Who do we fight this year?

Pepin savored their attention. "We leave on the morrow —for Saxony."

"Saxony. Good!" Heads nodded in agreement.

"Those Saxons raid our villages along the Rhine River," commented a nobleman.

"They rape our women."

"Destroy the crops."

Pepin spoke up. "The Saxons have not paid the tribute owed the Frankish crown for three full years!"

"They *will* pay!"

Men tapped hunting knives to shields in agreement.

The bishop's voice boomed across the gathering. "The Saxons are pagans. Worship false gods and idols!"

"Pagans!"

"Neustrians over the infidels!" shouted a captain to roars of approval.

"Austrasians over the whoring Saxons!"

Knife handles thundered on shields.

This is the way it should be, thought Pepin. Men in agreement to fight. Ready to follow their king.

As if on cue, the men—nobles, church leaders, captains, and foot soldiers—began chanting.

"Pepin, King of All Franks!"

"Franks for Pepin!"

"King Pepin!"

Pride swelled Pepin's chest at the accolades. That his sons were here to witness this affirmation by his followers, gave him great pleasure.

The Saxons fought hard—hacking and stabbing with their short swords. But they were no match for the flying axes that sailed from the solid block of Franks standing shoulder to shoulder, ten and twelve men deep. In closer fighting, the Franks' metal-tipped lances stripped Saxon shields from their hands, leaving chests exposed.

By the time the sun began slipping past midday, bloody bodies in grotesque postures littered the field of battle.

Pepin sat at a hastily erected trestle table flanked by noblemen and church leaders. Chieftains of the defeated Saxons stood before him, their hands bound behind their backs, ankles hobbled with leather thongs.

The stench of the battlefield assaulted Pepin's nose. The acrid, metallic odor of blood. The stomach-turning stink of excrement let lose from the bowels of dead and dying men.

We must dispose of the bodies, Pepin thought. But not until after the terms of defeat are accepted. Best the Saxons be reminded how much they have lost here today.

"You will take an oath of fealty to the Frankish crown," Pepin ordered.

The Saxons bowed their heads in acquiescence.

"As tribute, you will bring payment of three hundred horses to our *Champs de Mars* each spring."

The Saxon's heads snapped up. "But that is too much! We do not have—"

Pepin kept his voice calm, "Then we shall kill all of you and continue on to the next town. And the next, until three hundred horses *becomes* a reasonable payment."

The Saxons looked to their leader who sighed and shrugged his acceptance of the terms.

"And finally, you shall all be baptized Christians."

The priests smiled.

To a man, the Saxons shared their leader's look of dismay and alarm.

"But our gods—"

"Have no bearing on the matter," Pepin interrupted. "You lost. We won. Our Lord God is victorious over all. Through Christ you will be born again. Baptized, you shall be cleansed of all sin. Saved. New life in Christ. Or death forever. Choose. *Now!*"

* * *

That year Pepin and Bertrada celebrated Christmas in their villa. Late one night Pepin and Bertrada sat in their chairs of authority, sipping hot mead from tankards.

"The Saxons will fight again, but their defeat was total," Pepin said to his wife. "They shall be tame for a while yet. I have done what a king must—led the fight to strengthen our borders. Seen hundreds brought to Christ." Pepin swallowed a mouthful of mead, savoring the spicy flavor. "What more can a king— one who aspires to greatness—do?"

Bertrada shrugged. Smiled. "*Do,* m'lord?"

She laid a hand on Pepin's knee. An invitation?

Toward the end of winter, the usually healthy Bertrada began feeling poorly. Pepin worried as she became listless. Had no appetite. Could keep down nothing but the plainest of potages. "Rest," he urged her, his chest fluttering in alarm. "What in your pharmacopoeia can I fetch for you?"

"Perhaps some ground snakeroot rhizome," murmured Bertrada tiredly. "I have no idea what can be wrong."

By spring, Bertrada, with an almost apologetic smile on her face whispered, "I am with child. Again."

Pepin felt a sudden pounding of his heart. "My love. You never cease to amaze." He gathered her into his arms. "This might explain your illness over the winter. But, why? You never suffered so before."

"I was never so old before. Our "baby" Adélaide is twelve, Carloman sixteen, Charles seventeen, and the eldest, Rothaide, eighteen and married! How could I have another baby *now?*

Pepin took her hand. "My precious. My life. You must take care of yourself." *I cannot bear the thought of loosing you,* he thought, stroking her forehead.

When time came to leave for the *Champs de Mars*, Chlodomer brought Adele to stay with Bertrada. The two women had established a firm friendship, often visiting for several days at a time while their men were off on campaign.

Pepin stayed the summer within his realm, managing to come home every fortnight or so.

Bertrada remained fatigued. Her feet and legs swelled. She grew increasingly uncomfortable with the weight of the babe within. When cramps and bleeding started far too early for a safe birth, she took to her bed. The midwife joined Adele as a resident of the villa.

Pepin returned home to stay after the harvest but before the grapes were to be plucked and crushed. The feel of movement within Bertrada's womb encouraged him. The sight of his wife in bed terrified him.

When the birth began in earnest, Pepin paced the day room from end to end, listening to the muffled moans and cries coming from their upstairs chamber. "Please, God, save Bertrada and this babe she bears. I *cannot* live without her."

At last, hearing the baby's squall, he bound up the stairs. Adele barred his way to their bedchamber. "She is well, sire." She smiled, dimples appearing. "And you have a son. Will you name him Pepin?"

Pepin heaved a sigh of relief. *"Praise God!* Should Bertrada will it, this babe shall be my namesake."

Chapter Twenty-Nine

Pepin and Bertrada celebrated Easter of the year 760 at his ancestral home of Herstal, near Liége. Even this far north, spring had tenderly banished winter. Pepin and Bertrada sauntered along the path following the Muese River. They held hands like young lovers and breathed deeply of the crisp, fresh air, so welcome after the winter stench of the great hall. Young grasses sprouted at their feet. Above their heads, tree branches swelled with buds.

"A day like this makes me glad to be alive." Bertrada turned her face to the gentle sunlight. She closed her eyes and smiled.

Pepin raised her hand to his lips and softly kissed her fingertips. He was overjoyed that she had survived the birth of baby Pepin the year before. More than survived. Seemed her old self, but even more mellow.

They took a seat on a fallen log and watched the dark waters of the river flow swiftly by. Birds sang in the tree branches. From beneath her veil, a breeze blew tendrils of Bertrada's crown of braided hair to caress her cheek.

"You are beautiful and I am blessed." Pepin tenderly brushed a strand of hair back behind her ear. "Not for the crown—though that, too is God's blessing—but for such a wise and loving wife. No man could have better."

That year, Pepin changed the National Assembly from a *Champs de Mars,* to a *Champs de Mai,* held in May so bishops and abbots could celebrate Easter in their own dioceses and monasteries.

In the assembly held in 760, Pepin had no problem convincing his noblemen followers and the church hierarchy to conduct a campaign against Aquitaine.

"Since before my father's time," Pepin's voice rang loudly, "the Aquitanians have gone their own way. Again and again they have promised subservience to the Franks, then paid neither tribute nor provided supporting armies."

"True!" responded the men. "True!"

A bishop stood, gaining Pepin's recognition to speak. "Since the 743 Synod of Lestines, priests have been authorized to control their own church's wealth, freely giving a fair share to the crown. But in Aquitaine, Waifar takes it all, giving none to the Frankish crown, and neither allowing the church to keep what it needs of its own treasure and produce to accomplish God's work."

The murmur of accord grew, carried forth on a tapping of knife handles on shields.

Chlodomer stood. “Pepin sent envoys to Aquitaine. Waifar refuses to meet with the King of All Franks.”

“Refuses to meet?” questioned a nobleman.

“He will meet us at sword’s point!” cried a captain.

Filled with gratitude for their ready response, Pepin held up his arm, brandishing his hunting knife. “We are agreed? Go we then to Aquitaine?”

“To Aquitaine!” shouted his army.

“King Pepin for God and Church!” called out the bishop.

“King Pepin for God and Church!” roared the men.

Pepin recounted his successful *Champs de Mai* to Bertrada at dinner that evening. They sat on the raised dais, sharing a wooden trencher. The sounds of several dozen conversations swirled about them.

“Would you come with us? Pepin asked. “Bring the baby and travel with the Frankish army at least as far as Tours.”

“Why ever would you want me to?”

“When we battle the Saxons or any of those Germanii tribes, the Austrasians bear the brunt of the fight. But against Aquitaine, your Neustrians are closest to hand. I would have them solidly behind me in this campaign.”

“You think my journeying with you helps your cause?”

“As you are Neustrian, and your countrymen love you, yes, I do.”

"Then," Bertrada smiled, "I shall come with you and be glad of it. Not only to greet old friends, but to spend some part of the coming summer in your company as well."

Returning to Tours brought vivid memories to Pepin, who had been his sons' age when he first fought with the great Charles Martel. He remembered every detail of the sojourn in Tours before continuing south to Poitiers to face the dread Moslem army.

This day the city of Tours was bedecked with banners and flowers to welcome the king and his family.

They attended mass at the Basilica of Saint Martin of Tours, burial place of their family's patron saint. Pepin thought, as he did so often, of the story of Saint Martin, born in 316 to a military tribune. As such, Martin was expected to follow his father's footsteps and become a member of the Roman Legion. He was baptized a Christian at eighteen. On the spot, he shared his army coat with a beggar in Amiens, renounced the army, and became a monk.

At the end of the service, King Pepin walked alone to the tomb. Built of colored marble and decorated in gold and precious jewels, its opulence seemed in direct contrast to the man who had lived as a hermit before being elected Bishop of Tours.

Candles flickered, casting shadows and eliciting brilliant shafts of light from the riches of the tomb. Pepin knelt, glad the people had so revered Saint Martin as to endow his eternal resting-place with such treasure.

"Saint Martin," he prayed, "bless this venture. Bless me, your servant. Help me become a king whose reign is pleasing in God's sight. Amen."

If the Frankish army's arrival at Tours had been festive, their departure was uproarious. Pepin looked about him in wonder. No one—nobleman or villein, priest or craftsman, woman or child—had remained indoors on this glorious sunny morning.

Everyone waved colorful banners. Young maidens streamed outside the walls lined with cheering townspeople. They handed flowers to the soldiers lined up and ready to march forth into battle with the Aquitanians.

Pepin smiled fondly as he watched his sons on their first major campaign, blushing furiously when they tucked flowers in their tunics as they saw the older soldiers do.

He bent down from his horse to give Bertrada's hand a kiss. Her coming made the desired difference. Hundreds of soldiers had followed their noblemen from the farthest south reaches of Neustria to join Pepin's thrust into Aquitaine. Pepin gave his wife full credit for her countrymen's enthusiasm.

When at last the army moved out, they followed the Cher River south toward Auvergne. The summer sun beat down and Pepin missed the shady oak forests of Austrasia. On the other hand, he realized that Neustria's vineyards were of far greater value to his realm.

Pepin joined Chlodomer, wiping the sweat dripping down his face. "I can see why our Gallo-Roman cousins like this part of the realm. It feels nearly as hot here as Rome."

"Not quite, but warm enough," agreed Chlodomer. "Your sons seem to mind not the heat." Chlodomer glanced back to the line of soldiers.

Pepin followed his friend's gaze and felt a familiar surge of pride in his offspring. They walked among the footsoldiers with a good will. Faces red and perspiring, split by grins. Eyes alive, darting from side to side in fear they might miss seeing something new and important.

Pepin and Chlodomer had debated requiring the boys to begin as foot soldiers. True, Pepin and his brother Carloman had walked long before they were allowed to ride a horse at the head of armies. But they had not been crown princes. Nevertheless, Pepin figured his sons would be better respected as kings if they had shared the road with other footsoldiers as youths.

The Franks plundered outlying hamlets until they reached the ducal palace at Tedoad in Auvergne. Pepin laid siege to the compound, his army benefiting from the bounty of the fields and forests, while denying inhabitants of the palace replacements for their dwindling food supply.

One afternoon as summer was waning, a contingent of men approached from the south.

"My lord, Pepin," reported the Frankish captain who had ridden out to meet them. "Otbert and Dadin, emissaries of Duke Waifar, would speak with you."

"Have them enter our encampment, but warn our soldiers to remain alert and armed. This could be a ruse to distract our attention while reinforcements and food are smuggled into the palace grounds."

The emissaries and their party entered. Pepin placed the crown on his head as he took a seat in the only chair. The others took places on benches along both sides of a table.

"What says Duke Waifar?" asked Pepin.

"My lord, King Pepin," began the man called Otbert, "Duke Waifar would accede to your demands and return all church holdings to church and crown."

The bishops in Pepin's entourage smiled.

Pepin kept his own face impassive. "And?"

"And—what, King Pepin?"

The other man, Dadin, sighed and admitted, "Duke Waifar also sends gifts and treasure as demonstration of his willingness to grant all you demand."

Pepin allowed himself a smile and small nod of acceptance. "And what assurances does Duke Waifar give that he will keep his word?"

"M'lord, our duke gives you hostages, Adalgar and Either, noblemen both and treasured friends." At Otbert's nod, two men stepped forward from the group of Neustrians standing behind the bench.

Pepin judged them as true noblemen. They wore tunics of fine linen. Their hair fashionably short—fringed in front, shaved to the neck at the back—along with their olive complexion and dark eyes, combined to make them look every inch well-born Gallo-Romans.

"You may tell your duke we accept his word and his assurances." He looked to Chlodomer, the Bishop of Tours, and others seated at the table. All looked pleased with his decision. Even Villicus looked somewhat less antagonistic than usual. "We leave on the morrow, for Tours."

Chapter Thirty

The following spring, Pepin held his assembly at Villa Düren, between Cologne and Aix-la-Chapelle. Striding to meet with his troops camped in the meadow beyond the cluster of buildings, he had never felt more optimistic.

Peace—or at least armed truce—reigned between the Franks and their bordering tribes. The Saxons had arrived with their tribute of three hundred horses. Duke Tassilo of Bavaria strutted among the noblemen at last night's banquet, quite proud to be accepted as one among equals.

Duke Waifar and his army had not shown up for the *Champs de mai,* but that was just as well. His churches would send the crown's fair share of Aquitaine's ecclesiastical treasure and produce come harvest time.

Pepin took a deep breath of fresh spring air. He could wait before pressing for the tribute each Aquitanian should pay to their Frankish overlord. He would pull Aquitaine in, little by little, averting overmuch bloodshed.

This year, Pepin could remain within his realm, visiting towns and palaces, settling disputes, overseeing repairs, and assessing their crops for the winter to come. He savored the prospect of playing the magnanimous kingly role.

Bertrada would be pleased. She did her best to oversee the Frank's holdings in her husband's frequent absences. She would no doubt appreciate remaining in Quierzy. For this growing season, at least, she would not need to be away from Young Pepin who remained a somewhat frail toddler.

Everyone—from king and queen to footsoldiers and villains—would enjoy a chance to recoup from the hardship of campaigns and warfare.

Entering the flower-strewn field, Pepin was surrounded by his men. Chlodomer gripped his forearm in greeting.

Noblemen smiled and saluted. "Good morrow, sire."

Even Villicus' smile extended to his hazel eyes with something resembling warmth.

Footsoldiers stammered their greetings and blushed in pleasure when Pepin acknowledged them by name and inquired about their families.

From his chair at the head of the central trestle table in the middle of the meadow, Pepin announced there would be no campaign this year. Accolades for the king who had brought peace to the land greeted his pronouncement. Now they could concentrate on bringing prosperity to it as well.

Soldiers drifted off to improvised contests of skill and strength amid much shouting and laughter. Pipes skirled and drums beat in random bursts of sound. Meanwhile, Pepin officiated as his noblemen and bishops listened to complaints brought to this, the highest court in the land.

The pounding of hooves drew everyone's attention. A grimy messenger rode into camp, his lathered horse snorting for air, dripping foam from its mouth.

Startled, noblemen and bishops of the court stopped mid-sentence. Nearby soldiers turned to stare. Pipes and drums faltered, then silenced. Men quit their competitions, edging closer to hear what was happening. Pepin's heart pounded in alarm.

Willing hands held the mount while the messenger slipped off onto legs trembling with fatigue. "Sire," he gasped, "Waifar and his Aquitanians have invaded Burgundy! Burned and plundered as far north as Chalon-sur-Saône."

"Waifar!" A black anger boiled in Pepin's gut, thundered in his ears. "All promises of acquiescence made less than a year ago, broken so soon. By all that is holy we will teach that lying, scheming Gallo-Roman the consequences of trifling with Franks!"

"Our homes! Our families!" cried the noblemen from Burgundy. "We must be off to protect our own!"

"Waifar planned this from the beginning." Pepin's first hot temper quickly turned into cold fury. "That dog-worshipper attacked with cunning, knowing when you and your armies would be here at the *Champs de mai.* When better to gain the advantage?"

"Sire, have all of us from Burgundy your permission to leave immediately?" Willibald's voice choked. "We must save what loved ones we can."

"You shall not ride alone!" declared Pepin. "By Mithras, god of soldiers, we shall *all* go. I your king, and every man pledged to me, whether Austrasian or Neustrian, Saxon or those who follow Tassilo of Bavaria—all will ride to the aid of our cousins from Burgundy.

"And not only to save Burgundian lives and homes, but to destroy and plunder Aquitaine as well. We shall avenge our loses to the deceitful Waifar. By the bull, we shall!"

"To Burgundy!" shouted the soldiers who had drawn near to hear the news.

"Death to Aquitaine!" responded the others.

No one mentioned the joy all had felt when offered a peaceful summer at home. That peace no longer existed.

Scant weeks later, a benign summer sun shone innocently down on a scene of utter devastation. Pepin and his army of Franks stared wordlessly at the decimated remains of Chalon-sur-Saône. Piles of debris lay where huts had once sheltered whole families. Thatched roofs were reduced to ashes, sturdy timbers charred and fallen. Wattled walls of woven mats burned from within despite their protective coating of plastered mud and clay.

Beyond the huts, a skeleton of the great hall stood starkly against the summer sky. All that could be pillaged was long gone—the rest burnt beyond reclamation.

Even the church had suffered vandalism. Stone walls showed bruised smudges, resulting from smoke and flame where the wooden doors and roof had been set afire. In stunned silence, Pepin walked into the nave, now an empty shell open to the sky. Even the chancel appeared a gaping wound, everything of value carried off by the Aquitanians. He knelt at the altar, now reduced to a bonfire's cold ashes.

"Where *is* everyone?" From behind him, Willibald's voice was a bewildered whisper. "My wife. Children. Villeins?"

Feeling the loss as if it were his own, Pepin rose. Reached out. Laid a sympathetic hand on Willibald's shoulder.

"The entire town has been destroyed," gasped one of Willibald's footsoldiers. "Nothing left alive!"

"What should we do now?" cried another Burgundian.

"Stay here the night," Pepin decided. "Pray for those who died trying to defend Chalon. Then on the morrow we shall go forth, a mighty army seeking vengeance on those who did such a thing to us and ours!"

"Vengeance on Aquitaine!" The soldier stood taller.

Pepin declared, "And if hostages of Chalon be found alive, we shall rescue them and avenge their suffering!"

"Pray tonight. Campaign the morrow!" A bishop added his blessing to Pepin's plan.

"Pray tonight." Willibald's voice gained strength. "Fight the morrow!"

The Frankish army increased in numbers. Every Burgundian man and boy able to carry a weapon joined the cause. Entering enemy Aquitaine, they came upon hamlets from which everyone had fled. Pepin and his men gave vent to their wrath by burning and plundering the buildings.

"Pull up the grape vines!" ordered Pepin. "Pile them in the center of the vineyard. Set torch to their wine crop!"

They met the Aquitanians at last in Auvergne. They had gathered, determined to make a stand in the cluster of castles—Bourbon-l'Archambault, Chantille and Clermont-Ferrand—all of them within a day's ride of each other.

Pepin set up camp outside Clermont. "Let us see if Waifar and his followers dare come to battle honorably, face to face, out in the open. Or do they remain huddled, cringing inside the castle? Either way, by our might we shall prevail!"

Early the next morning, Aquitanians proved themselves willing combatants. The gates opened and out poured rank upon rank of footsoldiers, each protected by leather helmet, chain-link vest, shield, sword, lance and knife.

Pepin ordered his men into position, a solid block of fighting men in the center of the open field. "Saint Martin," he prayed, "make of us a worthy fighting force."

He arranged his soldiers as his father had taught him—most trusted on the outside edges in positions of greatest vulnerability, untried Burgundians next to seasoned troops, Saxons and Bavarians interspersed between armies from Austrasia and Neustria.

Slowly the armies approached one another. Pepin felt his heart race. "This is what a great king does!" he murmured.

From his position on horseback, he assessed the field of battle. "Hold axes until the last moment!" he cautioned.

Drums beat a tattoo, echoing his own heartbeat. He knew the Franks needed this battle to give vent to their anger. Pepin craved the chance to thrust his own sword into Waifar's chest. Cut his enemy's head from its neck with a single stroke.

"Now!" Pepin commanded.

A swarm of casting axes sailed through the air into the block of Aquitanian fighting men. Sounds of axes hitting shields were quickly followed by agonized cries of men wounded by the deadly blades.

In less than a heartbeat the two armies were upon one another. Swords clashed. Lances struck shields with resounding thwacks. Pepin watched, anxiety rising, as the Aquitanians tried to outflank his men. As the end positions fought back, he breathed a sigh of relief.

So intent was he on the battle raging along the front lines, he did not see another army of Aquitanians running toward him from the forest behind. Only at the last minute did he spot them from the corner of his eye.

"Franks! Defend the rear ranks!" he ordered.

This new enemy army swarmed over Pepin's standard-bearer. One Aquitanian soldier swung his sword toward Pepin's leg. Pepin hacked the man's sword arm, nearly severing it. His terrified horse whinnied, reared, nearly unseating him. Foot soldiers crowded in. He had no room to maneuver. Suddenly his horse was more liability than asset.

An Aquitanian stepped up, risking flying hooves. Thrust his sword deep into the animal's belly. The horse shrieked in pain and terror.

Pepin's mount crashed to earth, mortally wounded. Pepin was thrown to the ground. Stunned.

His foot soldiers sounded the alarm. "Franks for Pepin!"

Their king was in danger! "Saint Martin for the crown!"

Immediately, Pepin's own guard rushed to his aid.

Pepin gasped for breath. The haze enveloping his head cleared. All around him, men fought against the attackers with swords, lances, knives, and fists.

An arm reached for Pepin. Pulled him to his feet.

"Be you all right?" Chlodomer had brought his soldiers.

Pepin tentatively shook his head. Winced at the pain. "I think so."

"Good. Take your sword." Chlodomer handed him his weapon. "Back to back. We fight for honor—and our lives!"

The mid-day sun blazed punishing heat on the combatants. Dead and wounded littered the ground. The Aquitanians continued to attack.

Sweating and grunting, Pepin thrust and slashed. Countered with his shield. Thrust again.

Short Pepin had to hold his shield and stab his sword at a tiring upward angle. His arms ached. Trembled. Yet if he lowered his defenses for so much as an instant, he knew he was a dead man.

Early afternoon and the fight showed no signs of slowing. The Aquitanians kept attacking. The Franks held their own. No one dared stop to catch his breath, nor quench his thirst from the wine bag at his waist.

A giant of a man stepped over a dead body, sword held high above his head in two mighty hands. From his enormous height, he swung his weapon directly at Pepin's head. Pepin ducked. Thrust his own sword into his attacker's private parts.

The man screamed in pain and fell, crashing into Pepin's shoulder. The king sidestepped, barely avoiding being crushed. The ground shuddered as if a horse had fallen.

Chlodomer issued the killing stroke to the giant's throat, mercifully putting him out of his misery.

And still the battle waged on. The sun descended past mid afternoon. The majority of Franks remained upright, though exhausted. The Aquitanians refused to acknowledge defeat. Fought on. Determined to win or die in the attempt.

Shadows stretched across the battlefield, gently wrapping the dead in shade. At last Aquitanians no longer raised their swords. The Franks sank to their knees, gasping for breath, arms too tired to lift wineskins to parched lips.

Dazed, Pepin surveyed the scene. Flies buzzed over the dead, feasting on blood and excrement.

"We have no prisoners." Chlodomer's voice held a note of wonder. *"They are all dead!"*

"Let it be told, we put all who fought against us to death!" Pepin panted, still trying to catch his breath.

"But why?"

"If others hear we killed everyone, they may think twice about engaging us in war. Perhaps some will seek treaties rather than fight. The ploy may save lives. Theirs *and* ours."

Though Waifar survived, and men with him, the Franks destroyed the castles of Clermont, Chantille and Bourbon-l'Archambault. Pepin's soldiers ravaged their vineyards and burned whatever they did not pillage. Noblemen from several castles came to Pepin, begging for treaties, promising submission to his authority.

The Franks entered Languedoc, occupying the towns of Rodez, Albi and Toulouse.

A messenger caught up with Pepin in Toulouse. The king sat in the chair of authority in the great hall, surrounded by noblemen and bishops.

The dusty man knelt before Pepin. "Sire, even the monks have taken up arms!"

All conversation in the hall stopped. Pepin leaned forward, curious. The messenger continued. "Abbot Wulfard's men in the monastery of the blessed Martin have joined the fight against the Aquitanians. They have killed the Count of Poitiers, vassal to Waifar!"

"Praise God!" cried a bishop.

"God and church for Pepin!" responded the others.

Pepin and his soldiers returned home, exhausted but in good spirits. Pepin gloried in the fact they had met the Aquitanians in battle, and won. Young Charles could not contain his enthusiasm. He had fought hard and acquitted himself well. He reveled in the slaps to the back given him by other, older men. Carloman, too, seemed pleased, albeit less exuberant.

Though happy her husband and sons had returned uninjured and victorious, Bertrada remained quiet. "Young Pepin is worse."

The toddler, never robust, now occupied a trundle bed in Pepin and Bertrada's chamber. None of them got much sleep that night. Young Pepin coughed as though to rid himself of heart, lungs, and stomach. Pepin felt despair that his son should suffer so.

He gently pounded the lad's back to aid in the flow of mucus that dribbled out, thick and green.

Meanwhile, Bertrada made a tent of a cloth over bowls of steaming hot water for Young Pepin to breathe.

The next day, the cough subsided, but the babe burned with a fever. A page brought cold water. Pepin and Bertrada took turns wrapping their son in wet rags.

No sooner did the fever drop, than his lips turned blue and he shivered with cold.

His parents replaced cold, wet rags with warm blankets.

This cycle of fever and chills alternated throughout the morning hours.

At last Young Pepin slumbered, his breathing labored.

Bertrada and Pepin fell into exhausted sleep on their bed next to him.

As evening shadows lengthened, Pepin awoke to silence. He hurried to stand over his son.

Young Pepin lay still and silent, eyelashes brushing his cheeks. Pepin marveled that he slept so peacefully. Not until he gently brushed his son's face with a forefinger did he realize that the child lay in the peaceful sleep of death.

Tears streaming down his cheeks, Pepin carefully picked up his son and carried him to his mother.

Bertrada awoke. Understood in an instant. Reached to take her baby. Her keening cry pierced the quiet. Pepin gathered both wife and dead son in his arms.

Two days later, the entire estate attended the burial of the tiny prince. Pepin wrenched himself out of his grief and donned a soldier's mask as he gently lowered the tiny coffin into a cold grave. Bertrada had placed a tiny wooden toy horse in her baby's hands before they closed his casket. Now she clung to Pepin as they watched clods of dirt fall on the small box holding their son.

After what seemed an eternity, the last of the people left. Pepin and Bertrada walked arm in arm, back to where the freshly turned earth marked their baby's resting place. Pepin spread his cloak on the ground.

They sat there in silence. A bird song began to trill. A gentle breeze caressed them like a baby angel's kiss.

"I am no longer so self centered as to think God took Young Pepin as punishment for *my* sins," Pepin murmured. "But I cannot fathom why He would cause such a sweet innocent to die."

Bertrada sighed. Wiped away a tear. "Perhaps God had need of just such a sweet innocent in heaven. How could it be heaven, after all, without the sound of childish laughter?"

Chapter Thirty-One

Winter 763-64

Snow began falling before mid-winter's eve and continued through Christmas. Howling winds pushed it into drifts as high as the thatched roofs of huts scattered around the villa of Longlier, near Neufchâteau in northernmost Austrasia. Weeks later, neither the snow nor the wind showed any signs of abating.

Pepin stamped his feet. They had no more sensation in them than ice. He rubbed his hands, blowing warm breath on them.

The huge log in the center firepit of the great hall struggled valiantly, but lost its battle to heat the large open room. Cold drafts swirled in over the high threshold and through every crack and crevice of the wooden building. Wall hangings and leather curtains did little to hold out the frosty winter blasts.

The hall was crowded with people huddled under cloaks and blankets on the straw-covered floor. No one could have survived this winter in isolated huts. All had moved into the hall. Every once in a while, one of the low murmured conversations erupted into snarling acrimony, not unlike that of wild dogs fighting over a bone.

The hall, itself, smelt villainous. Too many people had lived too closely together for too long. Pepin ached to throw open the door and step out into sunshine and blue skies. He knew however, that beyond the door he would find nothing but snow, freezing wind, and darkness at mid-day.

His own spirits were equally black and cold.

He and Bertrada retired to their bed early in the evening. Although promising warmth, the bedcovers were as icy as the rest of the building.

"What troubles you?" asked Bertrada.

"The cold. The dark. This is the worst winter I can remember. Being cooped up is enough to drive a man mad!"

"And...?"

"Aquitaine." Pepin had no need to search for the answer.

"For four years I have led my armies against Aquitaine. At first it seemed Waifar and his followers were willing to grant us suzerainty, even though all they actually promised was legal distribution of the church's treasure.

"I am now..." Pepin paused, counting. "I am now forty-nine winters old." The thought made his head reel. "Nearly fifty! We have fought against Aquitaine year after year. Castle by castle. Town by town. But we make no lasting impression. Not one dent in their determination to ignore our superiority."

Pepin snuggled deeper under the feather-filled mattress with Bertrada and realized, for the first time that day, he was finally feeling warmth. "Where have the years gone?"

"What years?"

"Those since first we met. Were married, still awkward one with the other."

"Oh. Those." Bertrada seemed lost in thought while gently massaging Pepin's neck and shoulders. "They were swallowed up having children. Fighting campaigns. Not to mention being crowned king—the *first* in your family ever to do so. Why?"

"They seem to have gone so quickly. And I have yet to begin accomplishing all that I feel I should."

"Perhaps you have, and simply do not realize it."

"Think you not I would know, if I had?"

"Perhaps." Bertrada smoothed the tension from his forehead with her gentle touch. "On the other hand, you may always feel driven to achieve more, no matter how much you have already done. This ambition may simply be part of who you are."

Pepin felt contentment creep over him, along with the warmth. "Perhaps," he said. And yawned.

Pepin held his annual spring assembly in a meadow just outside Worms, on the west bank of the Rhine. Not everyone had come, and those who did were pale and thin. Most had coughs with runny noses, chills and fevers. Gaiseric kept busy from early morning until late into the night, ministering to the sick with teas and poultices.

The Saxons were among those missing, but one look at the Rhine River explained their absence. Swirling, muddy water overflowed the banks, washing over bridges that had stood since the Romans built them. Bringing the Saxon tribute of horses would have proved impossible this year—provided the animals had not all died of cold and starvation over the winter.

Nor were Tassilo and his Bavarians in attendance.

"My nephew would not be here even if the weather were warm and the Rhine low enough to wade across!" Pepin complained to Chlodomer. They walked among the dispirited troops who were sitting on rock outcroppings and fallen logs. The men were too worn by years of back-to-back campaigns and the harsh winter just past to engage in mock fights and contests.

"Tassilo," Chlodomer commented. "He is certainly his mother's son. And after you gave him Bavaria. Made him duke. For him to sneak away from Aquitaine last summer, taking his troops with him—I can scarce believe it."

"Believe it." Pepin felt bile rising. "He left. Feigned sickness to abandon us in the middle of a campaign after taking oaths on the bones of all the saints! By Mithras! He is a coward as well as a traitor!"

Just then, rain began falling from low gray clouds. Pepin sighed. "We may as well call the *conventus* to order inside the great hall."

Noblemen found places to sit on benches while footsoldiers stood, jostling for a place to lean against the walls. The sounds of coughs, spitting, and sniffling, as men wiped runny noses on their sleeves, filled the room.

"Go home, all of you," Pepin ordered. "Pray spring brings sun and good crops. Pray for health. No campaign will we fight this year."

The men smiled their relief, too listless even to cheer and beat knife handles on tabletops and shields.

Pepin and Bertrada celebrated Christmas of the year 765 at the villa of Aachen. Though this winter was less harsh than the one previous, scant food supplies made it a time of apprehension for all.

The king held his assembly the following spring at Attigny, where the Aisne and Meuse rivers met. He realized his countrymen were in no condition to carry on a military campaign, so for a second year none was planned.

By the end of summer, however, word reached Pepin. Waifar and his troops were once again plundering villages and destroying castles along the Neustrian border.

"By all that is holy!" Pepin declared, "next year we go to Aquitaine and settle the matter once and for all!"

Chapter Thirty-Two

After celebrating Easter in Aachen, southwest of Cologne, Pepin held the national assembly for the year 766 in Orléans. The march south through Paris and into the Loire Valley seemed no more than a pleasant outing. Bertrada again accompanied him, planning to summer in Tours. The men laughed and made ribald comments as Pepin plucked wildflowers to tuck into his queen's hair.

"I care not what they say," Pepin murmured. "You are more beautiful this day than when first we met. And I love you more deeply with each passing year." He kissed her fingertips before riding to the head of his troops.

Hundreds swelled to thousands, all camping in the meadows surrounding the town of Orléans. The men shouted greetings, challenging others to contests of strength and skill. A warm sun in a sky where naught but the smallest of downy clouds floated, guaranteed the *conventus* could be held out of doors.

From his chair of authority, Pepin felt his own spirits soar as he watched his army's exuberance. "We are strong. The weather remains fair. Join you with me in showing the Aquitanians who has the right to rule!" he challenged.

"The Franks!"

"Franks for Pepin!"

"Franks rule by might!"

"We *know* that." Villicus' voice carried over the tumult. "The Aquitanians know as well. Yet each year *we* claim victory. *They* swear obedience. We turn our backs and they attack us again! What good does it? We accomplish naught of lasting value!"

"True!" muttered several men.

"We should kill the lot of them," a soldier's voice was heard. "Then there be none left to again go false against their oaths!"

This last was met by laughter and pounding on shields.

"Hear me!" Pepin ordered. The men grew quiet, attention fixed on their king. "With this campaign we settle Aquitaine's subservience *for all time*. We shall put forth our whole effort. No longer will three worthless hostages be accepted as guarantee for their oaths! Before we return home, the Aquitanians all—every man, woman and child—shall be pledged and held hostage to their promise!"

"Franks over Aquitaine!" shouted a soldier.

"King Pepin for all!" cried another.

The calls rang out from all quarters. A loud banging of swords on shields filled the air with cacophonous clamor.

In full accord, the army of Franks would invade Aquitaine with determination. Succeed where before they had failed to quench that duchy's stubborn pride. Pepin's chest swelled at the acclamation his statement had received.

Pepin's army marched south from Orléans. Pepin made a determination to begin working to sway Villicus from antagonist to supporter.

He rode next to the nobleman and asked, in a quiet voice, "Villicus, why have you been so against me? From my first day as mayor of the palace you have expressed nothing but criticism and contempt."

Villicus looked shocked that Pepin had asked such a question. Had faced their enmity so openly.

"Why should I not?" he asked. "Why should you, an Austrasian, to be handed the office without merit, simply because you happened to be born of Charles Martel? No Neustrian was given the chance to earn the title.

"No wonder the Aquitanians fight so hard," he continued. They want not an Austrasian lording over them. Perhaps a Neustrian would stand a better chance!"

You *had* to ask, Pepin thought. Now you have your answer. What propose you to do about it?

He smiled. Shrugged. "It pleases me that your dislike is simply a matter of my birth. Nothing personal. Nothing over which I have any control."

Pepin held out his hand. Instinctively, Villicus took it, looking surprised as he did so.

Once again they camped at Tours where Pepin prayed at the tomb of Saint Martin. From there, Bertrada wished her husband and sons Godspeed and safe return from war. She, her retinue and guard would leave to tour Pepin's domain for him when the army marched forward.

Charles and Carloman, at twenty-four and twenty-one respectively, no longer walked with the footsoldiers. As heirs to the throne, each led his own contingent, as captains riding horseback. After much discussion with Bertrada and Chlodomer, Pepin had decided to assign Charles to serve a Neustrian nobleman, and Carloman one from Austrasia. The Neustrians were more difficult by nature, and Charles had, from childhood, exhibited a friendly, out-going temperament his younger, more volatile brother lacked.

First they traveled south, then east toward Auvergne. Within days they came upon all that was left of Argenton-sur-Creuse. As he had in Burgundy's Chalon-sur-Saône, Waifar had totally destroyed the castle and its outbuildings. All lay in smoldering ruins.

"Set up camp here," Pepin commanded. "The Creuse River will provide fresh water and fish. The forests shelter game for food. We will work together to rebuild the castle and compound of Argenton."

"Rebuild... but why?" asked Chlodomer.

"As a Frankish garrison on the edge of Aquitaine," Pepin answered. "We shall *force* Frankish domination, castle by castle, town by town. And in each we shall leave our own men to back up our suzerainty over Aquitaine."

"Leave... How long?"

"One year. Two. Three. Whatever it takes. We shall have a presence in Aquitaine *forever,* if needs be. They *will* recognize our right to rule. Our right to a share of their crops, crafts, and treasure. They will give us the king's share of *all* they own!"

"Set up tents there!" Chlodomer ordered. "Noblemen, meet with Pepin. We shall decide which troops provide food. Which clear away debris. Which will fell trees for rebuilding."

The men set to work with strong resolve. How strange it seemed to go to war and find oneself building rather than destroying. But they all felt a deep sense of satisfaction when fields were tended, castle walls set in place, and the huts rebuilt.

As soon as the town was livable, Pepin organized his garrison. "Willibald, you of Burgundy will be in charge, and all your men with you. Also you, Leuvigild of Neustria. You and your men enforce our dominance on this border area."

The men willingly accepted their assignments, realizing continuing presence by the Franks was crucial to long-term defeat of Aquitaine.

With crops and buildings restored, Aquitanians who had fled Argenton crept back to claim homes Waifar had destroyed. "Treat them fairly," Pepin ordered. "I would they accept our sovereignty as beneficial. Allow no insurrection. But neither antagonize them. I wish they hate not *all* Franks, based on ill treatment at *our* hand."

"Aye," agreed Willibald. "Most villeins care less who leads them, than that they be left alone to grow their crops."

"I knew I picked the best man to put in charge when I chose you." Pepin smiled and slapped Willibald's back.

Pepin, with the bulk of his army, moved slightly north to Bourges. With minimal interference he set up a garrison of Franks to oversee the running of that town. Little by little, he drew a line of defense beyond which the Aquitanians could not invade into Burgundy or Neustria.

With Aquitaine's northern border reinforced by Frankish soldiers, Pepin returned south the following year and moved his army to Aquitaine's southeastern-most corner. He reclaimed Narbonne, just inland from the Middle Sea, from the Muslims.

From there he traveled westward toward Toulouse on the Garonne River. Clovis had taken the town from the Visigoths over three hundred years before. It, like most of Aquitaine, had been under nominal Frankish domination ever since. Pepin was determined it should be under his *actual* rule as well.

Even before they saw the town, Pepin's army began passing small isolated farms, thatch-roofed huts surrounded by fields plowed and waiting for spring planting of wheat or barley. But no farmers sowed seeds. No wives tended kitchen gardens. Nor fed chickens. Nor gathered eggs. No telltale wisps of smoke straggled out the roof openings.

"Word of our invasion has preceded us," Pepin remarked to Chlodomer.

"I would guess they have all fled to Toulouse for protection."

"All the better," replied Pepin. "The more mouths Toulouse has to feed, the greater the strain on the town's food and water supply."

Soon the walls of fortified Toulouse rose in the distance. Time and again foreigners had swarmed over the Pyrenees Mountains from the south to invade the border town, Visigoths from long ago and Muslims as recently as in Charles Martel's lifetime.

"I have never seen such a well-shielded town." Chlodomer's voice held a note of awe. "Look you," he said to Pepin, pointing, "their log palisade circles the entire city! Not just the great hall with its outbuildings and bailey, but the church with its living quarters and gardens as well. Even the craftsmen's huts and living space must be crammed inside the walls."

Pepin nodded. Only a few huts had escaped beyond the protective enclosure to huddle nearby like chicks beneath a brooding hen. The one-room affairs boasted nothing beyond cesspits and pigsties. All other buildings were apparently within the fortification.

Beyond the straggle of huts lay plowed fields next to tidy vineyards and orchards, fresh leaves shining green in the early summer sun.

"Toulouse looks an impossible shell to crack," Chlodomer commented.

Pepin nodded. "Pray they choose to come out to fight. I see no way to get inside the walls to engage them."

While his army set up their camp surrounding the fields and filling the meadows beyond, Pepin surveyed the scene with foreboding.

The next day the Frankish army lined up outside the walls in rectangular battle formation—an invitation to honorable face-to-face combat. Slowly the sun sailed across a cloudless sky. They heard the church bells chime Tierce at mid-morning, then Sext at noon.

"Matins is early morning prayer,
At light comes Prime too soon.
Tierce comes mid-morning hence
And Sext is said at noon,"

Pepin murmured the childhood poem, noting the Canonical Hours, as the day became hotter.

"Nones is said mid-afternoon
At slanting of the sun.
Vespers is the evening prayer,
And when the day is done...
Complin's said.
And so to bed."

When Vespers chimed as evening shadows fell across the Frankish army, they broke off. Returned to camp and food.

"Toulouse knows better than to engage in battle when years of defensive practice and tradition caution patience," complained Villicus. He and Stilicho of Neustria had joined Pepin at his campfire.

"They are content to make the enemy wait in siege outside the walls," added Stilicho. "We may well grow weary and return home before those inside starve to death."

Although less a thorn in his side than Villicus, Stilicho had also long opposed Pepin.

"Their ploy works!" Villicus' voice said, 'I told you so!'

"Occasionally!" As king, Pepin had the last word.

On the second day, the Franks once again stood in a solid block.

Meanwhile the noblemen gathered around Pepin.

"How long wait we?" asked Stilicho.

Pepin pondered. His army could last indefinitely with abundantly available food and fresh water—both denied to those inside the walls. But his plan was to subdue towns and castles, then move on until all Aquitaine pledged allegiance to him. With those pledges secured by hostages and Frankish garrisons all across the troublesome duchy, Aquitaine would be his!

"If we wait too long," Villicus chimed in, "word will reach Waifar and he will bring superior numbers of troops to surround and attack us. Force us between the entire Aquitanian army and the fortified walls of Toulouse."

That possibility, too, had occurred to Pepin, but he wished Villicus had kept the thought to himself. What was he to do? Stay? Leave? Force the issue? But how?

"Give the order!" Pepin was surprised at the strength of his own voice. "Hold battle positions until Nones. Then, while the rest of the army remains ready to fight, let all from Burgundy tear up half the plants in the vineyard. Stack them on the road several paces back from the main gate. Come dark, set fire to them."

"I do not understand," said Chlodomer when he and Pepin were once again alone.

"We but tempt those inside a bit," responded Pepin. "How long can they resist defending what is theirs?"

At mid afternoon of the next day, Pepin ordered the Burgundians to chop down and stack half the fruit trees in the Toulouse orchards. That night their flames cast shadows as far as the main gate, some distance away. The gate remained stubbornly closed and bolted.

On the third afternoon, the Burgundians plundered anything left of value—foodstuffs, tools, clothes, furniture, bedding—then demolished as many of the huts as they could before the shadows of Vespers fell.

Come darkness, flames from *that* bonfire lit the sky and could be seen from a greater distance than the far side of the city.

Every morning, Pepin's army assembled in traditional battle formation. They stood thus until Vespers. With all his heart, Pepin hoped the citizens of Toulouse would become anxious enough over the destruction of their crops and property to engage in battle.

He looked over his shoulder frequently, hairs on the back of his neck raised, half expecting to see Duke Waifar and a full army of Aquitanians bearing down on them from the forests beyond. He imagined them overwhelming his standard bearer, disemboweling his horse, killing him—proud to eliminate Pepin, King of All Franks.

He could but help worry, too, about the fate of his sons if such an attack were to occur. On his death, Charles would be named King of Neustria, and Carloman, King of Austrasia. By killing his sons, the Aquitanians could eliminate the succession of his family's rule. Stamp out any hope of the great king's reign, should becoming *that* predicted monarch be the destiny of either Charles or Carloman. All hope gone. In one battle.

Frankish guards constantly patrolled the perimeter of the city, assuring that no foodstuffs or supplies entered, nor pleas for help escaped. Pepin could only hope Waifar was far away and had no knowledge Toulouse was under siege.

Dawn of the fourth day broke with a cool breeze blowing from the Pyrenees' snowy heights. Not one cloud marred the pale blue sky. Pepin watched as his soldiers lined up, once again, in the meadow just beyond the ploughed fields.

The Franks stood, vests and helmets on, lances, shields and casting axes at hand, by their presence taunting those of Toulouse to fight. The sun slowly climbed the blue dome of sky, its warmth overcoming the chill breeze.

Pepin felt sweat begin to gather on his face and neck. Under his arms. Down his back. Would that gate never open, spilling out the fighting men of the town?

When the sun slipped past its highest point and the bells of Nones rang across the land, the men from Burgundy left the solid block of army to saunter across the fields to the road and what remained of Toulouse's vineyard.

A mere handful of men began hacking away at the vines with their axes. The rest stopped in the middle of the road behind the vineyard, engaged in some sort of argument. They stood, backs to the town, faces angry, large gestures pointing this way and that. Pepin could not hear the words, but emotions were easily read.

While the dispute continued, those destroying the vineyard dragged bushes to pile in the middle of the road outside the barred wooden gate. From the looks of it, the entire balance of the wine crop would burn this night.

The handful of men returned to the vineyard to attack the next row of plants. Meanwhile the argument seemed ready to escalate into a full-fledged fight. The main body of Burgundian fighting men appeared oblivious to those cutting down the grapevines. Oblivious to Toulouse. Oblivious to the rest of the Frankish army who had turned away from the town walls to watch the altercation.

Pepin saw the heavy wooden gate open and fighting men of Toulouse stream out. They ran quickly but quietly, understandably hoping to catch the Burgundians off guard. They appeared intent on eliminating the threat from those of Burgundy before the rest of the Frankish army came to its senses. With this accomplished, the Aquitanians might well defeat the main body of Franks as well.

The fighting men from Toulouse bore down on those in the vineyard. The Burgundians, seemingly unaware what was about to befall them, hacked away at the grapevines. Meanwhile the argument grew to pushing and shoving. Soon fisticuffs and knives would draw blood. The army of Franks watched in fascination, gesturing and egging them on. Pepin did not move. Gave no command. Surveyed the entire scene.

As those from Toulouse were about to charge the Burgundians in the vineyard, intent on killing them with their lances, the Burgundians turned and flung their axes at the approaching army.

At the same time the dispute in the middle of the road abruptly stopped and the main force from Burgundy came to the aid of their brothers. Without a word from Pepin the Franks turned their attention away from the argument to address the main battle.

The Franks ran forward, splitting into two forces. Those on the left came to the aid of the Burgundians facing the Aquitanians. The rest dashed to the right, behind the Aquitanians. Cutting off any retreat toward the town gate.

Pepin grinned in triumph as he heard Chlodomer shout, "King Pepin's plan works!" With that Chlodomer swung his sword with both hands, disarming a soldier from Toulouse.

"Cease fighting!" shouted the nobleman of Toulouse. He signaled defeat by handing his sword to Pepin. Pepin ceremonially touched the point to the nobleman's chest.

"Kill no more!" Pepin declared. "Bind all Aquitanian soldiers, arms behind and ankles together."

When the prisoners had been shoved in submission before him, Pepin's soldiers cheered and banged knife handles on shields. Pepin's chest swelled with pride at this display of homage.

His plan to trick the enemy into leaving the sanctuary of their walled city had been successful. When it appeared the Franks were about to be caught off guard, his army had, in fact, been ready to fight and prevail.

"Every male of Toulouse from the age of twelve and up will accompany the Frankish army as hostage," declared the

King of All Franks. "You who look to Toulouse for trade and protection, accept *our* sovereignty."

"Every male?" the men of Toulouse raged. "You cannot take prisoner every male. How will the people survive without men to plant the crops? How are women and children to defend themselves against invaders from over the Pyrenees Mountains?"

"We shall take all males hostage—allowing them life—or take no prisoners at all!" thundered Pepin. "We have done *that* before."

The men of Toulouse blanched. Hung their heads. Remained silent.

"We shall leave behind the Burgundians to plant your crops, rebuild your huts, defend your women and children." Pepin glowed. Toulouse was his!

"Search Toulouse for any males over the age of twelve," he ordered. "Bind and add them to our hostages. If any be discovered in Toulouse past this night, kill them on sight!

"We leave on the morrow to conquer Albi."

Chapter Thirty-Three

After successfully conquering Albi, Pepin led what was left of his army homeward. Having assigned hundreds of Franks to garrisons throughout Aquitaine, his numbers were drastically diminished.

He and his army celebrated Easter in the city of Vienne on the Rhone River, south of Lyon. Immediately after, they traveled northwest, making a short stop to inspect Bourges, his main garrison on Neustria's southern border with Aquitaine. From there the army followed the Cher River, arriving in Tours less than a week later.

All Tours had heard of the Frankish army's victories over the Aquitanians. The entire town bustled in a frenzy of preparation as word came that the army, with King Pepin at its head, would arrive before Vespers that day.

With forewarning, Bertrada had returned to Tours to welcome Pepin and her sons. Although knowing all three of them were returning uninjured, she would not rest easy until she had seen them for herself.

Meanwhile she had her hair dressed twice before donning her head covering. She picked, then discarded three gowns, finally choosing one in a light, spring green. Her handmaiden helped her into a mantle of darker green, its long flowing sleeves ending at the elbow. Her handmaiden slipped a large emerald pendant on a heavy gold chain over her head.

Bertrada could not understand why she felt so overwrought. She was convinced Pepin cared not how she looked. Else he would never have taken her as queen. She, who was too tall and had feet of grotesque proportions.

More likely, she thought with brutal honesty, he would have taken her as queen for her influence in Neustria, and then raised a brood of illegitimate children with mistresses throughout the realm. But he had not.

If not her looks, what drew Pepin?

She answered her own question. Their joy in the bedchamber. The children she had borne him. But, he also trusted her opinion on affairs of the kingdom. Allowed her to represent him in all corners of the realm when he was away at war. He frequently had her by his side when he traveled from palace to town within his domain.

She realized herself to be a most fortunate lady. A strong pull of desire rose in Bertrada's lower regions and set her heart to beating wildly.

"Hurry, Pepin!" she quietly begged. "Hurry home."

Shouts from throughout the city rang in every nook and cranny of the royal palace. Bertrada knew Pepin and his army had been sighted!

Swept along toward the main gate with the crowd, she saw the army. Wide grins showed slashes of white teeth across faces covered with dust and grime. Her eyes flew to Pepin, then Charles and Carloman. In her eyes they had never looked more handsome.

She flew to the three men and was soon engulfed in a four-way embrace that smelt of sweat, dust, and horses. There is no more welcome fragrance, she thought.

That evening, Bertrada sat with Pepin on the raised dais in the great hall. With all the grime washed away, he looked tired and—Bertrada was surprised by the realization —old.

Her husband, usually so filled with vigor and enthusiasm, seemed to have had a candle snuffed from within. His long hair had more gray than red-blond. Smudges of fatigue underlined eyes faded from the vivid blue of old.

She touched his hand softly. He turned to her, and a reminder of the old fire glowed in his glance once more. The long campaign was to blame, she decided. Nearly two years. He would be his former self once he had a chance to rest.

Once in their bedchamber, Pepin quelled whatever concerns had niggled her as to his vigor.

By August, Pepin, health and vitality restored, ordered all who could bear arms to meet in Bourges. Pepin not only maintained a Frankish unit in this southernmost Neustrian town, he had sent additional soldiers to reinforce the army's presence, hoping to discourage Waifar and his Aquitanians from taking the offensive into Neustria.

"Would you recognize Bourges?" asked Chlodomer as they approached the garrison town.

"We have *indeed* made a difference," Pepin agreed. "Fresh new thatch-roofed huts. Workshops. The bailey cleared and expanded to accommodate soldiers' training and competitions. Why, even the great hall looks freshly daubed with clay!"

The fields were high with wheat and barley. Orchards glowed with fruit. Kitchen gardens showed green with cabbages, onions and the like.

"And what a bustle!" Chlodomer added. "When first we came, there were scarcely any people. We seem to have drawn farmers and craftsmen from near and far like flies to a feast."

Pepin nodded in satisfaction. "I would the Frankish armies' presence be a benefit to the people, rather than bringing tension and discord. Our nobles and their men have done well."

Once again, Pepin's army had grown from hundreds to more than a thousand. Tents sprouted. Banners flew. Men greeted each other with enthusiasm.

Pepin addressed the customary assembly on a fine summer day. He sat on the high-backed chair of authority, a gold crown glistening atop his long hair.

Noblemen sat nearby, benches pulled to trestle tables at which they would eat a mid-day meal later on. Captains and footsoldiers gathered as close as they could so as to hear.

"Where think you we should go now?" asked Stilicho.

Knowing the nobleman from Neustria would find fault with any plan, Pepin proposed, "March south. Capture the castles of Ally, Turenne and Payrusse. Proceed as far as the Garonne River to reinforce our suzerainty over Toulouse."

"Many live in caves in the hills above the river valleys in that region." Stilicho cleared his throat. Looked down his nose at the assembled noblemen. "I *suppose* you have a plan to dislodge them!"

"And we *still* have yet to face Waifar whose stronghold is farther to the west," needled Villicus.

"Waifar's battle will come!" Pepin slammed his fist on the table. "And *when* we face him, he will be denied armies from all the castles and towns we have captured and garrisoned."

Knife handles tapped on shields and tabletops.

This sound of affirmation renewed Pepin's commitment. "When we face Waifar, the victory will be decisive. And that victory will be ours!"

Men cheered. "Franks over Waifar!"

"Pepin for Neustria!"

"Burgundy for Pepin!"

"King Pepin over all!"

Chlodomer smiled at Pepin. "What threat castles and caves when the Frankish army is committed to victory?"

Pepin smiled back. "What, indeed?"

* * *

The Frankish army's confidence that fall remained contagious. Considering themselves invincible, they fought like madmen, looting and plundering every obstacle in their way. One by one the castles, hamlets and cave dwellers succumbed to Pepin's assault, no match for his followers.

He returned victorious to Bourges in time to celebrate Christmas. "Come the new year, we shall carry the attack to Waifar," Pepin pledged. "And *we shall prevail!*"

Chapter Thirty-Four

In Bourges, Christmas arrived with chilly winds and rain. Pepin and Bertrada sat in the great hall, the high backs of their chairs stopping drafts let in whenever the door was opened. An immense log smoldered in the center fire pit, warming their feet and faces.

Around them the palace hummed with the usual bustle. Pages and servants came and went on errands of their own. Soon trestle tables would be set up for the day's main meal.

"Do you not find it hard to believe there is no snow here in winter?" Pepin asked Bertrada.

Bertrada's face broke into a twisted smile. "With no snow to stop you, I suppose you plan to leave immediately on campaign into Aquitaine."

"As soon as the rest of the noblemen arrive with their armies." Pepin felt the familiar rush of anticipation welling. "This time we carry the fight to Duke Waifar himself. We have hedged him in with Frankish garrisons. Cut off sources of resupply of men and food. This time we *shall* defeat him."

"Would you see him dead?" Bertrada cocked her head. Raised one eyebrow.

"Only if he can be killed in battle. As did his father before him, Waifar often deceived the Franks. I trust not his declarations of subservience. But, I would not kill him as prisoner. That would serve only to make him a martyr for the Aquitanians to carry in their hearts when they make plans to rise against us yet again."

Pepin stared into the flames. Winning the war for an enemy's loyalty was indeed a tricky undertaking.

Bertrada sighed and patted Pepin's hand. "You will solve the dilemma of Duke Waifar. Of that I have no doubt."

Well within a fortnight Pepin and his noblemen sat at trestle tables in the midst of the army's encampment outside Bourges. A winter sun shone weakly through the veil of high overcast.

"We shall move southwest to Saintes." Pepin sat back and waited for the opposition sure to come.

"That and Bordeaux on the Garonne are strongholds of Waifar and his Aquitanians," Villicus challenged.

"By the bull! We all *know* that!" Pepin's voice was uncontrollably lacking in patience.

"We must face him sometime." Chlodomer looked eager for the encounter.

"I have heard his uncle, Remistagnus, is considering abandoning his nephew. He would back the Franks in exchange for our guarantee he could continue in possession of his estates." Stilicho's voice carried a note of triumph at being the bearer of such welcome news.

"Where heard you that?" asked Pepin. And why has the news not been conveyed to me before this, he wondered?

"From traveling merchants, or mayhap Neustrians who have cousins in Aquitaine. I cannot rightly recall the source."

"And you trust the information?" Chlodomer's voice held the doubt Pepin felt.

Stilicho laughed, mirthlessly. "No more than any other coming from Aquitaine."

"But still, Remistagnus' estate lies between here and Saintes," said Villicus. "We may as well start with him. He will either fight and be defeated or swear willing allegiance to Pepin."

"Which we will accept, but not trust," finished Chlodomer.

"Are we in agreement with Villicus' plan?" asked Pepin, giving full credit to his nemesis. "Remistagnus' estates first, then on to Saintes?"

"Agreed!" chorused the others.

Five days of hard marching later, Stilicho pointed toward a cluster of buildings surrounding a two-storied structure. "There lies Remistagnus' great hall."

The entire Frankish army stopped while Pepin took in the scene. No fortified walls, praise be. Though the hall offered sanctuary, the outbuildings—kitchen, blacksmith's shed, quarters for Remistagnus' soldiers, villein's huts and craftsmen's shops—would be easily destroyed.

"Don your leather vests!" he ordered. "And chain mail if you have it. Helmets as well. Carry shields, lances. Keep casting axes readily to hand."

A murmur and bustle met Pepin's commands.

"Supply wagons stop and let the foot soldiers through. We fight as soon as we arrive!"

"Pepin for Franks!" called a soldier.

"King Pepin victorious!" answered a dozen others.

The Frankish army, over a thousand strong, marched confidently toward the estate of Remistagnus. One unit began singing a battle chant that was quickly picked up by the rest.

All who looked to Remistagnus for protection had fled the fields and huts for safety within the great hall. Before the first Frank came close enough to pound on the huge wooden door, it opened.

Out came Waifar's uncle, gray hair cut short, leaning on a staff. A half-dozen men accompanied him. All carried white banners, denoting allegiance unpledged to any leader.

Pepin could see no weapons. Not even hunting knives.

"Put down your lances and shields, we pray you," Remistagnus called out. "We would no blood be spilled.

"I offer myself, my villeins, and my footsoldiers, to further your cause." Though he walked with a limp, Remistagnus' voice was clear and strong. "I willingly give you what information I have on my nephew, Waifar, as well!"

"By Mithras! I believe him less far than I can throw him," Pepin muttered to Chlodomer.

"Scribe!" Pepin called out. "Come record Remistagnus' pledge of fealty. All you Frankish noblemen and soldiers witness what is being promised this day."

After an uneasy night as guest in the hall, Pepin assembled his forces to proceed on to Saintes. In the line of march, he placed Remistagnus' soldiers between trusted armies from Burgundy and Neustria.

"I would I could go with you." Remistagnus' voice rang with regret. "However, my fighting days are over. I fear I would be more burden than aid to you."

"No. Remain here, on your own estates," Pepin responded. "You are of more value to me where you can urge support for the Franks among others in the area."

Pepin gazed at the huge army ready to move at his command. "You are *sure* Waifar's family is in Saintes?"

"His wife and children, along with his mother and at least one of his sisters are in the great hall there," Remistagnus assured him. "Though I know not with certainty whether the duke himself is there." The nobleman's voice cracked. Although the day was cool with a brisk wind, sweat ran down his face.

Pepin did not trust him. But he dared not leave a garrison there. The Franks might be walking into a well-set trap when they arrived in Saintes. He must take all his fighting men with him. Just in case.

"Wear vests and helmets!" Pepin shouted the order. "Keep lances, shields and casting axes ready to hand. Keep also your wits about you. If you must stop for any reason, call out to those ahead of you. Make them stop. Let no units be cut off from the full defense of those in front and behind.

"Keep an eye out for enemy soldiers at all times. Especially when we enter forests. The trees may well conceal an army or two, waiting to attack!"

Every man looked fearfully from right to left when the army entered a thick forest. Was that a shadow? Over there —did something move? Even Pepin felt his heart beat faster, every muscle taut with apprehension.

Exhausted, they emerged from the forest at last. Pepin saw Saintes long before they reached the town. The buildings rose from the flat plain, surrounded by cultivated fields and vineyards. A small river reflected the winter sun.

Not one Aquitanian could be seen as the army entered the hamlet. The people of Saintes, with ample warning of the Frank's arrival, had left their huts to seek safety in the great hall or the church.

"Those of you from Austrasia, as well as all who follow Chlodomer, Villicus and Stilicho, surround the great hall," Pepin ordered. "The remaining men from Neustria, Burgundy and Remistagnus' army encircle the church. Make no move to enter that building until ordered to do so. But neither let anyone leave.

"Captain, bang on the door to the hall with your ax handle. Let us see if they will come out to negotiate."

Thud! Thud! Thud!

Silence.

Birds sang. A horse snorted. Pawed the ground.

"Try hitting the door again," Pepin directed. "They may yet open and come out."

Thud! Thud! Thud!

Silence.

"Very well. The siege begins. Set up camp in the meadow," Pepin called out. "Stilicho, send men back to the forest to cut down a tree. We will batter down the door to the great hall."

Six men returned the next day, struggling to carry a large tree trunk. All branches had been trimmed except those to be used as handholds. Pepin again assembled his army.

Men vied to be picked to wield the battering ram. Pepin chose ten of the stoutest. With a shout, they picked up the trunk and ran full speed toward the door.

The army cheered them on.

With a thunderous *BOOM* the log smashed into the wooden door. The ram bounced back. The impact wrested the tree trunk from the hands of those who held it. The ram fell to earth with a *whomp,* scattering men in all directions.

"Again!" Pepin called out.

The soldiers picked themselves up, hoisted the log, and once more ran full tilt toward the heavy wooden door.

BOOM!

Although the log bounced off the door, felling the men who held it, this time the door shuddered and creaked with the impact.

"One more time!" ordered Pepin. "Army, be ready to follow the ram should it succeed in breaking the door!"

"Follow the ram!" shouted the captains.

"Into the hall!" responded foot soldiers.

"Death to the Aquitanians!"

Those manning the battering ram rubbed their sore hands and arms. With grunts and shouts they once more hefted the tree trunk. Ran full speed at the hall door.

BOOM!

Crack!

The door crashed open.

The log flew into the room carrying those who held it with its momentum.

The army crowded in, using the log as a shield.

By the time Pepin entered behind the first wave of footsoldiers, the battle was over.

Many of Saintes' defenders lay dying and bleeding on the matted floor threshings. The rest, flinging away their weapons, knelt with empty hands held out in supplication.

Women and children cringed, clinging to each other in the corners. Sounds of moans and sobbing filled the room.

"Where are Waifar and his family?" Pepin's voice carried more demand than question.

No one answered.

Observing closely, Pepin saw some of the Aquitanians glance up the stairs.

"Follow me!" he ordered.

He climbed the steps as rapidly as possible, a score of men close on his heels.

Four men stood guard outside a doorway at the end of the gallery.

Pepin and his men rushed toward them.

"Let us through!" Pepin barked.

The guards thrust out their lances.

Pepin ducked under the nearest lance, his hunting knife out of its sheath and in his hand without conscious thought.

He thrust it under the guard's protective vest. Quickly. In. Up. Twist.

The guard dropped his lance. Fell, mortally wounded. Blood flowing.

Meanwhile Pepin's soldiers made short work of the other three guards. A blow here. A thrust of a knife there. Soon four Aquitanian bodies lay in a bloody heap by the doorway.

Pepin was first to enter the chamber. He quickly scanned the room, searching for Waifar. For more guards. Although the room seemed crowded with people his first glance found neither Waifar nor guards. Only women and children.

His eyes locked with those of an elderly woman. She held herself proudly erect.

"And who might you be?" Pepin demanded.

"Duke Hunald's widow. Waifar's mother." She lifted her chin even higher. "And you, m' lord Pepin. Would you kill defenseless women and children?"

Pepin paused. Took a deep breath.

"No. I will not kill you. Though I doubt your son would be bound by such scruples, were our positions reversed."

The widow's mouth tightened, though she said nothing.

"And the others. Who are they?"

"My daughter and her children." Waifar's mother nodded to a young woman who held a toddler's hand and a babe in arms. "And my daughter-in-law with her children."

Waifar's wife, her two children by her side, returned his stare. A girl of about ten and a boy some two years younger looked out from eyes wide with fright.

No one made a sound, nor moved a muscle.

"Where, madam, might be your husband, Duke Waifar?" Pepin questioned.

"My..." Waifar's wife had trouble giving voice to her words. "My husband has left with his army for the south."

"Where south?"

"Toward the Garonne River. Per... perhaps Bordeaux. Or Mons? I do not rightly know, m'lord."

"Pack your belongings. My guards will assure your safety through this night. On the morrow they accompany you to a convent of your choice."

He was pleased to see a look of relief pass between his captives. He would not give the Aquitanians dead or raped women to look to as martyrs.

Pepin's relief nearly matched that of Waifar's family.

Chapter Thirty-Five

That evening Pepin met with the inner circle of his noblemen. Foot soldiers, captains and lesser nobles stayed in the meadow beyond Saintes. Waifar's family remained restricted to their upstairs chamber, guarded by Franks.

Servants cleared away trestle tables. Craftsmen of the hall and their families prepared their own pallet beds on the floor in far dark corners of the large central room. Pepin and his noblemen sat at the one remaining table, basking in the warmth and flickering light of the huge log burning in the fire pit.

"Now what?" Villicus' voice bristled with barely contained displeasure.

"Tomorrow morning a contingent of guards escorts Waifar's family to the nearest convent," Pepin replied evenly.

"The men should return by Vespers. The day following we continue south to the Garonne."

"Leave we a garrison here in Saintes?" inquired Stilicho.

"Think you we should?" asked Pepin.

"We have in the past," observed Villicus.

"But we did not at Remistagnus' estate," Stilicho was quick to point out.

"We leave ourselves vulnerable to an uprising by Aquitanians behind us as we move further south into Waifar's territory." Villicus acted like a dog worrying a bone.

"And we have no idea how many men we face in Waifar's army." Stilicho picked up the line of inquiry as if it were a hunting knife tossed between Villicus and himself.

"Do we even know where the Aquitanian army and Waifar *are?"* Villicus countered.

Pepin sighed. "We know not *where* Waifar and his army are. We have been told merely, 'south'. Perhaps Bordeaux or Mons. Certainly somewhere along the Garonne River."

With a wry twist of his mouth, Pepin acknowledged their lack of adequate information, as he continued. "Nor know we how many men follow him. We must assume a large army. The main body of Aquitanians."

"Our garrisons have only cut off his supply of men and equipment from the north and east of his realm," Villicus reminded the gathered men. "We have yet to touch his main source of men from Saintes to Bordeaux to Toulouse."

"Exactly!" Pepin exclaimed. "Therefore we leave no garrison here to reduce our numbers when finally we meet

Waifar. We may well need every man we have to vanquish the entire Aquitanian army."

"I like it not," Villicus grumbled. "Leaving ourselves vulnerable to a flanking action."

"Nor I," said Stilicho.

"Nevertheless, we depart *with every man* for Bordeaux, and beyond if necessary, day after the morrow." At least as king, Pepin knew he had the last word.

From Saintes to Bordeaux proved an easy journey along flat, open countryside. Here and there they passed a scattering of huts surrounded by fields, vineyards and fruit orchards. Everywhere, branches swelled with buds ready to burst forth. Winter, such as it was, giving way to spring.

Villeins plowed fields while women worked in vegetable gardens just outside their doors. As usual, children worked alongside their parents. They stopped what they were doing to watch as Pepin and his army passed—noblemen on horses, gonfaloniers carrying banners by their sides. Foot soldiers sang marching songs to the accompanying rhythms of drums. Supply wagons creaked and groaned behind placid oxen.

Pepin noted with puzzlement that no one appeared frightened of the huge Frankish contingent. None had left their homes and fields to seek safety. Though, to be fair, where could they go? No dense forests, great halls or stone church buildings existed conveniently nearby.

Pepin scratched his head. Mayhap word had reached them that the Franks fought and killed only when challenged. And took only what was theirs by right of plunder as victors. The thought pleased him.

Smiling, Pepin rode back along his army, having a word or two with the men he passed. He made it a point to speak with Villicus—asking his opinion on the campaign.

Crossing the Dordogne River where it narrowed, Bordeaux loomed ahead of them on the banks of the nearby Garonne. Even from that distance Pepin saw Saint Michel's Cathedral, newly built of glistening stone with its dark wooden roof, dominating the town.

"Don leather vests and helmets," he ordered. "Weapons ready. We know not what we might encounter when we arrive at Bordeaux. Mayhap Waifar with the entire might of Aquitaine fully armed and ready for combat."

To his surprise, the city gates remained open as they approached. "Be prepared," Pepin gave the order. "This may be a trap. Watch in all directions. Leave no man's back unprotected. Supply wagons gather in the open meadow."

He gazed again at the sprawling town only partially contained within its walls. "Soldiers take battle formations in front of the wagons until we learn the intentions of those inside Bordeaux."

With practiced ease, the long line of soldiers took their places in a solid rectangle of fighting men armed with lances, shields and casting axes.

Pepin rubbed his eyes. The situation was *most* peculiar. A conquering army—weapons at hand—stood in battle position outside the wall and yet no one came to engage in the fight. Nor had they closed and barred the gate.

Everyone waited, while Pepin looked about. He saw no one go to and fro from the fields. No carts carried supplies down the road to the wharf. No boats in the Garonne River loaded and unloaded cargo. No children ran and shouted.

The town remained silent, as though under a magic spell. "By the dog!" Pepin muttered under his breath.

When he could stand the tension no longer, Pepin, along with his personal guard, rode to the center of the road leading into Bordeaux. Although keeping his face impassive, his heart beat with great thumping pulses.

"Halt!" he shouted as they came within a few steps of the city gate.

Horses pawed the hard earthen road and snorted. Pepin rubbed his temple. Questions crowded his head. Where was the guard? Why was the gate open? What should they do now? How long should they wait?

As Pepin's head began throbbing, a group of men appeared on foot in the middle of the road inside the town. One moment the road was empty, the next filled with men.

More quickly than thought, Pepin scanned the assemblage for weapons. Saw none. No lances. Shields. Casting axes. A second glance revealed the men wore neither helmets nor protective vests. At last Pepin realized they were not guards or soldiers, but churchmen!

As he let out breath he had been unaware he was holding, he murmured to his men, "Stay alert, but touch not your weapons unless attacked."

The Bordeaux contingent walked at a steady pace, closing the gap between themselves and Pepin.

"God's greeting," said a tall man with hooked nose and serious dark eyes. He held out his arm, hand empty. "I am the Archbishop of Bordeaux. I bid you well come, Pepin, King of All Franks."

Pepin reached down from the height of his horse as he and the archbishop grasped each other's arms. The Archbishop of Bordeaux! "But where is Duke Waifar?" he blurted. "And the Aquitaine army?"

"Alas, I do not know," replied the archbishop. "We have not seen the duke since prior to Christmas last."

"Not seen..." Pepin tried hard to comprehend the meaning of this. By the Bull! he thought to himself. What kind of king must I be, if I cannot even *find* the enemy I have come to defeat?

The archbishop released Pepin's arm, but held his look, brown eyes compelling. "We have no army here. Your men may put their weapons away. No one challenges you. On that you have my word and the oaths of the priests who accompany me."

Pepin sat back on his horse. "Have you any idea of the whereabouts of Duke Waifar and his army?"

The archbishop shrugged. "I do not rightly know. Perhaps east along the Garonne. Or the fortification of Mons. Mayhap into the Perigord."

How, Pepin wondered, could the Duke of Aquitaine and his army of hundreds simply disappear like smoke into an evening sky? "We thank you for your assurance of peace," he replied, still perplexed. "If you and the others of Bordeaux remain within the walls, my army will bring you no grief. We camp here this night and leave on the morrow."

The Frankish army traveled as far as Mons on the Charente River without sight of Duke Waifar and the Aquitanian army. No one admitted knowing where the duke might be or how many men followed him.

Pepin shook his head, giving the men following him a lopsided smile. "This has been a most peculiar campaign. We left in apprehension over meeting Waifar and his huge army. In the months since, we have conquered the estate of Remistagnus, the towns of Saintes and Bordeaux, and the fortification of Mons—and have yet to set eyes on the duke or engage in a fight of any consequence!"

He added in an aside to Chlodomer, "By Mithras! I wish Waifar had been met and killed in battle!"

Chapter Thirty-Six

Pepin and his army returned to Neustria following Easter with his family in Sels. He convened his army in nearby Tours, and asked Bertrada to accompany them at least as far as Saintes.

"I doubt any Frankish queen has ever set foot in Aquitaine. Your presence there may well go far in changing their perception of us, from that of a conquering, marauding army to a people with whom the Aquitanians can live in peace. Once we have dealt with Waifar—one way or another —I plan Aquitaine to become a permanent portion of our Frankish rule."

He held her hand, looking deeply into her eyes. "However, if you feel apprehensive about going so far south, I would never ask it of you."

"Of a certainty," Bertrada assured him. "If you want me, I shall go."

From Tours, following the rivers to Poitiers, proved to be a pleasant journey. Trees were in full leaf and crops sprouted in the cultivated fields.

The army camped on the site of the decisive battle in which, years before, Charles Martel had defeated the Muslim army. In his mind's eye, Pepin, once again a seventeen-year-old, experienced his fear at the rushing assault of those turbaned soldiers. Saw them swinging scimitars from on back of fleet-footed horses. Felt the pounding of those long-ago hooves in the pit of his stomach. Heard the screams of mortally wounded men on both sides.

Now, all that remained was a flower-filled meadow between two rivers, the Vienne and the Clain.

The next day they set out again for the estate of Waifar's uncle, Remistagnus. "I doubt he will tell us anything of Waifar's whereabouts—if, indeed, he knows aught—but his estate lies on the way to Saintes and we may as well inquire," Pepin explained to Bertrada. "Besides, you may enjoy sleeping in a real bed and eating food prepared in a proper kitchen for a change."

"I have no complaints," Bertrada responded. "In many ways traveling with you, especially at this time of year, is rather pleasant."

As the army approached Remistagnus' estate, a sense of foreboding settled on Pepin's shoulders like a vulture's wings. A few women and children worked the fields unaided by husbands and fathers. Missing entirely was the normal bustle of activity between villeins' huts and the great hall.

Pepin rubbed his eyes. Where were Remistagnus and the portion of his army the Franks had left him? Why no greeting for the King of All Franks? Why had no one run to tell the lord of the estate, important visitors were arriving?

An old man with crippled legs sat on the ground in the shadow cast by his hut, sharpening a knife.

Without bothering to dismount, Pepin called to him. "Tell me, old man, where is Remistagnus?"

The man shrugged. "I be not knowing."

"Well, is he somewhere about the estate or has he gone far away?"

"He be gone." The old man nodded his head as if to confirm what he had just said.

"When did he leave?"

The man's eyes turned blank, as if trying to calculate. "It be a while back."

His patience stretched to the breaking point, Pepin demanded, "Did Remistagnus go alone or had he his army with him?"

"They all be gone. Every man and boy what could carry a weapon and walk on two feet." The old man looked at his own withered legs and sighed.

"Do they go to join Duke Waifar and his Aquitanians?"

The old man looked confused for a moment then shook his head. "I no think they be going to the Duke. They be going on they own to fight."

Little by little, Pepin and his soldiers pried information from the hamlet's remaining inhabitants. In direct contradiction to his oaths of fealty to King Pepin,

Remistagnus had taken his entire army to wage war upon the nearest Frankish garrisons.

Leaving Bertrada and a small contingent of soldiers for her protection at Remistagnus' estate, Pepin and the rest of his army left in pursuit of the treasonous nobleman.

When they arrived at the garrison, they found their fellow Franks engaged in an evenly matched battle with their Aquitanian attackers. Pepin's superior numbers quickly turned the tide in their favor.

"Capture Remistagnus alive at all costs!" Pepin ordered. "A quick death in battle is too good for the likes of him!"

The grunt and thrust and clash of battle lasted some few moments longer. Then silence, as Aquitanian soldiers put their weapons on the ground in front of them.

At last Pepin's men dragged Remistagnus and three of his captains to stand before where the king had set up court in the meadow. Behind him the Frankish army was busily making camp.

Remistagnus' complexion turned ashen at the sight of Pepin, crown on his head, sitting in tribunal surrounded by his noblemen.

"You seem to have recovered remarkably," observed Pepin. "When last we met, you required a walking stick and told me—told *all* of us—your fighting days were over."

Remistagnus said nothing. He stood, head bowed, avoiding Pepin's gaze.

"You pledged fealty to me!" Pepin's stomach roiled in anger. "Pledged for yourself and all who looked to you for leadership. And yet, the minute my back was turned, you sneaked out to attack *my* garrison! Have you nothing to say for yourself?"

"What can I say, my lord?" Remistagnus twisted his hands together. Looked up, fear apparent in his eyes. "My people fight to maintain their freedom. My nephew needed my help. They would not allow me to..."

"Your people! Your nephew! They... Jupiter's balls! Have you no pride? *You,* not 'your people'. *You,* not 'your nephew'. *You,* not 'they'. *You* are a traitor to your pledge. And *you* shall pay the price.

"Erect a scaffold," Pepin ordered his men. "Tomorrow we show the Aquitanians what happens to those who think to deceive the King of All Franks! *Tomorrow, you hang!"*

The next morning, Frankish soldiers forced every survivor who had accompanied Remistagnus on this fatal campaign to watch. The nobleman stood on an oxcart, hands bound behind him. The ox lumbered slowly toward the scaffold, where a noose cast an ominous shadow on the packed earth below.

Townsfolk and Frankish soldiers gathered to watch the hanging as well. Little boys shouted in glee at all the excitement. Many threw rocks and clods of dirt at the helpless Remistagnus.

As the sun climbed higher, the driver backed the oxcart into place under the rope. Soldiers hurried to lift the wooden railing from the back of the cart.

The garrison had no church. A traveling priest came but once a year for marriages and baptisms. Remistagnus would have to meet his God unabsolved by last rites.

"May he go straight to Hell," said Pepin without a shred of pity.

The guard grabbed the noose. Jerked Remistagnus' head up by his short gray hair. Lowered the rope. Pulled it taught against the nobleman's throat.

Remistagnus' knees buckled at the feel of the noose. He retched as if to vomit. A dark spot of moisture spread across the crotch of his pants instead.

"Let this be the fate of all who pledge falsely to the King of All Franks!" Pepin called out. "Let him hang. I hope his death comes slowly. He deserves to suffer!"

With that, the driver flicked his whip over the back of the ox that pulled the cart. The sharp-sounding crack of the whip, more than anything else, startled the placid animal into action. With a creak and groan the wooden wheels turned. The cart began moving slowly.

Remistagnus took a few quick steps, trying desperately to keep his balance. He stretched himself as tall as he could to ease the tension of the noose.

The cart moved forward.

One more shuffle and Remistagnus stepped off into nothing. The crowd cheered then grew silent. The rope creaked against the scaffolding. The nobleman's body writhed. Kicked. Eyes bulged. Remistagnus' face turned purple. His tongue protruded, strangely black and inhuman.

Little boys pelted the body swinging at the end of the noose with rocks, long after all life had departed.

By the time Pepin and his troops returned to Remistagnus' estate, Queen Bertrada had everything running smoothly. The hall had been swept clean and aired out. New rushes covered the floor. Freshly laundered linens filled the cupboards. Every pot and pan in the kitchen building sparkled, having been scrubbed with sand.

Outside, with the Frankish soldiers' help, vineyards and orchards had been tended, roads and bridges repaired. Crops sprouted in the fields.

"Weren't you afraid you would make a martyr of Remistagnus?" asked Bertrada once she and Pepin were alone together.

Pepin considered. "No. He was not the duke, symbol of Aquitanian rule. He was but a nobleman who had publicly pledged himself to me. That pledge may well have made of him a traitor in Aquitanian eyes. I think they will not mourn his loss overmuch."

"And perhaps make others think twice before deciding to play you false?" asked Bertrada.

Pepin gave her a knowing look. "Come here to me, woman. You are entirely all too knowing." He smiled. "Methinks it time we met, thee and me, on the field of that large bed over there in the corner. What say you?"

Without a word, Bertrada began taking Pepin's tunic over his head and untying the string holding his britches.

Chapter Thirty-Seven

Pepin left Bertrada in Saintes with a contingent of soldiers for protection.

The king rode beside Chlodomer as his army moved southward. "Mayhap the bishop of Bordeaux will have heard of Waifar."

"Think you the bishop will tell us where the duke is —even if he does know?" Chlodomer asked.

Pepin shrugged. "Perhaps not. I know not where the man's allegiance lies. Nor if everything told to him is considered a sacred trust. We can but ask—and hope."

As they approached Bordeaux, they overcame a straggle of Aquitanian men walking along the road. The men looked around as if for a place to run or hide. Finding none, they knelt in submission before king and army.

"Where are you bound? And from whence come you?" demanded Pepin.

One of the men dared lift his head and meet Pepin's eye. "We are for home, m'lord. From the Perigord." The man gestured off to his right. "Up the Dordogne River."

Pepin felt a surge of comprehension. "Army, halt here. Villicus! You and your men watch this rabble. Chlodomer, bring the Aquitanian and come with me farther on down the road. I would speak with him in private."

The three moved well out of hearing of the others. "By what name go you?" inquired Pepin.

"Theodahad, m'lord."

Pepin noted with satisfaction that Theodahad, while clearly frightened, answered in a strong voice. "Came you from Duke Waifar?"

Theodahad broke eye contact and shifted from one foot to the other. "Why ask you, m'lord?"

Pepin softened the harshness of his voice. "Because I wish an answer."

Theodahad shifted feet again. Wiped his palms on the sides of his course linen breeches. He looked from side to side as the silence lengthened.

"Well?" prompted Pepin.

Theodahad took a deep breath. Lifted his eyes to once again meet Pepin's. "Aye, m'lord." The answer cost him dearly. Indeed he looked to be close to tears.

"Good," Pepin commended. "And who was with him?"

"*With*, m'lord?"

"God's breath! *With Waifar!* Who thought you I meant?"

"I be not knowing, m'lord."

"Who was with Duke Waifar? How large an army?"

"An army?" Theodahad blinked. "An army?" he asked again. "Why none, m'lord. Leastwise, not so many as to count as such."

"No army with the duke? How could that be?" At Theodahad's prolonged silence, Pepin mused. "His wife and children safely out of reach in a convent. His chief supporters, including his uncle, Remistagnus, captured and hung—pitiable Duke Waifar! His army is now deserting him." Then a gruff question, "Am I right?"

"Yes, m'lord," mumbled Theodahad.

"So where is he now?" thundered Pepin.

Theodahad blanched. "He be dead, m'lord."

"*Dead?*"

Theodahad cringed at Pepin's shout.

"Are you positive?"

"Aye, m'lord. His body be in Bordeaux. To be buried. Any what wants can go see it for theyselves."

Pepin nodded, pondering. "Tell me, Theodahad, how did this come about?"

"We—me and the men—be meeting with some others of Duke Waifar's followers. We begin telling them how we hear the mighty army of the Franks be huge. Cannot be defeated by any we have in Aquitaine." He looked hopefully at Pepin.

"And..." Pepin demanded more.

"They be telling us they hear ye be fearsome in battle. H... hard in judgments." Theodahad swallowed.

"Both true. What else?"

"Us an' them be talking how ye rebuild what ye destroy. E...even what D...Duke W...Waifar, heself, destroyed."

"So, to what conclusion did you arrive?" Pepin found Theodahad's account of the soldiers' discussion more and more to his liking.

"Con...con... what, m'lord?"

"Conclusion. That means, what did you decide to do about this sad state of affairs?"

Theodahad looked frightened, but clamped his mouth shut. Remained resolutely silent.

"Know you who I am?" asked Pepin.

"Ye..." Theodahad swallowed. "be Pepin, King of All Franks, m'lord."

"True. If you displease me, what could I do?"

"T...torture m...me, m'lord. K...kill me."

"And if you please me, what then?"

A glimmer of hope filled Theodahad's eyes. "Let me go home, m'lord?"

"Oh, I could do more than that. I could let you go home well rewarded for your efforts. Do you understand me, Theodahad?"

"Yes, m'lord!'

"Now tell me exactly how Duke Waifar came to die."

"Them soldiers and us joined together, and we... we... k...killed Duke Waifar." Theodahad's look beseeched mercy. He plainly already felt the axman's weapon upon his neck.

Pepin smiled.

"Duke Waifar is dead!" he shouted as he returned to his army. "This man, Theodahad, has brought us the news. The duke's death ends the war! We have finally beaten Aquitaine!

Pepin reached into the girdle around his waist and withdrew his hunting knife. The Aquitanian's eyes grew round. A large garnet set in the knife's handle, sent bright red sparks into the sunlight.

"Garnets are believed to bring the wearer power, grace, and victory," said Pepin. "Appropriate for one who brought us news of our victory over the Aquitanians."

Theodahad dropped to his knees in front of Pepin, who touched the blade to his bowed head. "I give you this knife in gratitude. Use it well."

No sooner had the Aquitanians left, then Stilicho began complaining. "Our illustrious King Pepin never even *found* Duke Waifar! We fought no glorious battle. Have no grand tales to pass on to our children and their children's children. Nothing at all."

"God's death!" exclaimed Villicus. "Can you *never* be satisfied with our king? He defeated the Aquitanians by cunning and strategy. Without loss of blood. Is that not good enough for you?"

Pepin's jaw dropped. He exchanged amazed looks with Chlodomer. Then smiling, raised a hand in salute to Villicus. Mounting, he turned his army back the way it had come, toward Saintes.

* * *

The Franks returned to Saintes in high good humor. Pepin could barely contain his pleasure. He told Bertrada, "I have done, what I set out to do. Beaten Aquitaine!"

Bertrada, her face glowing with pleasure, held Pepin's hand to her lips. She cared not that the entire Frankish army watched.

The next day, Pepin sent out the order. "Gather what Aquitanian noblemen remain. Summon the Archbishop of Bordeaux and his fellow priests. We shall celebrate the defeat of Aquitaine and its inclusion in our realm with all due ceremony!"

In less than a fortnight, the Aquitanians had assembled in Saintes.

Queen Bertrada calmly oversaw all the necessary preparations. The great hall was aired and swept. Fresh rushes covered the floor. The king's banner and that of Saint Martin of Tours decorated the wall.

In the kitchen building, breads baked and pottage simmered. In the bailey, whole pigs browned on spits while sweating pages turned the handles.

In the hall, Pepin and his queen sat on the raised dais in high-backed chairs of authority. Aquitanian noblemen and their ladies along with the churchmen from Bordeaux joined the Franks on benches around the tables. Pages brought tankards of ale and flagons of wine.

When everyone had taken seats, Pepin spoke. "You Aquitanians have defied all conquerors with stubborn valor as far back as Caesar."

The Aquitanians, exchanging worried glances, sat a little straighter.

Pride filled Pepin. He had accomplished what even his father failed to do—conquered Aquitaine! This duchy was now a part of the Frankish realm. They were all, every man, woman and child, his vassals. Subjects of the King of All Franks!

"In recognition of your long history of self rule, I shall grant you your own law, the Breviary of Alaric, set down for you by your last Visigothic king."

The Aquitanians smiled.

"In exchange and recognition of your subservience, every one of you nobleman shall pledge your fealty to the Frankish crown."

One by one, they each knelt before Pepin, placed his hands between those of the king. Spoke his part in the age-old ritual.

This done, Pepin faced those gathered. "Because you are of great value, I promise to send my most reliable noblemen to Aquitaine as representatives of the crown. I shall open all abandoned churches. Grant the clergy full autonomy over their priests.

"In return, you will give me the king's share of your crops. The products of your looms and craftsmen's shops. The crown's portion of the church's treasure. In return, as King of All Franks, I pledge to protect you from your enemies."

The Archbishop of Bordeaux stood and raised his tankard, "To Pepin, King of All Franks!"

The rest of the Aquitanians stood. With grudging respect rather than the Archbishop's enthusiasm, all raised their tankards and drank to the conquering king.

Chapter Thirty-Eight

Fever struck Pepin with the swiftness of a thrown casting ax. One day he was celebrating his unprecedented victory over Aquitaine—and the next, without warning, he had not the strength to get out of bed.

As his body burned, sweat soaking through his under tunic, Pepin realized there had been subtle signs of impending ailment. Since before Easter he had experienced a fatigue that a solid night's sleep did nothing to alleviate. And the cough that had come and gone since the previous winter had returned with a vengeance. But his joy in victory and the anticipation of achieving his life's goal had blinded him to the symptoms.

Pepin groaned. His head throbbed as though several men were inside, pounding with lance handles. His eyes burned. Hot and dry, they seemed ready to burst from their sockets and run like molten lead down his cheeks. His throat felt as though slashed by sharp knives. He tried not to swallow.

His whole body ached. The sweating brought out a smell as though interior putrefaction streamed out through every pore. How could this be? He was never ill!

Gentle hands removed his tunic and drawers. Wiped his body with a cloth. Redressed him in clean, dry underclothes. Spooned soothing hot liquid into his mouth.

"Tea of willow bark," Bertrada murmured. "It should take away some of the pain and reduce the fever."

Pepin struggled to say, "Thank you." Could not tell if he had actually uttered the words or merely thought them before falling into a fitful sleep.

He awoke, sopping wet again, but far from feverish. Indeed he seemed covered with ice water. His body shook with cold, teeth chattering. How could he be cold—in Aquitaine in the summer!

Again Bertrada appeared from nowhere to dry his body. Changed his underclothes. Then tucked a thick comforter around him.

"My love," Pepin thought. Hoped he had said. Prayed Bertrada understood.

He had no idea how long he alternated between burning fever and icy chills. He knew only that each time he awoke, Bertrada was there, ministering to his needs like an angel straight from God.

Emerging at last, he felt pathetically weak. His head continued to throb with a dull ache and his throat was red and raw. The racking cough returned each time he lay down, so he slept sitting up, bolstered by pillows.

A fine soldier I make! he thought bitterly. Having to sleep, cosseted by pillows instead of flat on the ground!

Bertrada smoothed the hair off his forehead with a gentle hand. "Thanks be to our blessed Mother Mary, your fever has broken at last." She gave a weary smile. Deep shadows under her eyes made them appear even larger and darker than usual. "You worried the entire court."

"As soon as I am able, we must go to Tours to give thanks to Saint Martin for my recovery," Pepin declared. And if I am not yet fully recovered, to ask his aid in healing me from this illness, he silently added.

Traveling in easy stages, Pepin and his entourage took more than twice the normal time to cover the short distance from Saintes through Poitiers to Tours. Some days Pepin rode his horse, stopping to make camp when he became too fatigued. Others, he was forced to ride in a litter. Or travel not at all.

As they approached the city walls, he declared, "I will arrive in Tours sitting on my horse! God's death! I am King of All Franks. Victor over Aquitaine. I shall enter the city triumphant. *Not* in a litter!"

His arrival in that venerable city was riotous enough to lend him the strength he needed. He did, indeed, enter astride his favorite horse. Straight backed, he waved to the crowd. A flush of pleasure replaced his sickly pallor.

By the next day, Pepin's strength had fled. He was barely able, heavily supported by Chlodomer, to walk to the tomb of Saint Martin following Mass.

He collapsed, more than knelt, at the railing. "Saint Martin, patron saint of the crown of the Franks, bless me, I pray." He paused as a wave of nausea passed through him. "As thou hast healed hundreds before me, heal me of this sickness. I have much yet to do...."

You have accomplished all you set out to do, a voice inside his head reminded him. *Strengthened your borders. Conquered Aquitaine. Made the Frankish holdings bigger and stronger than ever before.*

Pepin continued his stubborn prayer. "But, I want to *live* to enjoy my success."

Feeling little better, Pepin began the long, torturous journey north through Orleans and Paris. In the monastery of Saint-Denis, Bertrada bade the monks give Pepin a cot in the private chamber of the infirmary so they could apply their healing arts.

There, in a scene reminiscent of his own father's death, Pepin gradually accepted the idea of his own mortality. With sadness he realized Saint Martin had, for whatever reason, withheld his favor.

Pepin and Bertrada discussed the division of the Frankish realm between their sons, Charles and Carloman. "I would give..." He paused, swallowing. "Charles that portion which I inherited from our father," he said.

"As Charles is the more diplomatic of the two," Bertrada agreed, "he should rule the more difficult Neustrians and Aquitanians. Though you have set him an excellent example. And even unconquerable Aquitaine is firmly under your control. God be praised!"

Pepin gestured for a cup of water for his parched throat. Bertrada raised his head, helping him sup the cooling liquid.

His thirst slaked, he waived the cup away. "My precious angel of mercy," he murmured.

Bertrada smiled.

Pepin felt her cool and gentle hand on his forehead. "And Carloman," he continued, "will be king of the rest. His is still the easier... Austrasia... our family's stronghold."

"Carloman will do well with that domain."

"We must have that scribed on parchment." Pepin closed his eyes, weary with just that short conversation. "Think you the noblemen will find fault?"

"I see no reason for them to do so. It is fair. Just. And follows precedent."

"I wonder," Pepin paused, then continued, "which of them is to be the great king?"

Bertrada seated herself on the edge of his bed. "Perhaps you have already filled that role."

"No. I think I would know if I were the one." Pepin laid his hand on his heart. "When I look into myself, I see only a man who tried. I get no sense of greatness."

He sighed. "Perhaps I am to be like Moses. After traveling for years in the wilderness, I can see the Promised Land, but will not be allowed to cross over into it."

Bertrada took his hand in hers.

Pepin slipped into a haze of half awareness. His head pounded. His mouth tasted foul. He gestured again for the cup of water.

Finishing, he murmured, "Which of the two, think you might be...?"

"The great king? I am hard put to answer." Bertrada stared off into space. "My children will always be children to me. When I look at Charles and Carloman, full grown and far taller than any who follow them, I see two little boys in a great hall, running wild, dodging in and out of pages and serving wenches, or tumbling in the straw flooring with a litter of puppies. Though they marry and start families of their own, they will always remain so to me."

Pepin smiled, seeing the boys as she had pictured them.

She held his hand in both of hers and kissed it. As his heavy eyes closed, he heard her say with a catch in her voice, *"Oh, my love."*

One afternoon, as the square of sunlight streaming through the wind opening moved slowly across the floor, the leather curtain at the doorway to his chamber flapped. A priest glided to the side of Pepin's bed. Looking down at him with compassion, he took Pepin's hand in his own.

Pepin watched as the priest took from the pocket of his robe, a small vial of oil, blessed months before on Maundy Thursday. *Is this...my time?* Heart pounding, Pepin hesitantly faced the first, faltering steps on the final journey of his life.

"As is written in the book of Mark," the priest intoned, "the rite of extreme unction was instituted by Jesus Christ, Himself. Mark says, 'And they cast out many devils, and anointed with oil many that were sick, and healed them.' In His footsteps, I so anoint you with holy oil, that you might be healed."

As Pepin confessed his sins, the priest anointed his eyes, ears, nostrils, lips, hands, feet and loins. With the confessions, the priest recited absolution for sins committed through each of these body parts.

"With this sacrament," the priest continued, "the Church teaches that though you be dying, you receive health of soul, remission of sin, and, if God wills, health of body. In the book of James is written the words, 'Is any sick among you? Let him call for the elders of the church; and let them pray over him, anointing him with oil in the name of the Lord. And the prayer of faith shall save the sick, and the Lord shall raise him up. And if he has committed sins, they shall be forgiven him.'

"With the power vested in me, I now pronounce you forgiven of your sins by God through the death of Our Lord, Jesus Christ. Amen."

Pepin watched the priest reverently put away the precious vial of oil, then kiss and fold his stole.

A while later, Pepin had the strange feeling he was not alone. Peering into the corner farthest from the square of sunshine, he saw a shadow become darker. More distinct.

"Papa!" Pepin croaked. "How came you here?

Charles Martel, looking much as he had during the Battle of Poitiers, moved forward to stand directly in Pepin's line of vision. He held the baby Pepin, smiling and rosy-cheeked, in his arms. "You found your grandson. I hoped you would."

Pepin coughed. "I know I am dying. Fifty-three. Almost the exact age you were... You chose not to become king, but yet wore a mantle of greatness. I wonder..."

Pepin struggled to raise himself. "Did I live up to your memory?" He gasped for breath. "I do not ask to have achieved the destiny of greatness you told us of on *your* deathbed." Pepin's fingers plucked at his coverlet. "Only that I did not squander my life."

"Why would you even *think* such a thing?" His father's eyes were filled with even greater compassion than had been those of the priest.

"You achieved the crown!" Martel's eyes glowed. "The crown now belongs to our family. To your sons and their sons to follow. *That* is a truly great feat!"

Pepin felt his chest expand. His body became lighter.

Charles Martel continued, looking deeply into Pepin's eyes. "Because of you—your life and accomplishments—your son has all he needs to become the king of the prophecy!"

"My son?"

"Yes, Charles. He will be the great king. His name will live on throughout eternity. Until the end of time he will be remembered as Charles the Great. *Charles le Magne. CHARLEMAGNE!"*

Pepin felt a tremendous sense of release.

The light, flowing through the wind opening, brightened as though the sun had come out from behind a filmy cloud into clear sky. The patch of light moving slowly across the floor became a brilliance, nearly blinding Pepin.

He turned his gaze to comment on the extraordinary light to his father. But the chamber appeared empty. Although the leather curtain remained in place and still, *Charles Martel, the Baby Pepin with him, had disappeared!*

Pepin smiled as he contemplated the message his father had come to tell him. My son. *Our* son. Bertrada's and mine. Charles will be the great king.

As late afternoon turned into flaming sunset, Bertrada quietly entered Pepin's chamber. She had spoken to the priest and understood her husband had precious little time.

Hesitantly, afraid of what she might find, she went to Pepin's side and gazed at his face. His eyes were closed. His lips curved in a smile. She had never seen him appear so at peace. Always before there had been an urgency about him, a striving that he had now, somehow, set aside.

Her hand to her throat, she noticed Pepin's chest rising and falling. He was breathing! Not dead. At least, not yet.

She took his hand, familiar and warm, into her own and brought it to her lips. He opened his eyes. His smile deepened in recognition.

"My father was here." Pepin paused to gather his strength. With a rattling breath, pushed himself higher on the pillow. "I saw him.

"Our son, Charles, is destined to be the great king of the prophecy. He will be known for all time as Charlemagne!"

"Charlemagne? He is to be Charles the Great? *Our* son?" The concept made Bertrada's head spin.

"Our son." Pepin pulled her hand to his lips. Kissed it. Closed his eyes.

Bertrada gazed at him. "History will doubtless refer to you as Pepin the Short. And to me as Bertrada Big Foot." She chuckled quietly.

"If they remember us at all, it will be only as the parents of Charlemagne. But in my heart, you, my husband, are the greatest king of all time."

Bertrada smiled as her tears fell, splashing Pepin's still face with their cleansing gentle rain.

Afterword

On the tomb of Pepin the Short in the cathedral of Saint Denis, is the simple inscription, *Pater Caroli Magni,* father of Charles the Great. But he did more. Much more.

Pepin took the Merovingian crown and placed it firmly on the heads of the Carolingians. With his coronations by Archbishop Boniface and Pope Stephen II, he established the concept of rule by divine right—that sovereigns derive their right to rule by their birth alone—a right based on their interpretation of God's law.

He subjugated the Bavarians and contained the tribes along the Franks' eastern boundary. He defeated the Lombards and secured territory for the chair of Saint Peter in Rome. "Pepin's Donation" was the prototype vision for the present Vatican.

Even with his obsessive hatred of Duke Waifar and the Aquitanians, Pepin earned a reputation as a fair conqueror and ruler. He was known, as well, as a just and capable administrator. In these endeavors, he was nobly aided by his wife, Bertrada, one of the few females in early medieval history whose life is recorded in any detail.

Pepin was more religious than his father, Charles Martel. The churchmen spoke of Pepin with warmth, while they condemned "The Hammer", even as they accepted his protection. Unlike many of his predecessors, no moral lapses are recorded during Pepin the Short's lifetime.

He was far more than simply the father of Charlemagne. He was a courageous and precedent-setting leader. As such, he is worthy of accolades—and an epitaph of his own!

Destiny's Godchild

A medieval legendary beginning for the House of Charlemagne

By Diana M. Johnson

1999 B.P.S.C. IRWIN Award in Fiction

ISBN 0-9661504-0-6
270 pages, $12.00

"Your life will change the course of Frankish history." So saying, the Master sends Young Egar to seek his destiny. Egar can earn his living with the harp music, juggling, and sleight of hand taught him by the Master. But change history? How could that come to pass? Entertaining in the royal palace in Paris, Egar meets nobleman Pepin de Vain, tutor to the prince. Egar the Magician sees a vision of a great king yet to come. Pepin assumes he is to be that king—an assumption that will land both Pepin and Egar in serious trouble.

"A beautifully lucid style makes ***Destiny's Godchild*** *a pleasure to read—cleanly written, briskly paced, with an interesting central character who gives the reader an unusual slant on the history of the period."*
Eve LaSalle Caram, Senior Instructor, The Writers' Program
UCLA Extension

*"****Destiny's Godchild*** *reminds me of the historical novels I read so voraciously as a young girl. I have not seen one of this caliber surface in many years."*
Carol Bachofner, Heartsounds Press

Pepin's Bastard

The Story of Charles Martel

By Diana M. Johnson

ISBN 0-9661504-1-4
294 pages, $14.95

"Neither you nor our child will have aught to fear." Charlemagne's pivotal reign is still some distance in the future when Charles is born, the bastard son of Mayor of the Palace for All Franks, Pepin de Gros. Pepin's jealous wife, Plectruda, will stop at nothing to see Charles dead, thus saving the power behind the throne for her own legitimate sons. Somehow, Charles must survive and gain the power to face the feared Muslim cavalry even now pouring over the Pyrenees Mountains, determined to wipe Christianity off the face of the land.

"A compelling and heart-stirring story of the triumphant ascent to power and glory by Charles Martel, grandfather of Charlemagne."
JoAnn Levy, Author of ***For California's Gold,*** A Novel of the California Gold Rush.

"I delight in the eloquently vivid writing. A glorious book to follow ***Destiny's Godchild.*** *My congratulations to Diana Johnson!"*
Betty Freeman,
Former California Writers Club State President